William Greene

Manuel Matamoros: His Life and Death

A Narrative of the Late Persecution of Christians in Spain. Third Edition

William Greene

Manuel Matamoros: His Life and Death
A Narrative of the Late Persecution of Christians in Spain. Third Edition

ISBN/EAN: 9783337086220

Printed in Europe, USA, Canada, Australia, Japan

Cover: Foto ©Raphael Reischuk / pixelio.de

More available books at **www.hansebooks.com**

MANUEL MATAMOROS:
HIS LIFE AND DEATH.

A NARRATIVE OF THE LATE PERSECUTION
OF CHRISTIANS IN SPAIN.

COMPILED FROM ORIGINAL LETTERS AND OTHER DOCUMENTS.

WITH A SUCCINCT SKETCH OF THE GOSPEL WORK TO THE PRESENT TIME.

By WILLIAM GREENE.

Third Edition.

" Is not this the fast that I have chosen ? to loose the bands of wickedness, to undo the heavy burdens, and to let the oppressed go free, and that ye break every yoke?"—ISAIAH lviii. 6.

LONDON :
ALFRED HOLNESS, 14 PATERNOSTER ROW.
GLASGOW :
R. L. ALLAN, 143 SAUCHIEHALL STREET.
AND MAY BE ORDERED OF ANY BOOKSELLER.

1889.

L I N E S

DR. A. N. SOMERVILLE.

———>•◆•<———

I LITTLE thought, else keen had been my pain,
   Those brilliant eyes should beam on me no more;
That scarcely fifteen moons should wax and wane,
   Ere death had sealed them by blue Leman's shore.

Dear MATAMOROS! no friend have I known
   Of soul less soiled with earthliness than thine;
In chains and exile, brave thy Lord to own,
   The victor's wreaths thy martyr temples twine.

Loving and lovely, gentle, guileless, pure,
   All base alloy thy lofty bosom spurned:
To lead thy bleeding Spain to Christ for cure,
   With life-consuming fire that bosom burned.

I loved thee, as did those of many a clime—
   Thy glorious race on earth seemed but begun.
The Lord "does all things well." In golden prime
   Thou servest now, where shines no setting sun.

And BRIDEL's * voice by Leman's lake is dumb;
   Its silvery tones on earth are hushed for aye:
The Great Belov'd has to His garden come,
   And, stooping, caught the lilies quick away.

---

* A Swiss Pasteur at whose house Matamoros lived during his stay at Lausanne.

IN issuing a Third Edition of the Life of Manuel Matamoros, I desire to express my thankfulness, first, to the Giver of all good things, who has permitted me to collect these truthful, though alas! imperfect, details of the Life and Death of one who was His faithful soldier and servant, and secondly, to those Christian friends whose wishes have been carried out in the republication of this little book, as their prayers, encouragement and pecuniary assistance have rendered it possible.

One of these friends, in speaking of the subject of this memoir, said to me, "How closely he followed in the steps of his Divine Master." This is his best and truest eulogy. May it please our God to raise up many such in Spain and in Britain, and may He give His blessing to this repetition of a weak endeavour to promote His Glory.

W. G.

CONTENTS.

CHAPTER I.

PAGE

INTRODUCTORY 1

CHAPTER II.

BIRTH. — CONVERSION. — SERVICE IN THE GOSPEL. — IMPRISONMENT 5

CHAPTER III.

COMMUNICATIONS FROM BARCELONA 16

CHAPTER IV.

IMPRISONMENT AT GRANADA 28

CHAPTER V.

DON FRANCISCO RUET 45

CHAPTER VI.

LETTER FROM REFORMED CHURCH AT GRANADA.—PROCEEDINGS OF FRIENDS IN ENGLAND 50

CHAPTER VII.

THE LOJA TRAGEDY 77

CHAPTER VIII.

LETTERS FROM GRANADA.—SPEECHES IN PARLIAMENT.— THE ENGLISH PRESS 84

CHAPTER IX.

EXTRACTS FROM THE DEFENCE OF THE PRISONERS AT MALAGA 135

CHAPTER X.

PAGE

The Spanish Press. — Letter from Matamoros. — Defence by his Advocate before the Tribunal at Granada 143

CHAPTER XI.

Letters from Granada 162

CHAPTER XII.

Visit of an English Clergyman. — Letter from Matamoros.—Conclusion 182

MEMORIALS OF THE LAST DAYS AND DEATH OF MANUEL MATAMOROS.

CHAPTER XIII.

A Visit to the Prison at Granada. —The Deputation of the Evangelical Alliance 191

CHAPTER XIV.

Matamoros's Release from Prison 207

CHAPTER XV.

Work at Lausanne.—Preparations for Evangelizing Spain.—Work organized at Pau, Bayonne and Bordeaux 212

CHAPTER XVI.

A Woman's Reminiscence of Matamoros . . . 224

CHAPTER XVII.

Failing Health.—Loving Friends.—Last Days.— Asleep in Jesus 230

CHAPTER XVIII.

Recollections of our departed Brother . . . 248

CHAPTER XIX.

Conclusion 257

MANUEL MATAMOROS.

CHAPTER I.

INTRODUCTORY

FEELING it at once a duty and a privilege, to give to the church a brief account of the life, labours, and imprisonment of that beloved disciple of our Lord Jesus Christ, Manuel Matamoros, I commence my pleasant undertaking by asking the aid and blessing of the Divine Counsellor, without whom nothing is strong and nothing is holy, and I look to Him for that guidance which He never refuses to those who feel their own insufficiency and who throw themselves on Him in their hour of need. Christ loved the church, and gave Himself for it, and it is for that church that these pages are penned; not only for those members of it now living, but also for those who may come after.

"It seemed good to me also, having had perfect understanding of all things from the very first," to give back to the flock what the Great Shepherd has entrusted to my keeping, even the detailed account of the sufferings and trials and untiring labours of our brother in bonds, with extracts from the many

B

long and interesting letters I have received from him, all which have been carefully preserved from the first.

God's superintending care over this servant has been unmistakably shown in many ways. He said to Israel by Hosea, "Thou shalt not be for another man, so will I also be for thee," and the dependence and whole-heartedness of the prisoner in being for the Lord, has been one of the secrets of the Lord's unceasing love and tender care for him.

I obtained a knowledge of the Spanish language during a residence of several years in Spain, where I was engaged in the laying out and construction of some of the many lines of railway that now intersect the Peninsula, and having been, by God's good provi-dence, led to know and love the Lord Jesus, I en-deavoured, while helping in the material progress of the country, to prepare that highway which is called the way of holiness, wherein the redeemed shall walk.

It was in the year 1858 that I left Spain, but ever since I have taken a deep interest and active part in the work of God going on there and latterly, have had the privilege of receiving and communicating to many Christian friends the prison letters of a faithful martyr.

As it is my intention to give to the church some information respecting the recent revival of truth in Spain, it may be interesting to know that a country-man of ours, Dr. Rule, of Aldershot, began some thirty years before to labour for the Lord in Andalusia; his message was honoured of God, and received by many Spaniards, and the schools which he then estab-lished in Gibraltar, in connection with the Wesleyan body, are thriving to this day. This learned and laborious servant of Christ translated into the Spanish language a tract entitled " Andrew Dunn," which has since been used by God in enlightening many.

The late Dr. James Thompson, an agent of the British and Foreign Bible Society, was the next sent by the Lord into Spain; he was at Madrid about the year 1845, as far as I can learn, where he lost his beloved wife; his prayers and activity for the advancement of the Lord's kingdom in Spain were untiring while he lived. He died about the year 1854. His efforts resulted in the formation of the Spanish Evangelization Society at Edinburgh, which continued for some time to labour with success.

At about this period, Mr. Parker, of London, brought out his modest publication, entitled the "Alba," printed in Spanish, with a view to enlighten the Spanish mind as to the errors of Popery, and to introduce the pure gospel of the grace of God. This little messenger did important service in Spain, and the "Spanish Evangelical Record," edited by Mrs. Robert Peddie, of Edinburgh, served to keep the people in this country informed as to the progress of God's work in Spain.

There are at the present time about 14,000,000 Spaniards in the Peninsula, and were we carried by the Spirit into the midst of the open country, we should see it full of bones and very dry, so that we might ask, " Can these bones live?" And then the answer of the Word is, " Prophesy upon these bones, and say unto them, O ye dry bones, *hear the word oj the Lord.*"

Already, with the feeble efforts that have been made, some results have been obtained, and a goodly. band of witnesses has been brought out, ready to testify to their countrymen the glad tidings of the grace of God. But we are only on the threshold, and the bitter opposition, by the adversaries, to the introduction of the truth into Spain, offers no obstacle to the "hosts of the Lord." There are separated unto our David, men of might and men of war, who by God's grace have faces like the faces of lions; He has his Gideons now as of old, to whom He has said, "The Lord is with thee, thou mighty man of valour." They have not been wanting in this first glorious campaign who "have jeoparded their lives on the high places of the field," neither shall they be wanting while there is one stronghold to be cast down, or one captive to be set free. The Red Sea is before us, mountains on the right hand and on the left, but the word abideth sure, "Stand still, and see the salvation of the Lord; the Lord shall fight for you, and ye shall hold your peace." Even so, Lord Jesus, be it unto thy servants according to *thy* word.

CHAPTER II.

BIRTH.—CONVERSION.—SERVICE IN THE GOSPEL. —IMPRI-
SONMENT.

THE name of Manuel Matamoros will, in the lapse of a century or two, hold an important place in the religious history of Spain.

In a letter I received from him, dated "Carcel. de la Audiencia, Granada, Feb. 12, 1861," he gives a brief sketch of his life in the following words:—

"I am twenty-five years of age, according to the baptismal record read by the tribunal from the place of my birth, Malaga; and, beloved brother, young as I am, nevertheless, ever since I have had the use of my reason, my life has been one continued chain of suffering. After studying three years in the military college of Toledo, according to the wish of my deceased father, who was a lieutenant-colonel in the Spanish artillery, I abandoned that profession, which was so much opposed to my tastes, at least as it exists in Spain, and I came to manage my property, consisting of seven pretty good farms at Malaga and its neighbourhood.

"A succession of misfortunes, which happened within a very short time, obliged me to sell five, leaving two remaining, of the value of about 10,000 dollars, which were mortgaged to free me from the military service which fell to my lot, and to help me to maintain my mother and her family, and move with them to Barcelona. I now see my poor mother in great straits, which weighs heavily on my spirit; she has hitherto been always pretty well off, but is now obliged to earn her bread by embroidering. May God bless her; she has many virtues.

"The reason of my leaving the service was through a notable circumstance, which placed me in a critical position, even endangering my life, and came about through the confession made by a corporal in my company to the chaplain of the regiment, who gave me much annoyance. To this corporal I had given a copy of the tract, ' Andrew Dunn,' and had succeeded in convincing him of the truth; he forwarded it to his mother, with the desire of effecting the same change in her mind, but she forced him to retract his opinions, and to confess to the priest, threatening that if he did not comply with her wish, he should lose her favour."

In the year 1854 there was a revolution in Madrid. At such times I was enabled to do things that I dared not do in ordinary circumstances, such as print and circulate gospel tracts, for doing this I should have been sent out of the country; but, making use of my opportunity, I got a quantity of valuable tracts printed. Then the difficulty was to put them into circulation. So I had recourse to the following novel expedient:—Knowing one of the leaders of the Republican party, and knowing their hatred of priestcraft, I proposed to this gentleman to receive packages of good gospel tracts and to send them to all the leaders of the Republican party in the different towns. He did so, and by this plan I had them efficiently circulated when I was utterly helpless myself. Probably it was one of these tracts that was blest to Matamoros.

It appears that Matamoros' first religious impressions were received from hearing the preaching of Don Francisco Ruet, an ordained minister, in the Presbyterian church at Gibraltar, as also by attending the ministry of a Señor B——, at Seville, a convert from Romanism in that town. These impressions, deepened by the reading of the Spanish tract, "Andrew Dunn," caused Matamoros to send in a formal protest against the errors of Romanism, and to inscribe his name in the books of the Presbyterian congregation of Gibraltar.

Don Francisco Ruet was born at Barcelona, and brought up for an advocate, but went to exercise his profession at Turin, where he heard the celebrated De Sanctis, the Italian reformer, preach, and became a convert to the pure faith of the gospel of Christ. He suffered imprisonment at Barcelona in the year 1855, but was afterwards, at the end of nine months, set at liberty, and banished from Spain. He went then to Gibraltar and preached, and was instrumental in convincing many Spaniards of the errors of the Roman Catholic faith.

The reception of the gospel of the grace of God by Matamoros was as seed sown in good ground; and from the day he accepted that grace, he became a willing follower of the Lamb: his first inquiry, it

would appear, on entering the service of Christ, was,
"Lord, what wilt Thou have *me* to do?" Ruet
directed the steps of our faithful brother to Malaga
and Granada, to preach Christ to those who, in those
towns, were sitting in darkness and in the shadow of
death; they have seen "the great light."

Before undertaking this dangerous mission, Matamoros understood well the immense difficulties that
lay in his path, and that bonds and imprisonments
awaited him; but he had counted the cost, and, like
Paul, had been enabled to say, "None of these things
move me, neither count I my life dear unto myself,
so that I might finish my course with joy, and the
ministry which I have received of the Lord Jesus, to
testify the gospel of the grace of God."

Malaga, his native town, was the place in which
he commenced his loving and successful labours.. In
one of his early letters to me he gives an account of
his first proceedings in the following terms :—"From
the moment I dedicated myself to the holy cause of
the gospel, I understood, beloved brother, that its
propagation ought not to be an isolated attempt, nor
reduced simply to the circulation of books, many of
which I have seen thrown into the fire, or used for
purposes completely different to those for which
they were intended; indeed, I observed that not more
than one in every thousand accomplished the end
in view; while I desired, on the contrary, that one
should be the means of enlightening at least a hundred
persons.

"As soon as I arrived at Malaga, and being still
in the army, I devoted myself to convincing my fellow-

countrymen, by discussing with them, and by comparing
and drawing deductions from the Word of God; but
principally among those persons in whom I had most
confidence. As soon as I had succeeded in convincing
them, I invited them to unite with the true church
of the Lord Jesus Christ; and when they decided
on so doing, I showed them the importance of writing
a letter, in which they expressed clearly and explicitly
their views, and these letters were signed and dated
in due order; by this plan we guarded against betrayal,
and interested them in the work, and knew with
more certainty the faith and conviction of the writer
of the document. Having agreed with Señor Ruet,
I directed them to write to him, so as to prevent a
surprise; and he in his turn answered them and encouraged them in further inquiries, and in deeper study of
the Word; sustained their faith; and his letters, being
read by many, produced a good effect, and gave excellent results.

"The protests thus obtained at Malaga were the
first commenced in Spain. In a short time, dear
brother, they became so numerous, that the instruction
of all was a task infinitely superior to my ability; nor
could I keep alive the faith of such a number of
people; so I determined to give an entirely new
organization to my labours. I formed a committee
from among the most active, best instructed, and most
evangelical of the believers, for the purpose of directing
and propagating our work on a more solid basis, and
for producing the most consoling and blessed results.
The total number of brethren were divided into as
many congregations as our committee was composed of

members, and these semi-missionaries were entrusted
with the instruction of these meetings. By this means
I succeeded in making our work go forward with renewed activity, and augmented the number of meetings
for edification. In a word, at every step we found
ourselves approximating more closely to the sacred
end to which the blessed cause of the Lord ought to
bring us.

"When I received some packages of books, I no
longer let them be given away at random, nor did I
allow them to be thrown in at the doors of some
houses, as ·had been done elsewhere, neither did I
place them in the hands of uncertain individuals;
but I handed them over to· the leaders, and as they
knew the exact state of the church and its wants, the
books were divided into as many parts as there were
leaders, and each member took that proportion which
he required for his congregation. The leaders, knowing
most accurately the wants of their respective congregations, distributed the books with the greatest prudence,
and thus in two or three days I saw a considerable
number put into circulation, all of which seemed to be
thankfully received. Never, beloved brother, have I
had too many books; on the contrary, I have often had
reiterated peremptory demands, and have not been able
to meet all the wants.

"It will be easy for you to see that this system
given to our work ought to give satisfactory results,
and so it proved. Speedily the leaders of the committee found themselves insufficient to carry on the
work of preaching; speedily the congregations were
firm in faith and well instructed, to such an extent,

indeed, that it would have filled you with joy to have witnessed those meetings for simple Christian edifica-cation.

"These meetings were commenced by fervent prayer for the presence of the Holy Spirit, and were concluded by thanksgiving, because there was daily manifested a visible improvement in them. I, poor in talent and oratory, and with but little instruction, devoted myself to preaching, which I did two or three times a week, and which did not hinder the members of the com-mittee from going forward with the separate classes, which was always desirable, as our meeting in large numbers was dangerous. One of these meetings was witnessed by Dr. and Mrs. Tregelles, at which there were about ninety-seven present, and among them my dear mother. . . . .

"All the members of our churches are in admirable contact, and know each other well; and immediately when one is unwell, a committee of three attend by turns at the house of the sufferer, visiting him at least once every day, and see after the wants of his family; and to the sick person no care is lacking so that he may be supplied, the expenses being paid out of the general fund of the church for this end; so that the spirit of fraternity is indeed a truth."

From Malaga, Matamoros proceeded to Seville, Granada, Barcelona, Jaen, and various towns of the province of Andalusia. In Granada particularly his labours were much blessed, and a large, numerous, and influential body of believers was gathered there. At Barcelona, our brother met again Dr. and Mrs. Tregelles, in the month of September, 1860.

Here it is necessary for me to say, that feeling that my knowledge of Spanish was a talent committed to me by God for which I was responsible, I felt desirous of employing it to his glory, and was impelled one afternoon to kneel down, and pray that He would allow me to use it for the good of Spain. The prayer was short, but it was heard, and was speedily answered. This was at my house at Abergavenny, in Monmouthshire.

In a conversation Mrs. Tregelles had with Matamoros, she mentioned my name to him, and recommended his writing to me, which he did in the month of September, 1860. In answer to this letter, I encouraged him to continue in his self-denying and glorious work, and promised him my sympathy, prayers, and support in every way. The second letter I received from him was from the prison at Barcelona, as follows:—

"*Prison, Barcelona, October 17th*, 1860.

"Respected and very dear brother in Jesus Christ,

"I have received with sincerest joy your kind letter of the 9th, which afforded me infinite comfort in this house of misfortune. The same day on which you were so good as to write to me—the 9th instant—at seven o'clock in the morning I was arrested for the single crime of being a Christian, and loving my fellow men so well as to desire that they also should know the Lord Jesus, by whom alone they can be saved. A charge laid against me in Granada induced the civil governor of that city to send a telegraphic order to the governor of this place for my arrest, and also for the minute examination of my house, etc. After a most rigorous and tyrannical search, there was found in my possession a packet of letters and papers from several places in Spain, and certain other documents which compromised me to a considerable degree. I was brought to this prison, and kept for eight days in a sad and terrible solitary confinement. After two examinations before the whole tribunal, I was relieved from my solitude, that is to say, I am now confined with criminals! I gave my answers without confessing anything but my own faith—so as not to involve others; that faith which shall save me when the one Supreme Judge shall sit upon his throne.

"At this stage of my examination a singular episode occurred—the magistrates believed that I should deny my faith, and that the sight of the enemies of Christ and my tyrants would overwhelm me, but they were mistaken. The questions and answers were as follow:—*Question.* 'Do you profess the Catholic Apostolic Roman faith; and if not, what religion do you profess?' *Answer.* 'My religion is that of Jesus Christ; my rule of faith is the Word of God, or Holy Bible, which, without a word altered, curtailed, or added, is the basis of my belief; and in this I am confirmed by the last few sentences of the Apocalypse, and the many distinct charges of the Apostles in their Epistles. The Roman Catholic and Apostolic Church not being based upon these principles, I do not believe in her dogmas, still less do I obey her in practice.' The tribunal appeared astonished at these words, and the judge said to me, 'Do you know what you are saying?' 'Yes, sir,' I replied in a firm voice, 'I cannot deny it; I have put my hand to the plough, and I dare not look back.'　The judge was silent, and the tribunal rose.

"Nothing, dear brother, alarms me for myself, but I do grieve over the arrests which have been made, both before and since mine took place, in various parts of Andalusia.　Oh! they will injure worthy Christian people, honoured fathers and virtuous sons!　Alas! this oversets my tranquillity of mind, and I shall not recover it for many days!　And again, my dear old mother, with my two little brothers, are left alone in this strange town.　Thus my position is very trying; I suffer, yes, I suffer much!

"Our mission, my dear friend, is not, and has not been, to separate believers from the Church of Rome; it has been to bring souls out of the Roman darkness, and from Atheism or indifference to the knowledge of Christ; to gather together intelligent and evangelical congregations; in a word, to form churches worthy of God and of the world.　As you will easily imagine, my spirit is not at rest, and I cannot to-day write you at length upon these topics; but I promise to do so shortly, and give you explicit details.

"You may do much for Catalonia; it requires and promises more than any other part of Spain.

"Although my imprisonment threatens to be a long one, that is, of some months' duration, yet I can labour here also, for the brethren visit me; and from this spot I can give you full information.　The work in Barcelona has not suffered in the slightest degree, for all depends upon me, and I would sooner die than cause any one to suffer.　In Andalusia they have received a fearful blow; but time will obliterate their panic, and all will go on as before. The seed sown has been abundant and good, and the enmity of Christ's foes is impotent. God is on our side.

"Later, I hope to send you the rules of our organi zation, but the basis of our existence is the Word of God—the Holy Bible.

"Adieu, dear brother. I would gladly be free to do all that you would wish; but, alas! in Spain, it is a crime to love the gospel! I trust you will soon write to me, you will easily believe that now, more than ever, your letters will be a comfort to me in my present sorrowful and trying position. Counsel and consolation from Christian friends is a necessary of life to me now!

"God be with you, dear friend,
"Your brother in Jesus Christ,
(Signed) "M. M."

CHAPTER III.

COMMUNICATIONS FROM BARCELONA.

ON the receipt of the last interesting letter, and feeling deeply for our brother in bonds, I wrote to him again to solace and comfort him, laying his case before the Lord in prayer frequently, and asking for especial wisdom and guidance. I watched anxiously, as may be supposed, for an answer, and received, in the beginning of November, the following reply:—

"*Prison, Barcelona, November 8th,* 1860.

"RESPECTED AND MOST DEAR BROTHER IN THE LORD JESUS CHRIST, OUR HOPE AND CONFIDENCE,

" My poor pen cannot describe to you the exceeding joy and gratitude which I felt on the receipt of your most kind and Christian letter. I can only say that it was a real comfort to me in my bitter trial.

" The Spanish clergy are thoroughly alarmed; the press, which is their creature, labours to aggravate the evils of our position—inquisitorial influences are pitilessly working against us, both in secret and in public. May God forgive them all for the evil they would do, and bring them into the path that leads to life!

Has the English press done anything for us? It is most desirable that it should do so; for that portion of the Spanish press which is favourable to us dares not speak out, and that portion which is against us is doing us much injury, by giving an utterly false colour to our holy cause.

"I purpose, dear friend, when I am brought before the superior tribunal, protesting before them and before the Spanish public against the injustice and cruelty with which they treat us, for the sole crime of being Christians. If I am condemned, I will protest, by the press of every country in Europe, against the injustice that punishes for the sole sin of professing Christianity. The world should know that the Inquisition still rules in Spain; the world should know that it is a crime in this land to love the gospel; the world should know that if the fires of the stake have been extinguished, the tortures of the galleys still exist. This protest I will send to you, that you may translate and publish it. It is no foolish pride that induces me to do this; I believe it is an act of Christian faith. I love the Lord Christ, and will confess his name; and will protest against the Church of Rome, which so unjustly assumes it.

"The Council of Granada summons me to appear there. I shall be forced to travel 200 leagues (about 700 miles) on foot, bound in a gang of criminals, and confounded in their disgrace in every town and village through which we shall pass, where my offence will not be known. My health is very delicate, and this journey and the cold, and the wretched prisons of the smaller villages on our road, will be all dangerous to me. Only by paying my own passage, and that of the two men who escort me, should I be permitted to make the journey by sea: of course this expense is quite beyond my power. Neither will I ask any fresh sacrifice from our friends in France. My family is in much distress on this account; in truth, my position is trying. My faith does not and will not waver, but I suffer physically.

"A thousand, thousand thanks to you for the love and favour which you express towards me in your letter. I do not deserve it, but I am grateful for your noble and Christian feeling; also I thank you for the succour you are sending to my family. God will repay you. He is blessing me with much quietness of mind on this account.

"I hope you will soon write to me. I can receive but one more letter from you at Barcelona. My family remains here. Pray to God for us, dear brother, as I pray for you.

"Ever believe in the love and gratitude of your brother in Christ, "M. MATAMOROS."

On learning by the last letter the summons of the Granada tribunal, and hearing of the very delicate state of Matamoros' health—brought on by his great exertions in preaching, and labouring for the good of souls—I feared that if he made this long journey on foot, and in the manner mentioned in his letter, his health would give way, and that he would never reach Granada alive. So I determined at once to send him what money I had by me at the time, and which I forwarded, amounting to £15. And here let me give an account of God's faithfulness in behalf of those that endeavour to serve Him.

The account of the imprisonment of a Spaniard at Barcelona appeared, I believe, in a London paper. My name was connected in some way with it. A lady residing there read the account, and immediately sent me a sum of money in aid of the prisoner. The amount which she sent me was precisely that which I had sent to Matamoros, and this without the least communication between her and myself. Indeed, no one but the God who had enabled me to send the money, and who had now returned it to me, knew of the matter. I felt deeply humbled, and very grateful to the loving Father who had thus ordered the steps of His children, and heartily set my seal to the words, "Doubtless there is a God that judgeth in the earth."

The following letter came at this time:—

"*Prison, Barcelona, November 27th*, 1860.

"RESPECTED AND VERY DEAR BROTHER IN OUR BELOVED REDEEMER JESUS CHRIST, THE ONLY MEDIATOR BETWEEN GOD AND MEN,

"I have just received your comforting and Christian letter of the 17th November, and with it an order for £15. Thanks! a thousand thanks, dear brother, to you and to your friends, for this good deed—thanks from the bottom of my heart, which my pen cannot express. But you and the lovers of the gospel, the true children of the Church of Christ who have joined you, will be able to appreciate the depth of my gratitude by the Christian joy you have experienced in succouring a brother in bonds for Christ's sake, a brother whose only offence and only crime has been loving and circulating the Word of God. . . . . .

"Dear brother, it appears that my tyrants seek to make my captivity daily more irksome, striving with each other for the pleasure of giving me pain. I have been examined *a third time*, and have been informed that I must obey the summons of the tribunal of Granada; but that besides this, the tribunal of Barcelona had determined to bring another action against me to discover and prove what I have done and attempted for the circulation of the gospel in Catalonia. So not only is one tribunal acting against me, but two—or rather three—those of Granada, Barcelona, and Malaga. The tribunal of Granada is so anxious for my appearance there, that in the space of a very few days I have been several times summoned, and my papers called for also. They need not be in haste—I am ready. My poor mother has petitioned the government to delay my journey, in consideration of the feeble state of my health; and some of the newspapers have supported this demand of hers. Will the governor grant it? We shall see; and I will let you know the result. My poor mother is suffering martyrdom. Her repeated anxieties have brought on a serious attack of illness; and she has been confined to bed for several days.

"I cannot recall without a shudder the sorrowful scene that occurred the day of my arrest. When my dearly-beloved and most unhappy mother saw me seized, she fell fainting and senseless to the ground; and my little brothers burst into tears and loud cries, for in their innocent and comfortless sorrow they believed that she was dead. I attempted to go to her assistance, and was not permitted. Cruelty! I shall ever remember that terrible moment with anguish. From that time her health has been so feeble that I am deeply anxious about her and on her account. I really dread the day of my departure. God's will be done.

"Spain is the grave of many martyrs, the victims of the Church of Rome. In her religious intolerance she has only changed in the external forms for the last two hundred years. The Church of Rome hates light and knowledge, and punishes us because we have learnt to know Christ. The Church of Rome despises the Word of God, and imprisons us because we love and respect it and hold it in our hearts as a sacred and saving possession. Let us take comfort, however, for we see that the rigour of Papal tyranny is impotent against us, and their satanic wiles are useless. Our imprisonment was needful, and has done much service to our holy work. All Spain knows that we suffer for Christ's sake; and so all may see, evidently, how far removed is the practice of the Roman Church from the precepts of God's holy Word. But whatever she may attempt against us now is already too late. The Word of God is in the hands of thousands of Spaniards, and the study of it has raised up hundreds of decided Christians, willing and rejoicing to spread the good news, and despising the gainsaying and the persecution of men, ready to take up the cross and follow Christ. So, though tyranny does not falter, neither shall our holy work. But tyranny is the work of man, therefore it

must cease. Our work is of God, and therefore ultimately it shall gloriously triumph.

"For myself, I am perfectly tranquil. Every
fresh suffering that my poor weak body endures,
every fresh delay which is interposed between me and
the day of my release, is a fresh motive to increase my
joy and confirm my faith. I glory in tribulations!
My imprisonment is a trial to the body, but not to the
soul. The slayers of the body are weak and miserable
enemies to the soul of a Christian. It can even
rejoice in its sufferings for Christ's sake.

"I cannot describe to you, dear brother, the happiness that I have felt since I received your letter,
and learnt from it that your noble fellow-countrymen
had interested themselves in my fate. Oh, give them
the assurance of my deep gratitude. How can I
repay so many favours, so much Christian love?
The reward is so great that I could never give it, but
God will repay it tenfold; and posterity will not fail to
keep a sacred niche in history for the sons of noble
and powerful Albion, who are ever ready to support the
good cause, and to defend the weak and the afflicted.

"May God enlighten you, dear brothers in Christ,
—may He take you under his special protection!
May He recompense, as He sees fit, your noble deeds!

"I have confessed Christ before the tribunals. I
do not, and shall never, repent of this. As I have
done at Barcelona I purpose doing at Granada. I
will confess Christ before the weak as before the
strong; before my brethren as before my murderers.
I shall suffer—and what then? Did not Christ suffer
for us miserable sinners? Did He not lay down his

life for our sins? Did he not redeem us by his death?
What are my little trials to be compared to the blessing that his words and his example are to me? Oh,
nothing! less than nothing! I knew well, when I
undertook my evangelical labours, that I was in the
midst of wolves. I knew the thorns and thistles that
would be under my feet, but I never forgot the words
of the Saviour, 'He that taketh not his cross and fol-
loweth after Me, is not worthy of Me.'

"Let us pray to our great Master, that He would
pardon our enemies and prosecutors. Let us pray
with sincere and humble faith that He would bring
them to His heavenly fold—that He would enlighten
and preserve them. I feel no anger against them.
I understand the motive of their inhuman cruelty, and
I heartily pity them for their separation from Christ.

" Farewell, dear brother; I do not yet know when
I shall leave this place. The journey to Granada is
indispensable; but the state of my health may occasion some delay. But you shall hear of my movements if possible.

" Your brother in the Lord Jesus Christ,
" MANUEL MATAMOROS."

Seeing that the money had been received in due
time, I felt a pleasure in praying much to the Lord
that He would continue to guide all things for the
best, and for His own glory, and for the advancement
of His truth in Spain. Before Matamoros left Barcelona, the intelligence having reached that city of the
sympathy of British Christians, a letter was forwarded
by him as follows, with forty signatures appended—

"*Barcelona, December* 26*th,* 1860.

" RESPECTED BROTHER IN THE LORD,

" We desire to use but few words in the expression of our deep gratitude towards your Christian fellow-countrymen, for their noble and generous conduct towards our brethren in Christ, who suffer persecution for their faith in this country, through the intolerance of our government and the influence of the Romish priesthood. We, the undersigned, have now the pleasure of declaring that we do not belong, nor will we ever belong again, to the Church of Rome, whose dogmas we consider to be opposed to the Word of God, which is our rule of faith now ; nor do we acknowledge any other religion to be true than that of Jesus Christ and his apostles. Having made the above declaration, you will understand, dear brother, how grateful we feel for the active measures taken by the distinguished deputation which waited on Lord John Russell, not only because of the good it will do to our brethren, but because of the incalculable benefit which will result to the Lord's work here. We have heard, also, of the generous assistance which Messrs. Newton, Tregelles, and Peddie have, with yourself and others, rendered to our dear brother, Don M. Matamoros, whom we love as he deserves, and for which we hasten to express our heartfelt gratitude. We feel confident that we express the sentiments of many Spaniards, and therefore we have not hesitated an instant in sending you not only our own thanks but also those of many who are like-minded with ourselves.

" We trust you will not be surprised at not seeing our addresses given, because of the fatal persecutions to which we are exposed in this unfortunate country. To you and all Englishmen who are interested in the Lord's work, we offer our sincere Christian love, sympathy, and affection, and are your brothers in the Lord Jesus." ·

[Here follow forty signatures.]

All having been prepared by God for our brother's voyage, he set sail on the 26th December, 1860, and I received a letter communicating the fact to me, as follows:—

"*National Prison, Barcelona, December 26th*, 1860.

"BELOVED BROTHER, MR. GREENE,

"In two hours from now I start for Granada in the steamboat as far as Malaga.

"I have just been visited by a body of the brethren, who have given me the accompanying memorial to forward to you. They had previously read the letters you wrote to me, which produced enthusiastic joy, and called forth the enclosed document, which, as you will perceive, is a most important one. It would be well to publish it, suppressing the names, the insertion of which would be quite sufficient to insure the immediate imprisonment of all concerned. The reason there is not double the number of signatures is because they wish to take advantage of my presence here to forward it. The enthusiasm is intense and indescribable. They have written to Malaga on the same subject, and I believe that they will also write to you.

"I shall have to be three days in prison at Alicante. My expenses will be greater than I expected, but there is no help for that now. I know that my friends are awaiting me on the pier, and 'will accompany me to the ship,' to bid me farewell. The Lord reward their love. What think you of the love of these brethren? I will send you my address when I arrive at Granada, and if possible will write to you from Alicante. I am writing to-day to A——, and yesterday I wrote to Dr. Tregelles. Farewell, dear brother; a thousand kind regards to your dear family. Adieu! may His Holy Spirit be with you.

"M. MATAMOROS."

About this time a valuable letter appeared, which, as it gave many interesting statements to the public concerning the imprisonments made in Spain, I have thought well to introduce here. It is as follows:—

"The following is a brief statement of facts connected with the still continuing persecution in Spain. It originated thus: A young man of about twenty years of age, named N. A——, belonging to a respectable family at Granada, was student at an ecclesiastical seminary, presided over by the archbishop of that province. Having made rapid progress in his studies, he became one of the favourite scholars of the rector, and a *protégé* of the archbishop. A friend presented A—— with a New Testament and two controversial works. He was reprimanded and kept in close confinement for a week; but his convictions remaining unchanged, it was resolved that he should be arrested. His Protestant friends having heard of this, advised him to escape to Gibraltar. He did so, and is now a refugee in England.

" José Alhama, a hatter at Granada, a man of high Christian character, and greatly respected by all, was suspected of having aided the flight of A——; he was suddenly arrested, his house searched, and himself carried off to a dungeon, his wife and family being wholly unprovided for. Among the letters found in Alhama's house were some from Manuel Matamoros, from Barcelona. A telegram was sent to that town for his arrest. At midnight, on the 6th of February, four gensdarmes with their sergeant and a constable entered the house of Alhama; his aged mother admitted them; they demanded all the keys to search the house. His wife was in bed, ill from premature confinement, brought on by distress at her husband's sufferings. They obliged her to rise, and searched the mattresses, boxes, trunks, beds, clothes, pockets; for two hours the savage search continued; nothing, however, was found to incriminate the family, but the terror was too great for Alhama's wife, and she fell down in an epileptic fit.

"Very recently eighteen persons have been arrested in Malaga; three out of one family, the father, mother, and eldest son, five little children being left wholly unprovided for. They were arrested at dead of night, and were carried off to a dungeon, where they still remain. More arrests have also taken place at Seville, and the head of one of the best public schools in that city is now in prison."

CHAPTER IV.

IMPRISONMENT AT GRANADA.

THE last letter left Matamoros on board the steamer at Barcelona, accompanied by his guards; the sympathy of the crowd on the quay showed how much they admired him, and the love they bore to the cause for which he was suffering.

Everything went on smoothly on board the steamer, and the voyage was performed most pleasantly, thanks to a merciful God, whose loving arm had been stretched out over His faithful servant. He arrived at Malaga in due course, as will be seen by the following extracts from his letter of January 8th, 1861:—

"I left Barcelona on the 26th, and reached Malaga on the 30th of December, where I was received by a considerable number of brethren, who came on board the steamer to see me. The same evening, when I was starting for Granada, numbers of friends and brethren accompanied me to the diligence, in which Sir Robert Peel was also a passenger. I arrived at Granada on the 1st of January, and on appearing before the tribunal was ordered into solitary confinement, and was accordingly taken to a different prison from that of our dear brother Alhama.

"This scandalous, tyrannical, and arbitrary action coming to the ears of Sir Robert Peel, he immediately presented himself with truly admirable energy before the authorities, and demanded that I should be released from this position, and also, that he, with Lady E. Peel and Lady J. Hay, should be permitted to visit me. The judge gave him a written order to visit me, but doubtless the tribunal were unwilling that I should receive visitors of such high rank in a filthy, damp, and dark apartment, where the only bed was a small mattress spread upon the floor. When removed, I had the honour of receiving a visit from these personages. We spoke very plainly together; they went all over the prison; they saw the cell where I was first confined, and where, thanks to them, I remained only two days. They also saw the cell where Alhama was confined for twenty-two days, the sight of which called forth an energetic protest from these good people, who could not comprehend why so much tyranny was exercised against a person for preaching the gospel, which is the duty of every good Christian. Lady Emily Peel and Lady Jane Hay went through the female ward, accompanied by the governor's wife, and comforted the unfortunate women by speaking kindly, and edifying them by wholesome Christian counsel.

"They so delighted these poor folks that they begged for another visit the day following. They left Granada, assuring me of their wish to return to London, so that Sir Robert might speak about this matter in Parlia-

ment. . . . . The spirit of the Barcelona and
Malaga churches is excellent, as is also that of
Granada, in spite of the terror the clergy have in-
spired.

"Let us go onward and upwards. It is necessary
to make use of this precious present time, and be
firmly assured that both Alhama and myself will stand
out boldly to the last. We know that Spain and
Europe have their eyes upon us, and we would prefer
to die in bonds sooner than appear to falter. Our
deep love for the cause of our divine Redeemer urges
us onward; what avails the anger of our tyrants, what
their threats? Nothing, nothing; we glory in our
sufferings. Alas! dear friend, how I miss the visits
of my mother and my family. They are ever before
my mind. I am getting my food from the hotel, but
it is much dearer than at Barcelona, and when I had
it from home I could economize greatly. The heavy
expenses of myself and guards from Barcelona to
Granada, and their pay back, has been double what I
expected, £24, and I am fretting about this. But
farewell, dear friend, I shall expect a long letter from
you to comfort me."

Thus far our dear sufferer has got on his thorny
way; but how bright will be his crown, and how the
good hand of his God has been upon him hitherto, is
fully manifest to those who have watched the movings
of the Divine hand in his behalf.

From Barcelona, Matamoros had written a letter to
A——, now in this country, an extract from which I
give as follows :—

" National Prison, Barcelona, December 13th, 1860.

" DEAREST BROTHER IN THE LORD,

"You have done well in writing to me. My thoughts have been constantly fixed on you since I left Granada. I have not forgotten you for a moment. I have prayed constantly to the Lord for your well-being, for the steadfastness of your faith, and for upholding you in every Christian grace. . . . . . .

" God will not forsake us; His Holy Spirit is constantly with us. In our poor country, tyrants rejoice in our sufferings; all their energy, all their desires, all their highest aims are to augment the fetters which bind down our liberties and blight our hopes. They labour, agitate, and hasten to present to us, with inquisitorial cleverness, horrible scenes, to annihilate us. But, unfortunate people, they do not understand that we are peaceful, satisfied, and proud of our lot.

"Rejoice, brother, for since the day of my imprisonment the enthusiasm in Malaga has increased, as in my letters I have exhorted them not to be weary. At first their hearts sank at the rigour of the tyrants; but since, they have understood that they must go forward with a double speed, and they have done so. Thirty-seven new converts have been added to the church, and the spirit of grace is every day more comforting and more deeply rooted in the hearts of that Christian band. Many prayers ascend daily for the deliverance of our church, now so fiercely persecuted by these enemies of Christ. They are bringing an action against us in Malaga at the present time, and notwithstanding, this only serves to increase our numbers, and to inspire us with new courage.

"Yes, dear brother, my physical forces are sinking rapidly; my weak flesh fails me, and the thread of life appears nearly spun out. The dampness of these prisons is killing me; but every step I take towards the tomb, every grain of sand that falls through life's glass, is a powerful, yes, an indestructible force, which strengthens my faith and my joy, and enables me to anticipate my last hour with rejoicing, and with a peace I was a perfect stranger to, until I found Christ.

"Oh! how I praise the supreme Creator for this benefit of his inexhaustible love. I have always felt an indestructible love and fear to the Lord before and since my imprisonment, and if it could serve in the least to forward our holy cause, I beseech the Almighty that He would prolong it to the end of my days. I beg you also will pray for this. Do, for I do not desire the well-being of my body, which is destined to death, and my greatest consolation would be to know that my sufferings had been beneficial to humanity. What signifies one day more or less here below? What signifies one more pang? Nothing, when it is for the greatest, for the only holy cause.

"Your letter gave me great comfort. I rejoice to see the just tribute which English Christians have rendered to your virtues and those of Alhama. But I deserve it not, and all that you say with reference to myself only makes me ashamed. I do not deserve such honour as these noble brethren have conferred upon me. I have done only what it was my duty to do. During the last fortnight there have occurred here things worthy of special mention. The Society of St. Vincent de Paul has exhausted every possible means to induce me to retract my declaration. The chaplain of that establishment, the notary in my case, and the president of that inquisitorial institution, have offered me their most cordial support for the recovery of my liberty if I will retract my declaration, and I have complained to the governor of their barbarous abuses. I rejected their propositions with contempt. I have told them plainly that they were insulting me, and that if they repeated their unworthy act I should feel obliged to refuse to admit them into my dungeon.

"I also sent a communication to the papers, which they have not inserted. You can hardly imagine with what sagacity and skill they have made these proposals to me. They were careful not to wound my delicacy, and made their offers hypothetically; but I, understanding their object, rose, and answered them in strong and suitable language, and retired without even taking leave. They began by reminding me of the orphanhood of my family, the state of my health, my resources, and the sorrowful future that lay before me. 'I am only sorry on account of my family,' I told them. 'The rest, gentlemen, is of so little consequence, that I would lay down not one life alone for the benefit of the gospel cause, but a thousand, if I had them.' They answered me with sagacity, and made the proposition to which I replied as I stated above.

"In spite of the state of my health, I must go shortly to Granada. I am only awaiting a letter from Mr. Greene, and from thence I shall write to him at length, giving him every intelligence.

D

"I must remain here no longer. I am injuring the
orethren imprisoned at Malaga, and above all, Alhama
and I am determined to go, but I do not think my
health will improve.

" I am waiting to be called before the superior tribunal with anxiety. I shall present myself before
them as the law permits, and shall defend myself
energetically. I desire to prove to them why I have
cast away tradition, the only support of the Church of
Rome. I desire to prove to them that my conduct is
worthy of a true Christian, and I will send you my
defence, which I shall write from Granada; and yet,
dear A———, I am sorry to leave this place. My room
is a little focus of gospel light. I have three converts
among the prisoners, whose protests I hold, and who
will, I trust, be virtuous Christians.

"Oh, how much an energetic, evangelic propaganda
is needed in this house of crime! The chaplain of the
prison is satisfied with celebrating the sacrilegious and
unbloody sacrifice of the mass. God rejoices in the
conversion of the most miserable. Our Lord came not
to save the righteous, but sinners; and in these prisons
his holy word should be preached with double fervour.

"Be diligent, dear brother; lay up a store of Bible
knowledge; and this, illustrated by your practice, may
yet prove a blessing to Spain. Write to me, for
though I may not be here, your letters will reach me.
May God be with you—may His Holy Spirit guide
you! I am tranquil, and strong in the Spirit. I will
never yield. Now and ever I will dedicate my life
and all my energy to the work of the Lord. I will
take no rest. You know me, and you know I will do

what I say. Let us be worthy of the blessed cause to which we have dedicated ourselves; let our one aim be the good of mankind, and the accomplishment of it the only recompense to which we aspire.

"Give, in my name, my most humble remembrances to Mr. G—— and Mrs. T——. I cannot tell you, dear brother, how I have cried over Mr. G——'s last letter. I have read it, perhaps sixty times—it comforts, and does not weary me. I am waiting for letters from the said gentleman, and Mrs. T——. I am only detained from starting by waiting for letters from them.

"Adieu, dear brother. Yours most affectionately,
"MANUEL MATAMOROS.
"To N. A——.

The last letter shows the deep and zealous spirit that animates this earnest disciple of Christ, and also how bonds are ever for the furtherance of the gospel, and for the deepening of His spirit in the regenerate.

The following letter from the brethren comprising the Reformed Church at Malaga, was forwarded at this time to Dr. Tregelles, of Plymouth, and is addressed to the followers of Jesus Christ in this country:—

"REVERED BRETHREN IN THE LORD,—
"Our hearts are filled with joy and well-deserved and fraternal gratitude; and we desire to express to you something of the holy Christian happiness which we have felt on hearing of the noble and generous

protection which you have extended to our dear brother, Don M. Matamoros, now a prisoner for the sake of the Divine Redeemer, the only Intercessor and Mediator with God.

"The holiest spiritual bonds unite us to this dear brother. Seconding the noble efforts of that worthy minister, Don F. Ruet, he formed in this town a church, whose members do not, and will not, recognize as chief or head of the same any but the Redeemer, the Lord Jesus Christ; nor will take as a rule of faith any other than the Word of God—the Holy Bible.

"The religion of Jesus Christ and of his apostles is that which we follow; we believe it to be alone true, and consequently we do not recognize the authority of the Church of Rome, but rather hold her to be the greatest foe to Holy Scripture.

"That we have found the fountain of the water of life, we owe to Don M. Matamoros. His constant and evangelical instructions have given to this little hidden church much of the Scriptural knowledge that it possesses, and by his energy and zeal so considerable a number of names has been enrolled in its ranks.

"Dr. Tregelles can give you an idea of our state, our hopes, and expectations. The noble attitude of the generous deputation which appeared in behalf of our suffering brethren, and the sacrifices which you have made for the benefit of Don M. Matamoros and Alhama, have determined us to address these few words to you, as a public manifestation of our gratitude. United with our whole hearts and by the bonds of an unwavering faith to the church of Jesus Christ, we cannot but protest against the devices and snares of the Church of Rome, and we witness with deepest sorrow, the sufferings of her victims, in this miserable land, while yet we cannot but rejoice to find that our English brethren unite with us in their sympathy.

" We trust that you will give publicity to this manifestation of our gratitude; but we beg that you will not publish our names, as a severe and certain persecution would be the result.

" We remain, your Brothers and Sisters,

- in the Lord Jesus."

(Here follow 130 signatures.)

And on January 19th, 1861, Alhama wrote to Don N. A—— as follows:—

" *Prison, Granada.*

"Dear N——, my beloved Brother in the Lord,

" With pleasure I take up my pen, though I have only sorrowful tidings to give you of the troubles that I endure; I am not allowed now to hear from you so often as I wish. I know how much you must have sympathised with me, for I know how much you love me. Yes, dear N——, I suffer very, very deeply. You will imagine all, if I tell you a little. If I tell you that my wife is now constantly recommended to obtain a divorce, because I am, as they term it, a Jew. Don R. C—— asked her if she was not ashamed to

have a husband who was a thief—a thief of men's
belief? People spit at me, and at my children in the
street. In short, wherever they go they are assailed
with insults and opprobrium from the superstitious
and priest-led part of the population. These priests,
who should be called ministers of Satan rather than of
Christ, alas! how can they be His priests, whose
last words were a prayer for the pardon of His
murderers, when they deprive innocent children of
their father, a wife of her husband, and a venerable
mother of her son, who was her blessing and her
support.

"Oh, my poor children! your father will probably
die the death of a felon and a galley-slave, but he
will die confessing his faith in the Lord Jesus Christ,
and scorning all vain traditions and the false teaching
of the imposter, King Pope. This will only add to
your misfortunes, for in this land no asylum will be
open to you. But we will put our trust in God, God
the refuge of the defenceless, the comforter of the
afflicted, and He will never forsake you; and your
enemies cannot take away your heavenly Father as
they are killing your earthly one.

"N——, the finger of God points to thee to be the
protector of my innocent orphans. You know, had
the case been reversed, I would gladly have succoured
yours. My poor mother will need nothing. At her
great age it is impossible that she can long survive
my misfortune. And my poor wife, who was only
just convalescent when I was arrested, has suffered
so severely since, that she is threatened with consump-
tion, and her life is endangered.

"I fear my letter will grieve you. I shall be sorry indeed for this, but I know you love me, and will allow me to unbosom all my griefs to you. R—— told me that you had written to him, and that you regretted deeply having been the cause of my misfortune. No, dear friend, be at peace; my family loves you as ever, and to me you are what you have always been.

"On the first of this month I had the pleasure of embracing our brother Matamoros. He arrived here in very delicate health, but, thank God, is getting better, although we are enduring much trouble, partly on account of our trial, of which we have very bad news daily. When Matamoros was first examined, the prosecutor told him that he would probably be condemned to ten or twelve years at the galleys. To-day the attorney has confirmed this, telling us that our case comes under the 125th article of the penal code.

"It is also unfortunate for us that the alcaide (or governor) of this prison is son of the housekeeper of the Cordovese priest, and this man is influencing the alcaide much against us, and therefore we are suffering from many annoyances. Our families and friends are not allowed to visit us, and the alcaide has informed the governor that he felt this step necessary, because we were conspiring with the Protestants for the subversion of religion. The wife of the alcaide said to me plainly, that she could not conceive why we were not confined in the courts (*patios*), for people accused of such crimes as ours might properly be with the worst convicts, and should not be allowed to com-

municate with anybody. Pray that God may forgive
them all as I do.

"They persecute us even in our dungeons, and we
must pray for them from thence. Is not this what the
gospel teaches us? Oh how good and pleasant a thing
it is to know the Word of God, which teaches us to
suffer with patience all that is hardest in our undeserved captivity.

"Never will I draw back from the holy work in
which I am engaged, nor will I utter one sigh of
regret, for God strengthens me. The Holy Spirit
enlightens me, and St. Paul sets me an example of
resignation in tribulation; so all the fury and cruelty
of these modern Diocletians shall be unavailing to
silence us. We will preach the Word of God in our
chains, as though we dwelt in palaces. In spite of our
rulers, and in their very presence, we confess the
truths of the gospel.

"Every time that I have been brought before the
tribunals, I have declared that my only crime has
been that I have striven to be a follower of Jesus
Christ and not of the Pope; and that the only result
of their persecuting us would be to add some fresh
names to the Christian martyrology. In truth, the
work in Spain has never excited so much attention
and interest as it does now. Ten years of preaching
would not have advanced our labour so much as our
imprisonment and trial are doing. All are asking,
'What is this new Protestant doctrine?' and they seek
after our books from simple curiosity; and when they
have read them, they cannot but condemn the cruelty

of the clergy, and confess that we teach the true religion of the Son of God.

"In Spain, Christianity will date a new era from our trial. The clergy have perceived this, though something too late, and therefore they are now doing everything in their power to represent us to the people as Jews. The Archbishop has issued a pastoral of thirty-eight pages in quarto, which treats only of the Protestants.

"Señor P—— has been at the expense of a 'Novena' to St. Joseph, and every evening sermons have been preached, and prayers made to the saint to intercede with God that we may be brought back into the fold of the Romish church. This pastoral contains confessions which the clergy have never before made. How can I send it to you? It is a powerful assistance to our propaganda. Our brothers are all firm. Daily the church grows both in members and in faith.

"At —— no arrests have yet been made. Evidently the weight of the trouble is resting upon Matamoros and myself. We put our trust in God and in the church of Christ, else our fate would be very sad—the galleys. Ours is a state trial. All Spaniards look to England in this crisis, and from England only can we expect any help. Our French friends are powerless in the hands of their government. . . . Hard labour on roads or canals, or in mines, is the sentence which the law passes on those who are condemned, as we shall be. This is horrible!

"Matamoros will be obliged to go to Malaga, to be

judged there, in the first place; but as that inferior tribunal 'depends, as you know, upon this one, he will return here to receive his final sentence. Our suit already covers 1000 pages of law papers, and it appears to be only beginning. The indictments will be read separately; but as we cannot receive different sentences for one offence, they will be considered together, and the maximum punishment which the law permits will be inflicted. The places mentioned in our several indictments are Granada, Barcelona, Malaga, Seville, and Cordova; but in Seville and Cordova there is little or no evidence gainst us. The Seville accusation only rests upon two unimportant letters found upon Matamoros, and the address of B——.

"Affectionate remembrances from all the brethren. Ever believe in the inextinguishable love of your brother in Christ, ·

"JOSE ALHAMA."

In this letter we see the strong and unwavering faith of the other patient and untiring witness for Christ.

March 12th, 1861, Matamoros says:—

"On the night of the 7th, after our five months' imprisonment, seven police agents entered our cell, and began to search it minutely, but with great rudeness and harshness of manner and behaviour. We strove to bear this with perfect calmness; and when they announced to us the object of their visit, we simply replied that it was a matter of complete indifference to us, and, sitting down, we left them to their work.

"But this attempt to preserve an outward tranquility was too much for the strength of two unfortunate prisoners, already weary with suffering and with guiltless consciences. The impudent rudeness with which they dragged about everything we possessed irritated us to such a degree that I energetically reminded them of their duties, and of the respect which is due not only to our misfortune, but also to our position in society, and even to the class of our accusation.

"After this they behaved at least with less brutal rudeness of language, though their actions continued to be as savage as before. Nothing, I repeat, was respected by them; our persons, our bedding, the sacking of our bedsteads, all were rigorously examined. Nay, they carried the absurdity of the affair to such a pitch as to empty the water in our pitchers and jugs. Indeed, it is difficult to say what they expected to discover—they know best themselves. On the table by my bed lay a Bible and a new Testament (the gift of Dr. Tregelles, and which I valued highly on that account), a copy of the four gospels with notes, a few controversial tracts, amongst them 'Andrew Dunn;' all these were seized. I told them very simply and plainly that I was a Protestant, that the study of the law of God as contained in the Word of Life was of the first importance and necessity to me and I besought and entreated them to give me back at least my Bible. But my reasonings, my supplications, and my wishes were equally unavailing. With this holy book, which was our daily study, we have both lost much of our tranquility and calmness."

Man may take away their Bibles, but he cannot take away Christ from them. "My sheep shall never perish, neither shall any pluck them out of my hand." "I am *persuaded* that neither death nor life, nor angels, nor principalities, nor powers, nor things present, nor things to come, nor height, nor depth, nor any other creature, shall be able to separate us from the love of God which is in Christ Jesus our Lord." Rom. vii. 38,

CHAPTER V.

DON FRANCISCO RUET.

THE following notices of the conversion and ordination of Don Francisco Ruet to the Spanish Protestant Church of Gibraltar is extracted from the Home and Foreign Record of the Free Church of Scotland :—

"Gibraltar, October 28th, 1858.

"An event happened here two days ago, which is altogether new in the history of the Rock, and which is of so interesting a character that I trust you will find a place for it.

"I refer to the full equipment of a Protestant Spanish Congregation in Gibraltar by the ordination of Señor Don Francisco de Paulo Ruet as their minister by the Free Church Presbytery of the North of Italy. It was the first time a Presbyterian ordination had taken place in the colony, and, in all probability, the first time that such ordination ever was bestowed upon a Spaniard. The congregation present on the occasion, therefore, was a large one, composed both of Englishmen and Spaniards, some of whom were compelled by curiosity, and others by higher motives.

"The members of the Presbytery who took part in the service were the Rev. Dr. Stewart, of Leghorn, who preached in English, and after the ordination addressed Señor Ruet on the duties of his office in Italian ; the Rev. A. Sutherland offered up the ordination prayer, and afterwards addressed the congregation on their duties in the Spanish language, and the Rev. David Kay, of Genoa, who, after a few kindly words in Italian to the newly ordained minister, addressed the English portion of the audience. The service was interesting to all, but many of the Spaniards were visibly affected by it.

" The history of this congregation is a very interesting one. It is wholly composed of Spaniards, either born on the Rock or who have come to reside here, and who are converts from the Church of Rome.

"The Wesleyans have maintained schools for the instruction of children in Spanish for many years in Gibraltar, and it is possible that the Protestant movement among a certain number of this new congregation may be the result of this early training. Mr. Sutherland, after his arrival here, about three years ago, speedily mastered the Spanish language sufficiently to converse with enquirers who came desirous of being instructed in the differences between Popery and Protestantism ; and the first formation of this Spanish congregation is, under God, his work. It already consisted of twenty members, whom he had instructed and admitted to communion when Señor Ruet arrived about two years ago.

" Señor Ruet's early career had been an eventful one. Born at Barcelona, son of an officer of some rank in the service of the Queen of Spain, he was sent in due time to the Bishop's College in his native city, with the view of becoming an advocate, where he continued for six or seven years. It was during this period that he had his eyes opened to the iniquities of the Romish Church, and probably getting involved in some of the political entanglements of the time, was obliged to fly from Spain. He went to Piedmont and continued to support himself, as best he could, by his own exertions there during eight years. In Turin he was attracted to the Waldensian Church, and became deeply interested in the preaching and teaching of Dr. de Sanctis and M. Meille, by means of which his heart was changed, and after being for two years a catechumen in M. Meille's classes he was admitted to the Lord's Supper in the Waldensian Church. When Espartero came to power, the Liberals, who had expatriated themselves from Spain, returned thither again, and Ruet among the rest.

"He began to harangue the people of Barcelona in one of the public squares of that city, declaring to them that true liberty was to be found in the Gospel alone, and that so long as the Pope remained in power, and shut out the true light, no advance in freedom could ever be made. He was soon arrested at the instance of the priests, and cast into prison, whence, after an imprisonment of nine months, he was banished the country, his passport declaring that he was at liberty to return again as soon as he became reconciled to Holy Mother Church! That satisfied Mr. Sutherland and other friends, that if he suffered as an evil-doer it was for the truth's sake and not for politics, for he made his way at once to this place.

" The Spanish work in Mr. Sutherland's hands had now taken such dimensions that he felt need of assistance, and after careful inquiries, he engaged Mr. Ruet to visit and to address his inquiring countrymen. The wrath of the Roman Bishop here was greatly stirred at such a piece of audacity ; and he had influence enough to enlist some of the *employés* of the government in the plan of banishing the firebrand, so that it required both prudence and firmness on Mr. Sutherland's part to secure for the exile, for Christ's sake, the asylum which had been freely granted to Spanish political exiles.

"An appeal to the Governor, Sir James Ferguson, settled the matter. Ruet has been at least for two years an inhabitant of the town, and except on the matter of his religion, no one can bring a complaint against him.

" As Don Francisco Ruet was the instrument under God of bringing Matamoros to a knowledge of the glorious Gospel of the Grace of God and thus delivering him from the trammels of the Romish superstition, some details of the links in this mysterious chain will be read with interest. I give the story as I heard it, and do not vouch for its complete accuracy, but what was communicated to me was, that a lady at Rome had given a tract to one of the most eloquent preachers of the Vatican, De Sanctis by name, and this treatise was on the importance of studying the Bible to come to an exact knowledge of the will of God and of the plan of Salvation. This tract made a deep impression on the honest mind of De Sanctis, and finally led.him to the study of the Book of Books, which, under the guidance

of the Holy Spirit, ended in his abjuring the errors of
the Church of Rome and embracing the truth as it is in
Jesus. De Sanctis went to many places of Italy and
also to Turin, where God had now directed the steps of the
Spaniard, Don F. Ruet, who was to be brought also into
the glorious liberty of the Gospel. He was in due time
converted ; returns to Barcelona ; suffers imprisonment
for the precious name of Jesus, and finally goes to
Gibraltar, where Matamoros was in due time sent by
the same spirit, and made the mighty instrument in
God's hand of opening the doors of Spain to the incalculable boon of an open Bible. I had long asked God
to send us one man with the true spirit of the early
church, and in due time Manuel Matamoros appeared
on the scene.

> " God moves in a mysterious way
> His wonders to perform,
> He plants His footsteps on the sea
> And rides upon the storm.
>
> " Deep in unfathomable mines
> Of never failing skill,
> He treasures up his bright designs
> And works his Sovereign will."

CHAPTER VI.

LETTER FROM REFORMED CHURCH AT GRANADA.—PRO-CEEDINGS OF FRIENDS IN ENGLAND.

ABOUT this time we received from the Reformed Church of Granada the following letter:—

"DEAR AND REVERED BRETHREN IN OUR BLESSED RE-DEEMER, JESUS CHRIST,

" We learn, by letters from Malaga and Barcelona, that our brothers in those towns have, through you, addressed the English public in terms of hearty grati-tude for the support which has been rendered to our persecuted brethren here.

" We rejoice to hear that the Churches of Malaga and Barcelona have adopted so wise a method of mani-festing their Christian thankfulness to the illustrious deputation which brought the case of our friends before Lord John Russell.

" If the sufferings of Don M. Matamoros and Don J. Alhama were not inflicted on account of their evangelical sentiments and their constant co-operation and eminent services in the Lord's work, we would silently lament over their miserable condition, and pray to the Lord to pardon and defend them. But their crime has been none other than the offence of being Protestants and preachers of the truth; and we seize this opportunity of protesting against the barbarous tyranny which has entombed them for four months in loathsome dungeons, which has associated them with criminals, and which has made them the object of infinite vexations and persecutions.

" We unite with the Churches of Malaga and Barcelona in thankfulness to those among you who have lightened the sufferings of our innocent brethren.

" In Don Jose Alhama we recognize the fervent Christian, the honoured citizen, the unwearied soldier of Christ, who formed and gave existence to this Church, sacrificing, in so doing, not only his worldly interests, but also his precious freedom.

" In Don M. Matamoros we recognize an equally worthy brother, a zealous fellow-worker and preacher of the gospel in many places, and the founder of the Churches of Malaga and Barcelona; on whose name, as on that of his fellow-prisoner, no shadow of a stain has ever fallen. Yet these are the only accusations which can be brought against these dear friends, and which, in substance, appear in their indictment. Yet, were they simple brothers in Christ, and not distinguished champions doing battle for his name, we would yet raise our voice of thankfulness to you, and our cry of loud protest against the tyranny of our oppressors.

" We protest, because our religious sentiments are identical with those of our suffering brothers—we are Christians. Our rule of faith is the whole Bible, and the Bible alone. We desire to be distinguished by our

pure and sincere faith, our love, and our trust in Jesus
Christ, our only Advocate and Mediator. And, there-
fore, we energetically protest against the Church of
Rome, which is the greatest and wiliest foe of our
Lord.

"We conclude with an earnest expression of our
gratitude to Sir R. Peel, whose energy and Christian
zeal were the means of greatly alleviating the sufferings
of our brethren, releasing Matamoros from the solitude
of his confinement by especial recommendation, the
jailers rendering the condition of both of these prisoners
of Christ less lamentable.

"It is useless to attempt to express by these few
words, our gratitude to you and the other eminent
Christians who are praying and watching for the well-
being of the sufferers; all Spanish Christians know
and venerate these names.

"Receive, dear English brethren, the expression of
our Christian love. May the Divine Spirit dwell with
you and yours for ever.

"Your brethren and sisters in the Lord Jesus,
"THE PRESIDENT (in prison).

[Here follow one hundred and sixty signatures.

"To Messrs. Newton, Tregelles, and Greene."

A letter to me from Alhama gives some faint idea of
the sorrows of these brethren :—

"MY DEAR SIR, AND BELOVED BROTHER IN CHRIST,

"With great joy and hearty gratitude I take up my
pen to write you a few lines. I have read the letters

which you have addressed to the worthy Christian soldier and brave gospel champion, Don M. Matamoros. I have read in your last letter the passage in which you so kindly wrote of me. Oh, dear brother, your letters strengthen our faith, and give peace and consolation to our spirits. Truly, the conduct of the Pope's Christians and of Christ's Christians is widely different. The Pope's Christians torment us, body and soul; they speak ill of us; they anathematize us; they represent us as the vilest criminals, that the people may hate us; they cast us into filthy dungeons, separating us from our dear families and from our brethren in Christ, thus bringing the former to the verge of destitution, and filling the hearts of the latter with fear and mourning; and all this they do for the honour and glory of God.

"What! Does the love of the gospel lead men to ruin an honest and honourable family? Is it to the glory of God to rob innocent children of their father, and deprive them at once of his paternal affection, and of the means of subsistence? Is it in the spirit of the Lord Jesus, who pardoned the adulteress and prayed for his murderers, to cast into dreadful prisons, amidst the lowest felons, those whose only offence is, that they have preached the gospel and taught men to love as brethren, and strive to instruct them in those divine truths which God through his Son Jesus Christ has given to us for our learning,—truths which can alone make nations happy and release humanity from its curse?

"And the children of the gospel, how do they act? They fortify our faith; they wipe our tears; they comfort us in our afflictions; our children are their children; they pray for us; they pray for our enemies; and we from our doleful prison daily do the same. Eternal glory be to Jesus Christ—glory to his holy gospel—glory to those Christians who teach and practise the Word of God, and who unite faith and charity.

"I thank God for my conversion. I thank Him for having permitted me to read His Holy Word, for having learnt from it to convert hatred into love, to pardon and pity those who do me wrong, and to endure with resignation and faith the troubles of this valley of tears. . . .

"Until to-day I hoped that dear M. Matamoros would have been able to answer your kind letter himself, but the state of his health makes me fear that he may still be some days before he can do so.

"For the first fortnight of our stay here I trusted that he would be completely restored to health, but, alas! these hopes have not been realized.

"The unhealthy condition of our prisons renders his recovery but too doubtful. Nevertheless, I trust in God that he may be spared to us. . . . He sends to you and your dear family a thousand kindnesses. May the grace of the Lord Jesus be with you all, is what I pray.

"Your brother in the Lord,
"JOSE ALHAMA."

It may not be generally known that at the time of the irruption of the barbarians, the Vandals took possession of the southern portion of Spain. Hence the word Vandalucia, the *v* having been dropped it remains Andalucia. Matamoros, from his complexion, evidently belongs to the race of the Vandals, whilst Alhama is supposed to be of Moorish origin, sundry circumstances indicating this, and particularly the Arabic prefix to his name, *Al*, which is found in many Spanish words, and is easily accounted for by the 800 years of Moorish rule in Spain.

The English public were not idle during this reign of terror to Protestants in Spain. Deputations waited on Earl Russell, Minister for Foreign Affairs. The newspapers joined to help, and daily the voice of public sympathy became more audible. Petitions were sent to the Houses of Parliament. Prayer was made, but the Lord's time to deliver had not arrived. His way is not as our way. We are so short-sighted. One of the petitions sent to the House of Commons, after detailing many of the sorrows and persecutions of our brethren, concluded by the following words:—

" That your petitioners are informed that by the law of Spain there is but one religion permitted—the Roman Catholic—and no other form of worship is tolerated ; and that if any one quit the Roman Catholic Church, he therefore renders himself liable to several years' penal servitude at the galleys.

" That your petitioners fear that the present severe persecution of Protestants in Spain by the Romish priesthood is likely to exterminate, if possible, the Protestant faith in the land.

"That as Roman Catholics have in this country full liberty of worship, your petitioners earnestly pray your

honourable House to adopt such measures as may seem
advisable for the purpose of supporting Her Majesty's
Government, by co-operation with other Protestant
Powers, or otherwise, in making such a representation
as may obtain from the Spanish Government, by
pacific and friendly action, an assurance that such
persecutions will be stopped. And your petitioners
will ever pray."

The *Morning Post* newspaper also had some excellent articles, an extract from one of which we tran-
scribe:—

"I may add that the health of Matamoros, always
delicate, is fast sinking under the rigour of his confinement

"As the subject is likely soon to be brought before
Parliament, I am anxious, through your columns, to
draw the attention of members of both Houses to the
facts. I need not inform you that it is a distinct
principle of international law that nations may interfere on behalf of their co-religionists when severely
persecuted. Not that any ask for forcible intervention; but might not the English Government (if *their*
remonstrances are despised) induce other Governments
—Prussia, Holland, Sweden, Belgium, and probably
France—to unite with them in the endeavour to
induce the Spanish Government to rescind the law
which punishes Protestantism as a crime? And might
not our consuls and vice-consuls in Spain be instructed
to show as much sympathy with those persecuted for
Protestantism there, as our consuls in Syria and elsewhere in the Turkish dominions have been directed
to show to the persecuted in those countries? Suppose

that in this country we were to pass a law condemning to the galleys for eight years every one who professed himself a Roman Catholic, would not all Catholic Christendom be aroused? A convention exists with Spain touching the slave trade; is a convention with her impossible for the abandonment of that which is virtually the Inquisition? Zeal, earnestness, and pertinacity in reiterating applications and remonstrances often effect great things.

"It is very probable that Matamoros and Alhama may be worn out with protracted suffering, and die, but it must not be supposed that the question will expire with them. It will revive in a hundred other cases, and we must be prepared to meet it.

"It has been said, and I believe on the best authority, that the Spanish Government would gladly wash their hands of these persecutions, but they yield at present to the pressure of the priesthood and the Court. If this be so, it is an additional reason for pertinacious effort on our part. I enclose my card, and beg to subscribe myself your obedient servant,

"*Feb. 25th.*"   "ANGLICANUS."

Speeches were made in Parliament by Sir Robert Peel and Mr. Kinnaird; but the days of action in favour of God's truth have passed away among our rulers, and of us nationally it may be written, "Thou hast praised the gods of silver and gold, of brass, iron, wood, and stone, which see not, nor hear, nor know; and the God in whose hand thy breath is, and whose are all thy ways, hast thou not glorified." While all this want of action and sympathy was seen in our Government, the oppressed continued to groan and sigh, "and their cries have entered into the ears of the Lord of Sabaoth."

In February, 1861, Matamoros writes, "After the silence of a few days that have appeared years to me, I take up my pen to write to you. My imprisonment rapidly weakens my strength of body, but there is compensation, for my spirit is strengthened, my faith is assured, and I am passing through the happiest time of my life. It is now a quarter to two o'clock in the morning while I write to you, and I have been obliged to rise from my bed to do so, for during the day it would be impossible; we are much exposed, for there are many treacherous persons watching over us. I am very ill, but no other result could be expected from the effects of many privations and the unhealthiness of the prison on my already feeble constitution. Even men of robust health suffer here. The expense of my correspondence in Spain and abroad is considerable, but besides that, to be allowed to speak with a friend, to receive a visit, to send the most trifling message, or to procure the smallest comfort, all costs money. Such is the morality of the Spanish *employés;* even in the prisons they live upon the fears of the prisoners; they flourish in the shade of their griefs, and will not grant them the slightest alleviation unless it is paid for with money which their victims may save by depriving themselves of necessaries, or selling the furniture of their houses."

In the month of June the following tidings reached us.

"Prison of the 'Audiencia,' Granada, June 11, 1861.

" RESPECTED AND DEAR BROTHER IN THE LORD, OUR HOPE, TRUST, AND ONLY JOY,

"Three days ago I completed eight months of my sad and dismal imprisonment, and to-day at length I hear that my case is to be tried.

"The petition of the 'Promoter Fiscal' has been notified to us. I gave you, some time ago, some account of this man. He asks for nine years at the galleys for us three who are imprisoned at Granada, and four years at the galleys for those who were let out on bail, and who are now here for their trial, whose number is about ten. Advocates have been chosen for us; three from among the most eminent of Granada, as follows :—For Alhama, Don Antonio Moreno Dias; for Don Manuel Trigo, Don Mariano Lederma; and for me, Don Juan Rodriguez de la Escalera. The case will be defended by them this week before the inferior tribunal.

"I will send you, dear brother, a copy of the sentence, and the defence of our advocates, and any farther facts worthy of notice. Believe me that these things do not alarm me in the least. Absolutely in no wise has it changed, nor can it change the complete tranquility that I enjoy, both in my spirit and in my conscience as a Christian. I despise the rigour of the tyrant; and the physical sufferings I am undergoing are impotent in causing me to vacillate for a single moment.

"No, a thousand times no! My life has been but a chain of sorrow, entwined with thorns which have lacerated my heart; but our sufferings for the cause

of the gospel are and ever shall be an eternal satisfaction to us. I am not shaken, nor shall I be. I
live happy under continual suffering; and this happiness is mine by faith in Christ, who I ask to pardon
my enemies. Good-bye for the present, dear brother;
I cannot now write more; but let me remind you that
your unwonted silence, and the remembrance of my
dear mother, are the only things that make me a
ittle sad.—Yours ever in Christ,

"MANUEL MATAMOROS."

Six of Matamoros' letters had been intercepted,
which caused us great anxiety about him; and not
until the latter end of June did we know any details,
when the letter explaining the delay was received.

"*Prison, Granada, June 15*, 1861.

" VERY DEARLY-LOVED AND RESPECTED BROTHER,
"I have never experienced more difficulty in con-
veying to you my sentiments of love and gratitude
than I do at present. I have never rejoiced more
fervently at the receipt of your letter than I did when
your last was delivered to me; for, for six weeks I
had not heard from you, though I have written to
you six times. And what a miserable time has this
been! These last six weeks have been full of sufferings to me. Annoyances, many and various, have
tormented my enfeebled frame. My life is one of per-

petual agitation. It is like a tempest which threatens my existence, as a little boat tossed on the breakers would be imperilled by a storm. My constitution is failing under the weight of these repeated blows. But with all this I receive the most powerful assistance, the most precious help, which leads me to a haven of salvation; which converts grief into joy; suffering into peace; and changes all that is gloomy into all that is bright. My invariable faith in the Lord, our dear Redeemer, does this for me.

"But life has its necessities, and one of the chief to me at present is to receive your letters and those of Mrs. Tregelles; and during this unfortunate time I have not received her letters either. Consider my condition and you will pity and pardon me.

"Your letter of the 4th has made me uneasy concerning mine to you. You say you have not heard from me since a certain date, and I have written *six* times to you without receiving any answer. Oh, may God touch the hearts of our enemies, and if the letters have fallen into their hands . . . . .

"I pass on to another point which will give you and your family much sadness of heart. The punishment which has been awarded to us was officially announced to us on the 13th. Alhama, Trigo, and myself are to be condemned to eighteen years' punishment: nine at the galleys, and nine more under the constant vigilance of the civil authorities. Besides this, we are to be declared for ever incapable of holding any office or political position, and also of teaching or instructing. This is horrible, inquisitorial, and inhuman.

"Of this nine years of convict labour I need say nothing. You can fancy what they will be in Spain. But the other nine of surveillance are also very severe and trying. We shall be obliged to present ourselves once or twice daily to the authorities. . We shall not be allowed to leave the town in which we sojourn; but in case we should do so, we shall be obliged to travel by a route which shall be appointed for us, and also to have a note of infamy upon our passports. If we fail in any of these points the remainder of our sentence must be fulfilled at the hulks.

"Nine of our brethren are sentenced to seven years of the galleys, and D. N. N. to four. In all, twenty-one brethren are involved in this affair in Granada alone; and, with the exception of a few against whom the charges were not proved, are all doomed by the tyranny under which we groan to a dark and disastrous future. We read calmly the sentence of the Fiscal which imposes so barbarous a punishment upon us, and it should be made known throughout Europe as a specimen of the tyrannical spirit which influences the Spanish laws, and their inquisitorial rage against those Protestants who desire to propagate their faith.

"This sanguinary document is yet a curiosity, and is worthy of all our pity. It is a document written by a Roman Catholic to demand the punishment of men who are children of God, but are Protestants. This is sufficient to give you an idea of its form and its spirit. It is specially severe upon me. I am considered as a criminal of the first magnitude, and of a deeper dye than any of the rest. I am repeatedly called the chief of the organization, the instigator and director of all the rest. I am declared responsible for the *crime* of forming the churches of Malaga and Barcelona, and guilty also of evangelizing in these and other parts of Spain; and this, as well as my declaration of faith before the tribunal, demands a severe and heavy punishment.

"Amongst other little things, it is remarked in this document that my imprisonment has not answered the purpose of converting me; but that I have constantly been striving to propagate my heresies even in prison. In fact, nothing that could prejudice the supreme tribunal against me, or compass my total ruin, has been forgotten. But with all this, one point is very remarkable: the Fiscal confesses distinctly that this Protestant organization may one day change the religion of Spain. What a confession! And if it is true, how can they say that their religion is the true one? and if it is the true one, why do they fear and persecute the Protestants so much?

"Our dear Alhama is accused of various crimes; the chief of them being, the having assisted A——. in his escape; being president of the Granada committee, and, therefore, responsible for all its doings. His sentence will be the same as mine, as the accomplice of a crime is as guilty as the perpetrator; and, besides, other heavy charges are laid against him.

"The Fiscal has been completely and deeply to blame in his accusations against Don Miguel Trigo. Every one of the charges against him is unjust and inspired by revenge. The Fiscal has been for years a personal enemy of Trigo, and has now an opportunity of exhibiting and satisfying his vengeance; for although several of the lawyers believe that the superior court will release him, in the meantime he will have to endure the sufferings and pain of captivity. I would dwell at greater length upon these points, but that I purpose sending you a copy of the sentence in the course of a few days. It consists of twenty pages of MSS.

"The more liberal portions of the press, though themselves Roman Catholics, are horrified at the severity of the sentence. The *Clamor Publico* is taking an attitude which is worthy at least of the century in which we live, and touches upon this disgraceful affair in a few eloquent passages, which have been copied by other newspapers.

"But, dear friend, though I am sure this letter will make you grieve, yet you will see in all this matter the hand of Providence, which has determined that Roman Catholicism should throw this dark stain upon her name, to prove once more how different is her teaching from that of Him who would not permit Peter to strike His enemies; who healed the wound which His disciple made; and whose last words were to ask for the pardon of those who had shed His blood, and given Him gall to drink; and whose whole life taught humility, gentleness, charity, and fraternal love.

"Be fully persuaded, however, that courage, resignation, and tranquility have not failed me, do not fail me now, and never will, to bear with Christian resignation whatever afflictions weigh down my weakened frame. Neither in prison, nor before the executioner, will I ever retract; wherever I find myself, there they shall see me tranquil and rejoicing; there they shall see me disposed to confess my faith in the Lord, and to protest against the Church of Rome, his implacable enemy.

"Our beloved Alhama has suffered from a robbery of goods in his establishment to the value of 1000 reals, or £10, through a person in charge there. The replacing of these goods has cost him more than the value of the lost ones, that he had bought on favourable terms from another workman. This, added to the great wants of a numerous family, of which he is the only support, to the supplying of rich goods for the season, and to the wants that are produced from day to day by the prolongation of an eight months' imprisonment, has caused that the sums received by him have not covered his necessities. Besides this, Señor Alhama has not omitted, as far as his means would allow, to assist Trigo and other unfortunate brethren, who, having been taken prisoners with him, are now in want, and some donations for Malaga, the total sum of which, since the month of March, amounts to some 600 reals, or £6.

"I say nothing of the content which your sympathy has produced, and the love shown in your desire to see me, because my unworthy pen is too weak to do so; but, suffice it to say, that you make me happy with such significant proofs of Christian love. I do not think we shall be allowed out for a long walk. However, if you settle upon your journey, I think perhaps it would be more opportune, and of greater interest to you to do so, in time to hear

F

the final sentence, when the defences are made in public, when our crime, and the reason of our punishment is shown, and I think this would be important. . . . . .

"I think the final sentence will come on towards the end of the year; the circumstance of the birth of the new Infanta would be now very favourable for the ambassador to do much. Do you know if he has done anything?

"I shall receive the pictures to-morrow by the diligence, and I await with impatience for this great pleasure; I send you a thousand, thousand thanks for your generous condescension. Alhama feels equally grateful, and also sends you repeated thanks.

"Count always upon the eternal affection and gratitude of your unworthy brother in the Lord,

"MANUEL MATAMOROS.

"Alhama participates in the same eternal gratitude with me, gives you thanks for all, and offers his respects to your family."

"*Prison of the 'Audiencia,' Granada, June 22*, 1861.

"MOST BELOVED BROTHER IN THE LORD,

"The pictures are in our hands! Oh, with what anxiety I opened the envelope that contained them! How much I desired to see your likeness, whom I do not know, as I know the greatness of your heart! My eager gaze has been fixed upon it a thousand times; . . . . They are hung up on the strong wall of my prison, over the table at which I am now writing, and I fix my eyes on them every moment; and those sacred remembrances console me so much, they are a soothing balm to my tried spirit.

" But in what an opportune occasion your edifying letter reached me. This morning dawned upon a fatal day for me—one of those days that take away years of life—a day of extreme trial. The Fiscal's petition, in which nine years of imprisonment and other penalties of an afflictive and disgraceful character, were demanded against me, has traversed Spain like an electric shock. I had wished that my dear mother and the poor prisoners in Malaga had not heard of it; it will rend their sorrowing hearts; however, the press has taken upon itself to cross my desires, and has carried this news to the remotest corner of the Peninsula. But with what anguish to me!

" I have received various letters from Barcelona, Malaga, and other places, full of tender grief; but, alas! a dear friend in Barcelona has overcome me. He tells me my dearest mother is inconsolable, that she has almost lost her reason! My God, my God, shelter her, as Thou dost shelter me, giving me strength to be able to endure! . . .

" Two of the prisoners of Malaga have fallen sick in their wretched dungeons. My poor brothers! This is my situation to-day, think on it, and pity me. I do not suffer on my own account; no, I suffer in thinking that the beings I love most suffer; I suffer in thinking that they perhaps believe that I suffer, when, on the contrary, this epoch (that others, perhaps, may think sad) is to me the happiest epoch in my life.

" I feel my physical strength weakening under nature's hard laws, but my moral being grows ever more robust, ever more firm; yes, more firm, because there are no chains in the world, no sufferings sufficient, no torments capable of making me draw back. All the earthly power of the Church of Rome, with its stakes and scaffolds, would not be sufficient ever to intimidate this poor prisoner, the most unworthy of all the Spanish Christians.

"I know what I owe to my beloved Jesus, I know what I owe to his holy and immortal church, and that which I owe to myself, so as not to appear timid before the horrible torments of tyrants. What are their rigours to me? Nothing, nothing. I only hold as supremely important that which is acceptable in the eyes of God. It is true that I suffer, knowing that my brethren in the faith, and my virtuous and incomparable mother suffers; but this grief is produced by sincere Christian affection; it is the natural feeling of a son who loves a mother to whom he owes tender affection and care; but it is not the suffering of my distressful situation, which I would not exchange for the felicity of Pius IX.

"The translation of the notable discourse of Sir Robert Peel has been published in a Spanish newspaper. I pray you to tell him in my humble name that I offer him my sincere thanks for his noble, worthy, and magnanimous efforts; poor Spain owes him much, much, beloved brother, and our gratitude towards such an eloquent orator is engraved in the depth of our hearts.

"To the excellent Mr. Newton, offer in my humble name my respects; tell him, also, of my eternal gratitude, my warm Christian love; and assure him in the most positive manner of my constancy, my unvarying desire of sacrificing even my life, if necessary, for the cause of the gospel, and of my perfect tranquility in the midst of so many sad and repeated blows.

" I received yesterday a notable, expressive, and most eloquent letter, signed by different amiable and charitable brothers and sisters in Dublin. My state of health and my occupations prevent me from answering it immediately; however, perhaps I may be able to do so to-morrow.

" The blessing of the Lord be with you constantly, and with all your family. Alhama, who participates in equal gratitude and love towards you, begs me to assure you of it in the warmest manner.

" Your brother in the Lord,
" MANUEL MATAMOROS."

A short time before the reception of the above, a meeting had been convened at St. James's Hall, London, presided over by Lord Shaftesbury, and attended by a highly influential and respectable audience. On this occasion Sir R. Peel made a long and powerful speech, bringing before the public the horrors that these Spanish Protestants were obliged to suffer. After introducing the subject at some length, he continued by saying:—

" What have these violent persecutions cost Spain in the past? What lost Spain the Indies? Its miserable persecutions. What lost Spain the Netherlands? Mr. Motley, in his charming work, recently published, says:—' The great cause of the revolt which in a few years was to break out through the Netherlands, was

the introduction of the Inquisition, and the persecution
which Philip of Spain, in 1561, had arranged for ex-
terminating that religious belief, which was already
accepted by a large portion of the Netherland subjects.'
Let Spain take care that its intolerance even now, in
these days of revolution, be not pushed too far. When
Matamoros was at Barcelona, he was dragged to Malaga,
and from Malaga to the dungeons at Granada. I, in
company with two ladies, travelled with him into the
mountains of Granada to the prison cell of that town.
I learned to admire his simple piety; and I and the
ladies with me were determined to use every effort,
although we were strangers, to ameliorate his condition.
Now let me read you one or two extracts from letters
written by these men, Alhama and Matamoros, by
which you can judge whether they are suffering because they are excited Socialists or because of their
religious belief. Matamoros says, in one of his
letters :—

" 'The tribunals in this place are acting in a satanic
and inquisitorial manner with us; my physicial powers
are rapidly sinking, and the thread of my life appears
nearly spun out. The dampness of these prisons is
killing me; but every step I take towards the tomb
strengthens my faith.'

" Is that the language of a Socialist or a political
agitator? I have here a letter from Alhama, which is
still more touching:—

" 'Yes, I suffer very, very deeply. You will imagine
all if I tell you a little. They are constantly trying to
make my poor wife ashamed of her husband.

" 'I suffer with patience all that is hardest in our

undeserved captivity. Be firm; grow in faith; we put
our trust in God.'

"I will read one other extract:—

"'Of our misfortunes and sufferings here in prison I
will say nothing. The cruelty they practise upon us,
the extreme severity they treat us with, is almost without an example in the annals of tyranny. The jailers
have received strict orders not to allow us to speak in
the prison. The governor calls us heretics. The other
prisoners frequently wish to speak to us, but they are
told to pass by. Formerly we were allowed to see our
friends, and my patient Alhama was permitted to see
his mother, and wife, and children. All the prisoners
still have this liberty, be they even robbers or assassins;
but we are allowed nothing, and are not permitted to
speak to any one. I asked to walk a little while when
the sun was shining, and was refused. The jailer said
he had strict injunctions to use all rigour towards me.
Indeed, were I to write many pages, and to use the
strongest language, I could not explain all that I am
suffering.'

"I ask, is not that the language of a martyr? Matamoros has heard that the government pretends that
they are Socialists, and this is the way he answers the
charge:—'Our cause has nothing of a political nature;
it is completely separated from every political and
worldly movement; it is the holy cause of the gospel.'
That is the answer, that upon this platform, in the
presence of a thousand free Englishmen, I give to the
Government of Spain when they dare to taunt these
people with being imprisoned for their connection with
secret societies. I have seen these men in prison with

my own eyes.   Their cell was no larger than that table.
I paced it in three steps.   They had no light—no table;
everything was denied them.   Do you recollect Byron's
description of the prisoners of Chillon?   One of them
is dead, another is chained to a pillar, and the third is
dying.   The description conveys to my mind what I
should imagine to be the feelings of these men.   The
man chained to the pillar says of the other one:—

> "'He, too, was struck, and, day by day,
> Was withered on the stalk away.
> Oh, God! it is a fearful thing
> To see the human soul take wing,
> In any shape, in any mood:
> I've seen it rushing forth in blood,
> I've seen it on the breaking ocean
> Strive with a swoln convulsive motion,
> I've seen the sick and ghastly bed
> Of sin delirious with its dread:
> But these were horrors—this was woe
> Unmixed with such—but sure and slow;
> He faded, and so calm and meek,
> So softly worn, so sweetly weak,
> So tearless, yet so tender—kind,
> And grieved for those he left behind:
> With all the while a cheek, whose bloom
> Was as the mockery of the tomb.'

"That is what I saw in the dungeon of Granada.   I
have seen in my own experience the terrors of the
'heaving ocean.'   I have been with four other men
upon a plank in the mid ocean, the sole survivors from
a terrible shipwreck.   I have seen men, one by one,
perish at my side, but it did not move me: I awaited
my destiny.   It was horrible, but it was not woe.   I

have seen the battle-field of the defeated: it was horrible, but it was not woe. I have seen the prisoner expiating his offence, and receiving his last sentence for his defiance of the laws of God and man: it was horrible, but it did not affect me. But I have seen the prisoners in the dungeon at Granada, and I admit that I felt, perhaps as many of you have felt often, or, it may be, only once in your life—felt

"'What I can ne'er express, yet cannot all conceal.'

"Would to God that any words of mine could remove one iota of the burden that presses down these poor fellows in Granada! But they shall be relieved. We have a patriot minister who knows how to interpret the feelings of his countrymen, and he will be prepared to carry out the desire not only of the metropolis, but of every province of this empire, that Her Majesty's Government should take some step in the matter. We do not ask to go to war with Spain. The power of this country does not depend upon earthworks and barricades, and lines of defence. The power of this country is in the exercise of its moral influence. It was so in the time of Queen Elizabeth. For twenty years she never fired a gun, and yet England had then a character and *prestige* in Europe. Never was this country so much respected abroad, as in the time of Cromwell. Why was it? Not because of sanguinary wars, but because Cromwell knew how to maintain the character and *prestige* of his country amid the nations of Europe. So shall it be now. We ask that the moral influence of this country, as a friendly power, may be exerted in alleviating the sufferings and calami-

ties which have befallen these poor Christians in Spain,
whose doctrines are not those of a mere sect, but the
doctrines of many millions in this country and in
Europe.   The resolution I have the honour to move
will, I am sure, meet with the assent of every man and
woman in this assembly, and will receive the support
of public opinion not only here, but throughout
Europe.   For, by the friendly sympathy of a free press,
which is the worst enemy of oppression, the sentiments
we here express will be carried far beyond these walls,
and will animate the hearts of many in Sweden, and
France, and Germany, and I believe in Spain itself.
We would have them know, that as our institutions
secure unlimited liberty to every class of professing
Christians, so they give us an indisputable right to
intercede with other nations in favour of our fellow-
Christians who are suffering—not for their political,
but for their religious opinions —a persecution which
is not only an insult to Europe, and an outrage to the
spirit of the age in which we live, but which to my
mind is totally incompatible with the mild and charitable principles of Christianity."

The sympathy evinced by Sir R. Peel at the time
of the imprisonment of Matamoros, his great exertions since, and many things that have come under
my notice, impel me to bid him God speed, and to desire, as I do most heartily, that as by God's providence
he has been chosen in the first instance as the instrument of advocating the cause of our persecuted
Spanish friends, he may never dismiss this matter
from his thoughts until he sees an end put to this
persecution in the deliverance of the captives, and in

the proclamation of religious liberty in priestridden Spain

But it was not only in the palaces of our nobility that the story of the Spanish sufferers had become a matter of deep interest. It had already been rehearsed again and again in all the length and breadth of Great Britain, and over the continent of Europe; on the banks of the Ganges and in the United States; and better and higher still, we love to think that the sorrowful sighing of the prisoner has come into the ears of the Lord of Hosts. In all their afflictions *He* is afflicted. He has heard their cry, and will help them.

But simple imprisonment was not sufficient punishment in the eyes of the enraged ecclesiastics of Spain for those who had dared to preach the truth in the midst of the classic land of superstition. A more bitter cup was still their lot, as will be seen in the sequel. But in the midst of these deep waters, God was day by day adding to the number of the ministering children, who ministered to the afflicted of their substance, and words of sweetest consolation. Among these may be mentioned the Rev. B. W. Newton, of London; Dr. and Mrs. Tregelles, of Plymouth; Geo. Müller, of Bristol; and the Rev. R. Govett, of Norwich, to say nothing of a host of others whose untiring and prayerful sympathy has been invaluable. The Rev. Mr. Dallas and Mr. Eade went from the Geneva Conference to pay them a visit in prison. General Alexander went out at the instance of the Evangelical Alliance, with a mission to General O'Donell, the Spanish Prime Minister at Madrid, but in spite of all his remonstrances, the bars and the bolts still firmly secured their persons. A sum of nearly £1000 went from this country to pay for the heavy law expenses, and for the support of the numerous families of the imprisoned in Malaga, Granada, and Seville; this money, laid up in heaven, bears good interest here in showers of blessing, and those who thus use their substance shall find that when the Chief Shepherd shall appear, they shall receive a crown of glory which fadeth not away. "Inasmuch as ye have done it to the least of these, my brethren, ye have done it unto *me*." In the midst of all these persecutions we see a better day in store for Spain, in answer to the prayers of these sufferers. Before Germany was made free, Luther had to be bound; before England enjoyed an open Bible, Cranmer must suffer; before France enjoyed the same, centuries of sorrow were the forerunners. The Madiai in Italy were heralds of blessing for their land, but they must submit to the will of the Lord first in bonds, and shall we say that the same laws do not apply to Spain. Away with the thought. "They that sow in tears shall reap in joy," He has said who cannot lie; and we will wait on Him for the fulfilment of the word.

CHAPTER VII.

THE LOJA TRAGEDY.

OWING to the interception of six letters from Matamoros, already mentioned, many of the facts connected
with the diabolical scheme concocted at Granada, to
inculpate him in the political insurrection at Loja,
would not have appeared in the present work were it
not for the recent publication of a brochure by Messrs.
Nisbet, from which I give the account of this infa-
mous tragedy:—"In the beginning of July, 1861, an
insurrection broke out at Loja, a quiet little town
situate between Granada and Malaga. Nine thousand
men, displaying a republican standard, and proclaim-
ing democratic principles, appeared in arms. At a
given moment they destroyed the telegraph, intercepted the post, and cut off all communication
with Granada, and the rest of the chief cities of
Spain.

" When first intelligence of these things reached
Granada, public opinion was unanimous in attri-
buting the movement to purely political motives,
but the enemies of Protestantism in Granada, taking
advantage of the surprise and excitement of the

public mind, wrote immediately to the government
papers at Madrid, affirming that the insurrection,
besides being republican in its character, bore evident
marks of a Protestant origin, the rebels having
raised the cry, 'Death to the Pope.' The public
feeling being very much opposed to this sudden and
unexpected outbreak, the reports industriously spread
of its having originated with the Protestant party,
affected most injuriously the cause of the prisoners,
which was beginning to be regarded with interest and
favour by the more enlightened portion of the public.
Availing themselves of the panic produced, the
enemies of Matamoros resolved, if possible, to incriminate him and his fellow-prisoners. For this purpose the authorities had recourse to a wretched convict, condemned for robbery to seven years at the
galleys, to whom they promised liberty and 8000 reals,
if he would supply information against the Protestant
prisoners. This man, fetched back for the purpose
from the galleys, was employed to carry food and
water to the cells of Matamoros and Alhama. Whilst
thus engaged he contrived to steal a letter written
by, and others addressed to, Matamoros, all of which he
carried to the authorities. These letters were purely
of a religious character, and contained no allusion to
politics, yet they were used as a pretext for action.

"Early on the next day, July 8th, Matamoros was
roused from his bed and hurried off to a most loathsome dungeon. Alhama, too, and Trigo were removed from the cells they were occupying, and
placed 'incomunicados.' At the same time the governor of the prison and ordinary officials were sus-

pended, made prisoners, and shut up; new officials being appointed by the military fiscal, who was one of the most bitter enemies of the Protestants. These officials were to exert themselves to find among the prisoners some who, on a promise of a free pardon, would come forward as witnesses against Matamoros and the Protestants. But to return to Matamoros. He, as has been already said, was hurried off to a loathsome den, without daylight or air, where the filthiness and stench, together with the distress and anxiety of his mind (for he knew not of what he was accused), so affected him that he fell ill of violent fever.

"For three days he struggled on, but on the night of the 13th of July he was so ill, that he begged for medical aid; it was refused; he asked for medicine, that also was denied him. For eight days he lay there unable to rise, but at last, through God's mercy, the fever abated, on the thirteenth day of his imprisonment in this place. On July 25th, at five o'clock in the morning, he was dragged out to be examined by a military commission. He was eleven hours under examination, and for the first time, by the questions put to him, he discovered of what he was accused.

" The accusations against him were :—

" I. That he had, in his prison, projected and planned the insurrection at Loja, and that the leader of the insurrection had visited and held a conference with him in the prison.

" II. That he had furnished the insurgents with large sums of money.

" III. That he had intended to put himself at

the head of the insurrection in Granada, and to have given liberty to the prisoners, with the cry of 'Death to the Pope.'

"IV. That in order to effect all this, he had bribed the former governor with the sum of 30,000 reals (£300), and had likewise suborned the rest of the officials.

"V. That two persons who had visited Alhama on the 6th and 7th of July were conspirators. That one of them had an interview with Matamoros, in order to arrange with him what cries should be raised in the revolution, and that the other had brought to him large sums of money.

"The means resorted to for obtaining evidence in support of these charges may be judged of from the following incidents :—

"On one occasion, the convict aforementioned, who had been appointed to attend upon Matamoros, came to his cell, accompanied by the newly-appointed deputy-governor. The man told Matamoros that it was to the deputy-governor he owed the privilege of being visited, and that he deserved some acknowledgment. Matamoros accordingly gave him a gratuity. The deputy-governor went immediately to the fiscal, whose agent he was, showed him the money, and declared that it was given him by Matamoros as a bribe to silence him, as well as to secure through him the silence of certain criminals whose evidence he feared.

"These wretches, having been previously instructed, when called upon by the deputy-governor, immediately corroborated the accusation. At another time,

Matamoros, being in need of some food and some cooling drink, employed his convict attendant to purchase it, giving him some money for the purpose, and a few reals additional as a recompense for the service. The man, who was employed as an informer and spy, carried the money to the fiscal, and declared that Matamoros had given it as a bribe to prevent his coming forward as a witness against him.

"On another occasion, this same man stole a handkerchief from Matamoros, and carrying it to Alhama's wife in token that he had been sent by Matamoros, asked for the letters and manuscripts that Matamoros had committed to her care. She replied that she had none, that Matamoros had not committed any letters to her care. The man, disappointed in his scheme, went nevertheless to the fiscal, declared that she had the papers and would not give them up, and succeeded in obtaining her arrest and imprisonment, as well as the imprisonment of Alhama's aged mother.

"Some difficulty being apprehended in consequence of the agreement of Alhama's declaration with that of Matamoros, the following means were adopted to destroy the value of this accordance. Alhama's cell was under that of Matamoros, but had no communication with it. One night the deputy-governor came to the cell of Matamoros, and caused a small aperture to be made through the floor into Alhama's room below, then went to the military fiscal, and reported that there were means of communication between the cells. While these things were taking place, the leader of the insurrection at Loja was yet at large. A prisoner named E—— came forward and declared that he had not only seen the chief of the insurrection conversing with Matamoros before the rising at Loja, but that since that event he had again seen him talking with Matamoros through one of the windows of the prison.

"When called on to describe the rebel chief, he gave a description which agreed closely with that which had been published in the newspapers. There was also in the prison a parish priest named R—— S——, imprisoned for various robberies and crimes of a disgraceful nature. This priest being cited by E—— in his declaration, came forward, and not only corroborated what E—— had said, but added fresh charges. . They accused Matamoros of having endeavoured to induce the prisoners to rebel against the military fiscal and governor of the prison. Twenty prisoners were called forward, who, to the consternation of Matamoros, all confirmed the testimony of E—— and the priest, one man showing the money which he declared Matamoros had given him. But the good providence of God was watching over Matamoros. The cause was not decided by the military tribunal, it was passed on to the civil court. There the chief evidence, the person on whom the enemies of Matamoros chiefly rested, turned against them. E——, conscience-striken and repentant, after making two attempts at his life, made solemn recantation before the civil tribunal of all that he had said against Matamoros, and gave a clear and explicit narration of all that had been carried on against him in the prison, and told of the bribes and instructions given by the military fiscal and his agents. It scarcely

need be said that the result was the triumphant acquittal of Matamoros and the Protestant prisoners.
The military fiscal, who, before the unexpected failure
of the cause had been rewarded (somewhat prema-
turely) with promotion, was now disgraced and
sent away from Granada. Here, then, there was an
opportunity for the government of Spain to have
come forward and recompensed Matamoros for his
unmerited suffering by frankly abandoning the religious charge. Their agents had conspired against
his life. If the political charge had been established,
he would no doubt have been put to death. But the
government whose agents had woven around him that
complicated web of falsehood, felt no shame, no con-
trition. They in no respect recognized themselves
his debtors. His reward was continued imprisonment, and in prospect aggravated, not lessened,
punishment."

CHAPTER VIII.

LETTERS FROM GRANADA.

IN September I received again news from the prisoner. Matamoros says:—

> *The Prison, Granada, Sept. 7th,* 1861.

" Perhaps, dear brother and indefatigable protector, this letter may reach you before the very sorrowful one which I wrote to you last week. How long I have been hindered from corresponding with you (twelve weeks), and without hearing anything of you or my worthy English and Irish friends! This is a great trial to me—greater than my imprisonment; than the fury of my implacable enemies, or than my physical sufferings, which are, nevertheless, severe. The best and most consoling and greatest news you can give me, is what you tell me of the Christian solicitude and zeal and holy love, with which our friends and brethren in the faith ask after us, the prisoners of Christ. And, believe me, it is not pride or presumption that makes me so much rejoice at this, but rather I rejoice at the manifestation of our holy union as the ' body of Christ ' which is thus made so evident. Oh! when you reply to these dear friends, speak to them of my gratitude in the most lively and expressive terms. Be very sure that you cannot exaggerate it.

"If the proposal for a day of prayer on our behalf throughout England, Ireland, and Scotland has not yet been carried out, I beg of you to use your legitimate and fraternal influence that it may take place. The prayers of the saints are of more value to us than anything else in this world. These supplications will be heard by the great Head, and He in His mercy will give us strength to bear so much suffering, so much torment. Pray for poor Spain; for this unfortunate country, sunken in error and slavery by Satan's hand, and these prayers will be heard by our loving Father, who will grant all that we ask for His own glory. I have not yet received the last sums which you mention as having been sent to me. I received £20 in June; half was distributed in Malaga, and half was divided amongst ourselves here. Since that time I have not received any money, and am now in want. The position of the prisoners at Malaga must be terrible; they must be in severe trouble, and this breaks my heart; the more so, as I cannot but feel that the sacrifices made by our British friends are already very great.

"In Malaga two more arrests have been made. The defence made for Alhama and myself I hope to send to you soon. Our lawyers asked for our liberty, but it was refused. Alhama's advocate made a brilliant and lucid, as well as a courageous, defence, saying, amongst other things, after having professed his Catholic belief, 'That for a society in the state of corruption of so-called "Catholic" Spain, he would prefer the faith professed by his clients, though called Protestants; for its tendencies, apart from the question of faith, were eminently moral and noble.' My advocate, and also Trigo's, made good defences, and the affair is now in the hands of the lawyers of those of the accused who are at liberty on bail.

"I will not tell you anything, dear brother, of all that I have suffered. I could fill many pages with horrible descriptions; but in my captivity I have begun to write a sort of sketch of my life since my conversion. If possible, I will send it to you when it is finished. You say that you hope to hear me preach the gospel in Spain. Oh! it is my only aspiration, my highest ambition. I long to complete my classical studies; and then, poor, very poor, but rich in faith, I would preach unweariedly wherever I could be heard. Believe me to be, dear brother, your attached though unworthy friend,

"MANUEL MATAMOROS."

"My grateful respects to all our brethren in the Lord,

. "JOSE ALHAMA."

I received many sweet letters from Christians in England, and, after translating them, sent them to Matamoros, and they helped to wile away the sad time, and were as a sweet cordial in the cup of his deep and protracted sorrow. One of these, from Mr. Leonard Strong, of Torquay, was as follows:—

" Brampton, Torquay, S. Devon, England.

"MUCH BELOVED AND HONOURED BROTHER IN OUR
 LORD JESUS CHRIST,

 " Grace and peace be multiplied unto you from God
our Father and our Lord Jesus Christ. The Lord
permitted us a few days since to hold a meeting of
believers in Jesus Christ for worship, prayer and
mutual edification by the word, in this town, and
between our worship meetings we partook together of
a social meal or tea drinking as before our Lord,
during which a letter from yourself to some Christian
brethren at Kingsbridge (a town in South Devon)
was placed in my hands, with a request that I would
read it, which I did. The expressions of faith and
love therein contained, the joy in the Lord Jesus, and
willingness declared, through grace, not only to be
bound, but to die if need be for the name of the Lord
Jesus, in connexion with your present sorrowful
circumstances, called forth from us all the warmest
sympathy for yourself and dear family in these heavy
trials through which it has pleased God to bring you;
and as it drew from our little assembly at the time a
few offerings of love, if they may assist in any way to
ameliorate your condition, I herewith transmit them
through the kind hands of a dear brother in the Lord
who, I am informed, has some means of communication
with you. It is a very small sum, only £3 sterling,
but dear, afflicted brother, it is sent to you with much
love and many prayers that after you have suffered
awhile and made a good confession before governors,
magistrates, etc., you will come forth free, as our

Italian brethren before you, to worship God in Spirit
and in truth, rejoicing in Christ Jesus, none making you
afraid.   We, who at present enjoy so much liberty in
this respect, are especially enjoined to remember them
that are in bonds as though bound with them, and as
we are exhorted to make prayers for kings, and all
that are in authority, that we Christians may lead a
quiet and peaceable life in godliness and honesty, we
do especially remember your afflictions before the Lord,
and ask Him to turn the heart of the queen of Spain,
her ministers, advisers and associates in government,
that liberty of conscience and worship may soon be
allowed, as in other European governments.   I can
also say, dear brother, that we are not afraid for you,
but glory in you for your patience and faith in all your
persecutions and tribulations that you endure, seeing
God is counting you worthy of the coming kingdom
for which you also suffer.

"Let us call to remembrance the former days, how,
immediately after poor sinners were *illuminated*, they
endured a great fight of afflictions, and took joyfully
the spoiling of their goods, knowing in themselves
that they had in heaven a better and an enduring
substance.

"Now, dear brother, thou art, with others, made a
companion of them, cast not therefore away thy
confidence, which has great recompense of reward, for
to you it is *given*, not only to *believe*, but also to *suffer*
for *Jesus' sake*.   Cheer up, then, dear brother, for yet a
little while, and he that shall come will come and will
not tarry.   The Lord says, 'Leap for joy.'   He putteth
thy tears which flow from the weakness of the flesh

into His bottle, and He will refresh thy spirit and soon deliver you all out of your bonds. I am with much true sympathy and with confidence in the love, and in the mighty arm of yours, and my Lord Jesus,

"Your Brother in the hope of Glory,

"LEONARD STRONG."

"Prison of the 'Audiencia,' Granada, Oct. 8, 1861.

"BELOVED AND RESPECTED BROTHER IN OUR DIVINE REDEEMER, JESUS CHRIST, OUR JOY AND OBJECT OF OUR CONSTANT FAITH,

"Mr. Greene has just given me one more proof of Christian zeal in translating your important letter of June the second time, and sending it to me, impelled by the desire of comforting me, understanding clearly that it would produce in me most wholesome effects of Christian edification. I received with the greatest pleasure your very important letter—important to me in many ways—and which I now hasten to answer; but this I cannot do as I would wish, as, though my heart earnestly desires to do so, my intellectual powers are insufficient; but be it as it will, in whatever I do say my heart shall speak.

"Beloved and respected brother, if to man on earth it is given to be happy, I enjoy this benefit in a super-lative degree. My soul is filled with lofty and permanent recollections of Christian joy; the history of my life, during the past year, having been the means of procuring them for me, and founded prin-cipally on the magnificent spectacle that the Church of Christ has presented to the eyes of God and of the world, in watching, with pious and evangelical atten-

tion, over the wants of their Spanish brothers. The
continual and eloquent proofs of this love which I am
daily receiving will always leave in my soul grateful
and profound impressions.

"I see the day approach when my country will be
happy by the triumph of the gospel in the hearts of
its inhabitants. The honour has fallen to my lot to
suffer for having preached the kingdom of God, and
for having exhorted men to have faith in Christ, who
I know and love with all my heart. I see by the
love which you profess for me that He has not forsaken
me, that He accepts my sincere Christian desires;
and tell me, dear brother, is not this the truest
happiness that we can enjoy here below? Have I not
good reason then to be happy, and for calling myself
so? Yes, assuredly. Well, such is the ground of my
joy, the motives I have for glorying. This happiness
would have been a stranger to me had I been still
living in darkness, as is the Church of Rome, that
eternal enemy of Christ.

"Your pious and interesting letter refers, beloved
brother, to the sentiments that I had the pleasure of
expressing to the brethren of Kingsbridge; and that
humble expression of faith, you say, has produced in
you the most lively sympathies. Pray give, in my
poor name, to all who have honoured me by hearing it,
the fullest assurance of my Christian love. Beloved
brother, while young, very young, at the age when
generally all are left to run after some illusion of fancy,
some pleasure of a day, at that in which the deceitful
attractions of the world fascinate the heated imagination of youth, the infinite goodness of our heavenly

Father saw good to grant me the consolation of knowing
Himself through His Son Jesus Christ. I knew Him,
and knew at the same time my ancient errors of having
followed, as a blind automaton, the Romish Church,
which lives so widely distant from Him. I abandoned
that path which leads to perdition, and I proposed to
follow firmly and decidedly our Lord Jesus Christ in the
path laid down in His holy Word. I desired to teach
people the truths which I had believed, to teach my
unfortunate countrymen who live in sin, and to this
Christian end I dedicated all the time which has elapsed
since my conversion to Christianity up to this moment.
Comprehending that this high mission was superior
to my feeble strength, to my poor talents, and to my
scanty faculties (but the Lord says that he who lacks
wisdom let him ask of God, who giveth willingly and
upbraideth not), I asked Him from day to day, from
hour to hour, and I found that my humble efforts
gave a blessed result, that the Lord did not abandon
me; and I followed on untiringly, and will ever follow
the path traced out by my faith. This was, yea, this
is, the crime I am guilty of, and for this crime have
they buried me in a miserable dungeon, providing
for me at the same time these happy hours of trial.
My sorrowful prison, intended to intimidate me, opened
for me a door of hope on the one hand, as well as a
path full of trials. Of hope, for it was the proof of my
faith ; of trial, because it led many families to bitter
weeping and tears. Never have I dreaded my own
sorrows ; but I have been grieved much by those of
my many and virtuous brethren. In presence of the
stern and unbending tribunal, I had the honour of

maintaining my faith as a Protestant, my faith in Christ, and my eternal separation from the Church of Rome, His enemy.

"But, beloved brother, if men have traced out for me a path of sharpest thorns, since that day my heavenly Father has portioned out for me one of infinite pleasure. What signify the sufferings of the body? What the blind rage of an enemy who neither forgets nor forgives, and who, making use of the power of brute force, rejoices in the sorrows of a Christian who cannot be convinced by his arguments, nor be intimidated by his horrible punishments? Nothing ought, nothing can, avail for the man who, despising the world, fixes his eyes upon His Lord, and, committing his soul to his Maker, determines to follow Him. They may augment my punishment, but they will also augment my joy. They may augment their rage, but it will be manifest to the world, and the world will know them and separate from them.

"Not one life but one thousand would I sacrifice willingly in the name of Christ, and for His holy cause, and for the extension of His holy kingdom on earth. My enemies will find me always disposed to sacrifice all for my faith. There is no bitter future to intimidate me with, nor reasonings to convince me. My reasoning is all taken from the Word of life, and my invariable aim is to acomplish the will of the Lord, who exhorts us to imitate Him.

"The pious remembrance of our beloved brethren in the faith, who offer fervent prayers in our behalf, is invaluable; it is the greatest benefit they can confer upon us; and whatever you tell me on this head

leaves on my mind a sweet and enduring record, and on
my soul the happiest impression.

"You exhort me, dear brother, to bear in mind the
sacred memorial of the martyrs of Christ and of their
tribulations. I give you my best thanks for so doing.
Some of those glorious martyrs left behind them, even
in dying, the footprints of victory. Oh, may the
Supreme Being grant that our sufferings may open the
gates of my country to the Word of God; and if this
is to happen, they may do their worst to me. I have
been too long, and I have tired myself in writing,
but it was necessary to my peace to manifest my
gratitude towards you. My companions in suffering
salute you.
                    "Your humble servant in Christ,
                              "M. MATAMOROS."

"I ought to add, that the £3 that you kindly sent
has been received and distributed, and it is quite
unnecessary to say anything about our gratitude, as
you can imagine it. Please make this known to the
contributors."

On looking through these lovely letters of our
brother, I am constrained to see in all his sufferings
the hand of the Most High, and I believe they will
prove to be a consolation to many a Christian who
probably may be comforted by them in endeavouring
to follow in the same path of trial. "A garden inclosed is my sister, my spouse; a spring shut up, a
fountain sealed, a well of living waters, and streams
from Lebanon;" and such would Matamoros have remained to us in England, had it not been that in this

long and tedious night through which we are passing, God had afflicted one of the members of the body in order that His grace might be manifested. He has blown upon the garden, His Spanish garden, that the spices of it may flow out. But though the church in England has had a sort of first-fruits of the blessing of these bonds suffered in the name of Christ, surely Spain shall have the full harvest of the good results. If large sums of money had been expended, much labour given in evangelizing, the work of the Lord would not have been half so effectually promoted as by the bonds of these brethren. As Paul wrote before, so may we repeat in truth, "I would ye should understand, brethren, that the things which happened unto me have fallen out rather unto the furtherance of the gospel. So that my bonds in Christ are manifested in all the palaces and in all other places." And the following lines will go to substantiate this :—

" Prison of the 'Audiencia,' Granada, Nov. 23, 1861.

"MY DEARLY-LOVED AND NEVER-TO-BE-FORGOTTEN BROTHER IN THE LORD,

"The day begins to dawn, the first splendours of the morning, entering in by the clefts of the wretched shutters of the old window of my dungeon, announce to me that it has been the will of our beloved Father to spare my life to this day, in spite of the will of tyrants. It is about a quarter of an hour since I finished my morning prayer, which I always make immediately on rising from my bed, be the hour what it may. A melancholy silence reigns in this distant dungeon, and I take advantage of these hours to write to you, and answer some questions in your welcome letter. You, beloved brother, have asked me if Christian principles progress steadily in Spain. In this unfortunate country, where the voice of the press is silenced, the publication of every periodical that is not Catholic prohibited; the distribution of the Word of God the signal for persecution, as also that of every book that tends to show the true religion preached by Jesus; the enchaining of as many Christians as possible; the burning in the public 'plazas' of Barcelona and Cordova, and that recently, an infinite number of books, for the sole cause of their not being in accordance with the ecclesiastical court of Rome, and with the principles that it sustains and defends; drawing forced interpretations from the elastic laws of Spain to the prejudice of the Spanish Christians; and, in short, having recourse even to the ignoble weapons of crime, they try to obscure the truth.

"However, against these barriers that tyranny presents and sustains with unwearying zeal, you noble and decided soldiers of Jesus have presented yourselves a grand, worthy, and magnanimous vanguard of Christianity; sonorous echoes of the Christian spirit, representing its wishes, and making our government see that Christianity established in the earth demands for itself the fullest liberty of conscience.

"However, dear brother, if civilization has not opened, as it ought to have done, the doors of this poor dejected nation, if even it has not been able to shed its light on this soil, on a scale that, if not entire, might at least be in a measure; its spirit, nevertheless,

is not a stranger to the land, and thanks to it, and to
the age in which we live, it breaks the chains, come
from whence they may. The nation feels the necessity
of seeking the truth ; and in this study, in this medita
tion, in this search, so inherent to the nineteenth
century and to its worthy sons, the triumph is secure;
the triumph of truth, yes, of Christian truth, is secure.
He who wishes to come to the true knowledge of the
secret of the religious tyranny sustained in Spain
alone, finds it in the certain danger of the church of
Rome, and the positive welfare of the church of God
whose numbers are increasing.

" Within my prison I have had the indescribable
pleasure of hearing persons of a certain position in the
literary and scientific world, of sufficient worth and of
sound judgment, support my poor reasonings, and emit
new and brilliant judgments on this important question, founding their opinions on history, and on the
conversations of those whom they may mix with daily,
whether on the public promenade or the evening ' ter-
tulia.' Public opinion has occupied itself much upon
this question, hitherto dormant in Spain, and, in
general, has given its opinion that there is a future
for Spain. Yes, a bright morning will shine upon the
evangelical work in this land.

" If the fear, and a very well-grounded one, of this
letter being intercepted did not prevent me, I would
give you the names of those persons who have suppli-
cated me to take an active part in the work of evangelization. I would tell you what their influence is, what
their social position ; and assuredly you would rejoice
infinitely, as I have done, at this fruit of your efforts,

blessed by our dear heavenly Father. I could show you a long catalogue of the fruits of your Christian carefulness that has reached the ears of all, and produces its effects on all souls. A day never passes almost without my receiving letters from different ' points of the peninsula, in which similar desires are manifested.

"In —————— I have the positive assurance that the work of evangelization will develop itself both rapidly and solidly, as well as in an eminently consoling and Christian manner; and that it will be like an electric spark for all the province of ——————, and will have a great effect in Spain, through the great moral influence that the opinion of that part of the country (without doubt the most civilized in Spain), exercises throughout the peninsula. I could have wished that my imprisonment had taken place a year later; oh! only one year; and 14,000 or 15,000 Spaniards, declaring themselves Protestants, would have petitioned the Cortes for liberty of worship and the toleration we need. Do not doubt it, this gigantic step would have been made to the astonishment of Europe and the shame of tyrants. This step will yet be taken, do not doubt it; but at present it is premature. Spain is not a sterile country to sow the gospel seed in; I have been to the humblest dwellings, and among some people of elevated position; I have mixed with the humble, and with the proud; I have explored, in short, all that was possible to me, and the evidence has shown me sufficient to know what may be hoped from this unfortunate nation.

· " However, to-day more than ever, I hope much for the future. Do not doubt that that future will be very flattering for the work of the Lord in this classic land of tyranny; your efforts, made patent to the world, promise much prosperity to the holy cause of the gospel. At that time we shall make more progress in one month than at other times in a year. Do not doubt, in short, that you will have the consolation of rejoicing in the rapid progress, and, perhaps, in the complete triumph, of the great work prepared for this poor nation, in which you have had so large a part, and this joy you shall very soon feel, with the protection of the Lord.

" You tell me that you note more confidence of my gaining the victory in my letter to A—— than in any of my others. Oh no, a thousand times no, my hope increases every moment, every minute that passes; and if in some letters I have lamented, these lamentations have not been, by any means, the result of discouragement; no, discouragement is impossible to me! Believe it implicitly, I have never known what it is, and I hope never to know it.

" The battle is gained, be the result what it may; tyranny has received a fatal blow in Spain; the life and magnitude of evangelical work is every way more secure, and my liberty or my imprisonment are alike for its good; my liberty, because thus tyranny shows its impatience; my imprisonment, because thus it shows its only way of sustaining itself, and announces from its own mouth its approaching end.

" May peace, grace, and the fellowship of the Holy
Spirit dwell in you eternally.

" Your humble brother, friend, and son,

" MANUEL MATAMOROS."

The days of our prisoner were by no means spent
in idleness. On the contrary, an activity almost
unparalleled seemed to animate him. In one of his
letters, received about this time, he writes, " I have
just received my correspondence. One long and
eminently consoling letter from Mrs. Tregelles, yours
of the 14th, the enclosed notable one from Miss
Whately, three from Gibraltar of importance, four
from Malaga, and one from Barcelona. These
have come by this morning's post, and I hope for
some also by the evening's delivery. The letter
of —— is very valuable, and is written so sweetly,
with so much purity and feeling, that it has edified
my spirit, and filled my heart with joy. I can write
no more to-night; my eyes are sore, and my head
aches. I must go to bed, for it is already three
o'clock in the morning, and I have some things still
to do."

In another part of the same letter he adds, " One
of our brethren in Christ has fled to Gibraltar. He
was a great helper in the Lord's work, and was
well off at Malaga; and after going through repeated
trials, he is now serving as mason's labourer. This
breaks my heart. I really don't know what to do.
The life which I pass is not *life*. My own position
does not affect me in the least, but these tidings are
too much for me; they affect me profoundly, and,

believe me, that more than all the rest, they are helping to kill me."

Deep sympathy was one of Matamoros' leading characteristics, but many were the other graces that adorned this loving and faithful man. "How beautiful are thy feet with shoes, O prince's daughter! How fair and how pleasant art thou, O love, for delights!" His confidence in God is seen in his letter of February:—

"Prison of the 'Audiencia,' Granada, Feb. 26, 1862.

"VERY DEAR AND RESPECTED BROTHER IN THE LORD,

"You judge most truly when you suppose that the continued and eloquent proofs of Christian love, manifested towards us by your various correspondents, give me much true consolation. You tell me that England will do what she can with France for us. This is, indeed, a source of material comfort; but I must be plain and frank with you on this score.

"I believe that whatever efforts have been or shall be made on our behalf may, perhaps, be fruitless. But I have always striven to set aside the idea of what may be beneficial in the unimportant matter of my personal liberty, which is really of very little consequence to the world and to myself. The only slavery which appals me is the slavery of sin. But my slavery for the love of God makes me happy; and surely this happiness could not be increased by the addition of some physical comforts for an already weak and contemptible body; nor can its liberty be compared with the liberty, the happiness of the soul.

" You know I have never desired the noble efforts of the church of Christ for the sake of benefits conferred upon myself. I have greatly rejoiced on account of the advantage to that which concerns the salvation of the world, the salvation of my poor nation. In this sense, all that the church has done or may do for me gives me great pleasure; her attitude and her efforts have filled me with Christian joy.

"The exertions of a Catholic nation in my favour might be successful. I believe they would; but I repeat I could not rejoice in them. For me the Spirit that animates you and the loved and loving brethren has infinitely more importance and value than all the political movements of France and the whole Catholic world. . . . From the hour when I read ——'s speech, I feared his want of energy, and that it would only add strength to tyranny. In effect the neo-Catholic press has adopted his arguments as its text, and has made use of them to assure our condemnation. If *La Correspondencia* is correct in the report of the Duke of Tetuan's answer, I perceive that this answer is really identical with that given to Sir R. Peel in the House of Commons.

" And now, without reference to this diplomatic question, this wisdom of this world, what have been the commands which Divine love has issued to the church of Christ? To be unwearied in well doing, ceaselessly to invoke the mercy of the Eternal upon us, to hasten to our relief, and to display perfectly the picture of its Christian love. Then let diplomacy follow on its course, defending its own interests, and let the church of God follow hers; they will ever be widely distant the one from the other. Finally, nothing disturbs me nor violates my tranquility. I desire a happy termination of this matter, for there are many destitute families concerned; but our heavenly Father, who has seen the end from the beginning, will bring it to the conclusion which He sees fit. His holy and divine will be done, be it what it may. .

" The most honourable moment of my life is drawing near. In a few more months my enemies will have achieved their victory, and I shall enter upon my convict life. I shall no longer possess the rights of citizenship. The moment the sentence is pronounced against me I shall be a criminal, and only a criminal, in the eyes of society. My rights will be the rights of the parricide, of the thief, of the assassin. There will be no difference there. There will be one law, one regimen, one rule for us all.

" Not only shall I be deprived of my clothes, my hair cut off, and the happiness of seeing my beloved and tender mother denied to me; but I shall be absolutely prohibited from writing. Your letters, consoling, loving, edifying as they are, will not reach me then. Of course, it will be impossible for you ever to hear from me. Then, dear friend, if those sad but honourable hours are drawing so near, I entreat you to make use quickly of the time that remains for my consolation. I trust you will not delay in writing to me.

" Your letters are very necessary to me, yet now I can hardly hope to receive more than four more of them. All the trouble that I have caused you is now nearly over. I know I have often unreasonably imposed upon your love, but I feel a real want of your comforting letters, and I cannot resist the impulse to tell you so.   Pardon one who loves you heartily, and feels that he encroaches on your kindness.

"A few days ago, on the 17th, one of the authorities of Granada came to the prison at about 10 A.M. He asked directly for me, and was immediately conducted to my room by the chief of this establishment. I was in bed; feeling even now far from well.   He took his hat off immediately on entering, and, in spite of my repeated request, would not replace it.   With the most lively interest he inquired after my health, and begged me to tell him if I wished for anything.   I thanked him, and said I wanted and want nothing.   On the table beside my bed lay two copies of the Bible, the one Valera's version, the second Scio's.   The first attracted his attention, and he said to me :—

"'Have you the Bible there?'

"'Yes, señor,' I answered.

"He took it up, and before he opened it he asked, 'Is it English?'

"'It was printed in London in 1853,' I answered.

"'Do you read much in it?' he asked.

"'Yes, señor, at least twice every day; it is my greatest comfort in this place of suffering.'

"'Do you profess yourself a Protestant?'

"'Yes, señor.   I was interrogated by the tribunals of Barcelona and Granada, and not choosing to deny, I confessed the truth.'

"All these questions were asked with great politeness, and then laying down the Bible, he turned to another table where I had more books, and asked :—

" ' Are those tracts or religious books ? '

" ' No, sir, excepting a copy of the Liturgy. The rest are the History of the English Revolution and some other books which have been lent to me, but which I have not had time to read, and must return.'

" He then examined with extreme, almost exaggerated, attention the likenesses which I have hung up in my cell. He dwelt long upon yours, and asked if you were English. I replied ' Yes,' and he then looked at that of my mother, and he told me her name without my asking.

" When he had left me, with an injunction to let him know if I wanted anything, he desired to be shown our exercise-ground, asked the hours at which we are allowed to see our friends, and finally inquired into the position of our case, and gave orders for what was to be done if General Alexander came, and how he was to enter. He also went to the apartments of Trigo and of Alhama ; was exceedingly polite with them also, and asked many questions concerning their treatment in the prison.

" A few days ago, the following scene occurred in the alcaide's house, where I was spending the evening : --An old lady, with less prudence that fanatical love to Popery, insisted on opening a discussion with me on matters of religion. As the conversation advanced, the good lady took advantage of the privileges of her age and sex to insult rather than to reason with me. When I was allowed to speak, I took occasion to show her that she was more likely to wound my feelings, perhaps involuntarily, than to convince my intelligence by such a mode of proceeding. My little brother

Enriqué was standing by, and did not lose a word of the conversation. The old lady, having somewhat moderated the tone of her argument, we began to discuss the question of the Eucharist, and after some general remarks, the good lady concluded by saying to me, 'Do you see how wisely the Inquisition acted in burning all heretics? Your words are more evil and dangerous than fire. Look at that little angel (pointing to Enriqué), he is listening to every word, and at last will be a Protestant like yourself.'

"'I believe you,' said Enriqué. 'I don't mean to go to hell with you and the Pope!' This sally of my little brother's drew forth the laughter of all the guests, and the renewed wrath of the old lady.

"I have just learned that to-morrow our case passes into the hands of the royal fiscal, by his own demand. There are two assistant fiscals, who do nearly all the business; but it appears that the royal fiscal desires to take our case into his own hands. We shall see. He is, I believe, the most liberal member of the 'Audiencia'; for the rest, nearly all old men, belong to the old school, and are thoroughly priest-ridden. The English ambassador has lately asked for, and immediately received from —— the fullest details respecting our case.

"Señor Marin, of Malaga, has been very ill in prison, and his daughter also. Both are now better, and the latter has been ordered change of air and water for a few weeks.

"My mother is very well. Alhama and his family continue well. Trigo also is in good health. I am as usual, but with good heart. All send you a thousand kind regards. In answer to your exhortation to stand firm, I must tell you that I purpose to be stedfast to the end, be that what it may; you will not see me shrink. I ask of the Lord the powerful aid of the Holy Spirit, and I fear nothing for the body while I am so happy in my mind.

"Onward, dear brother—onward and upward! I cannot tell you all I feel towards you. You have a high place in my heart. I pray that God may fill you and yours with peace, grace, and the communion of his Holy Spirit.

"Your loving brother in the Lord,

"MANUEL MATAMOROS."

His deep attachment to his mother was another sweet trait in his character. She indeed proved a mother to him in this long night of sorrow, and had it not been for her untiring care, he must have succumbed to his bodily sufferings. Perhaps I may be wrong in speaking thus. Would it not be wiser to say of him, as he would have said himself, "The Lord God is my strength, and He will make my feet like hinds' feet, and He will make me to walk upon my high places." His unflinching stedfastness on hearing the royal fiscal's demand against him is manifested in his next sweet letter. Of him it may be said—

> If on my face for Thy dear name
> Shame and reproaches be,
> I'll hail reproach and welcome shame,
> For Thou rememberest me."

Matamoros wrote again on the 17th of March. The following are extracts from his letter:—

" The results of the accusation and the demand of the royal fiscal is, as you know, the sentence of eleven years at the galleys, and other accessory punishments. This ferocious outburst of intolerance has not sur. prised me. After a year and a half of such and so many vexations, after so many troubles and trials, the three prisoners of Granada are to be condemned to eleven years of penal servitude, for the sole offence of their Christian faith. This is the maximum punishment indicated by the penal code; and if the accessory penalties are confirmed, it will be an infinitely severer sentence than the framers of the code ever anticipated.

" The demand of the royal fiscal generally indicates, with tolerable certainty, what will be the sentence of the superior court. There may be trifling variations—as increase or diminution of penalty, but they are usually slight. In this suit, the belief of the judges has been evidently influential. They have thought the greater our martyrdom the greater their merit.

" Four days before the fiscal's accusation the archbishops sent hastily for the secretary. They say it was to ask the number of the accused. Possibly. It is only too certain that on the following day the case had taken an unfavourable turn. The accusation was settled in consultation by the four fiscals, lawyers of the 'Audiencia,' every one of whom is a bigoted Roman Catholic—nay, belongs to the party who still defend the Spanish Inquisition. It seems

as if they sought to make my future as dark as
can be. No matter; I forgive them with my whole
heart, and I pray to God that my sufferings may be
the means of one day making them remember and
repent, and that, in their repentance, they may seek
the truth of Christ, and faithfully follow it. May
our God have pity upon them!

"A similar penalty has been demanded for Alhama and Trigo, but I hardly think it possible that
it can be confirmed against the latter. For those
prisoners who have been at liberty on bail, a term of
eight years has been demanded. In fact, the whole
accusation breathes our slaughter, threatening, hatred,
vengeance.

"Onward! onward! They demand the maximum
penalty against us. Is not this the maximum of our
honour? I will go forward, and will fulfil the word
that I gave to the judge at Barcelona, when he
desired me to withdraw my confession of Protestantism. I repeat now what I said then: 'I
have put my hand to the plough, and will not look
back.' This is the road that my faith points out.
I will never waver. To me to live is Christ and to
die is gain. I will go forward and onward. The
disciple is intimately united with his Master. That
Divine Master *sought* his cross, and voluntarily shed
his blood for us; He died to give us life. Well
then, if I desire to follow Him, shall I fear what
Jesus did not fear? No! If I die in Christ, and for
Christ, I shall live eternally with Him. The will of
God be done in all things

" Your assurance of the continued prayers of many saints on behalf of the prisoners fills me with happy joy. Give to all my hearty thanks, and the assurance of my gratitude and love. My dear mother consoles and sustains me in these trying circumstances by her courage and resignation. Yesterday some friends called, and expressed their sympathy on the result of the fiscal's address, and said, amongst other things, that our enemies, in addition to the penalty, sought to brand the Spanish Protestants with the infamy of the galleys. Steadily my mother answered, ' They are deceived; my son ought to be proud of it. I, his mother, shall glory in telling that I have a son at the galleys for his Protestant faith; and if children should survive him, this remembrance of their father will enoble them.' . .   . . .

"The prisoners of Malaga have added a glorious page to the church's history. Three days ago, they declared before the tribunal that they were not Roman Catholics, but Protestants by faith and conviction. I believe some of them had answered ambiguously at their first interrogation, and could not rest without this fresh step to satisfy their consciences. May God enlighten them and me also! . . . .

" I earnestly aspire to a fair and brilliant future for myself! My will and my soul are bent upon this point; nothing disturbs me or alters my tranquility, save the idea of involuntarily straying from my chosen path—this terrifies and confounds me. This path is not that which the world opens to me. So widely apart are the two, that now, although I recognize pious and eminently evangelical zeal and love in the efforts which you and your friends are making for my liberty; yet, I believe that *I* ought not to strive for it.

" I read in the Book of Life, that the Lord knew that his hour had not yet come; that He knew when it had come, and that He advanced as it were to meet His fate, although it was one of anguish. It is true that He withdrew from a place where He was persecuted, but only because His time was not yet come; when that hour arrived, He—life of our life— went to seek the scene of His martyrdom!

" I have given myself entirely to God, through the most sweet name of Jesus. I am His. He will open the door of my prison, if He sees it meet for me and for all. Or else, He has another lot in store for me which I cannot imagine, the end of which, as far as this earth is .concerned, I shrink from contem- plating. But my end and aim is Jesus, and being so, ought I to shrink from or refuse to bear sorrow or persecution for His name's sake? No; for He sought out His sufferings for us. No; for the pathway to heaven is the pathway of the cross. Well, then, I know not if it is for the advancement of the cause of my freedom, that my poor and humble but sincere letters should be published. But I do know that the publicity which has been given to the story of the sufferings of Jesus has saved my soul; that the publicity given to the constancy and piety of Paul has given me a bright example; and that the publicity given to the Book of Life has given me life, for it has taught me to worship God through Jesus, in spirit and in truth. Now, who can say whether the publication of my sufferings for my fidelity may not bring some soul to the gate of salvation? Might it be so? Yes, then let that soul be saved, and let my body perish in the hands of my tormentors. So many saints have died, but their souls have been witnesses of the truth before the world, and have been saved by Jesus. For he who loses his life for His sake, the same shall find it.

"This publicity has been for nineteen centuries wounding to death the power of the evil one, witnessing against his impurity, destroying his kingdom, step by step driving back his hosts. Light has sprung up in the dark places, and in the region of error enters eternal truth.

"My letters are poor and weak, but as they are the expression of the vehement and sincere desire of my heart, some who read them may be led to ask the reason of my joy in tribulation, and he who cannot understand it by faith, may strive to fill the void that my words will leave in his heart by the study of the Book of Life, which is my strength and consolation, and this study may give health to the soul which is sick with doubt or indifference. Perhaps, also, my weak but sincere words may confirm in the way of life some one who is walking or beginning to walk feebly in its glorious path. My pen is very weak and ignorant, but my desires and wishes are in no way weak or feeble; they are solidly written in my heart, and to carry them out, I will go on unweariedly, firmly, and steadily to the end, to the last moment of my life.

"I must repeat and reiterate to-day what I have said for a year and a half now; to-day, that the passions of my enemies appear like an overflowing river; which is that, by God's grace, I will go forward and onward with yet greater joy and decision. I am, as ever, most thoroughly resolved not to lose one moment or one opportunity to show forth all my wishes, their grounds, and the deeply-rooted sentiment that produces them, or to declare to my foes that they will never succeed in conquering or in punishing me. For earnest faith is unconquerable, and against such there is no law.

"This is my soul's necessity, or rather the natural effect of my faith in God. He gives me life, joy, peace, spiritual food for my soul's health. But on the other hand, I only look forward to increased wrath on the part of my enemies: fury, that grieves me on their account, but that is to me a sweet pledge of my sure rejoicing in Jesus. But once again. When I shall have entered upon my term of punishment, I cannot but look forward to my death, perhaps very close at hand, for the flesh is weak; but in this I shall find my joy. The hand of the all-wise God, the gentle hand of my gracious Father, will be in this. If I am faithful unto death, He will give me the crown of life; and being faithful, I must die under my punishment, for this will be for the advancement of the holy cause; welcome then, this death! This is the future to which I aspire, as I told you before. Therefore, I must not struggle for liberty. The will of the Lord be done in all things. And you, His faithful children, act as seems fittest."

At this time (March, 1862) the prisoners at Malaga addressed to Matamoros the following assurance of their faith having been strengthened by his constancy:—

"DEAR FRIEND, AND OUR LOVED BROTHER IN CHRIST,

"We have received your Christian letter, and we confess frankly that we were anxious for the moment to arrive, because we are always delighted by your correspondence, and because our souls receive by it the efficacious consolation which keeps faith alive in our hearts, and gives us the aid we require to suffer patiently persecution and disgrace. We find much to admire, dear brother, in your letters; much to respect and follow. In them we perceive what pure ideas animate you; what unwavering faith and what holy love to the Lord Jesus, and that this love is exalted in proportion to your sufferings for His name. We see by your letter that you have not flinched to confess before the tribunal the creed you profess; that your principal wish is that the Protestant religion be propagated in our benighted country, by spreading the light of truth, and making all know the maxims contained in the Book of Life. All these things we respect, and we cannot do less than render our just tribute of admiration to the indefatigable propagation of such holy truths. Up to the present we have kept you informed of our declarations, acts, etc., which have been given in our trial, and the faithful observations that concerning them we have received from you have so deeply moved us, and have caused such a deep sensation in our minds, that

I

having repented from the bottom of our hearts for
having wavered in confessing our faith, we have
resolved to go before the tribunal that is trying us,
and with all clearness to amplify our declaration;
manifesting to them, that owing to certain untoward
circumstances foreign to our character we held silence
for a length of time, which now causes us remorse,
for we are Protestants to the bottom of our hearts,
and we have propagated and will propagate the
maxims and doctrines contained in the Holy Bible,
and imprisonment is not sufficient to quench our
ardent faith, nor shall it tear from our bosoms those
ideas which are our chiefest glory, and which we
pray to the Eternal may be diffused through the
length and breadth of Spain. Also we desire to
inform you that our one desire is that the truth be
propagated, and that all may receive the divine light
of the gospel, and may be made acquainted with the
true doctrines that Jesus taught upon earth. We
also desire to say that in this step we have not been
moved by any human interest, but simply from the
conviction that the Reformed religion is the right
one; and believing, as we do, that all the creeds
which differ from it are either false or adulterated,
we abandon the maxims that the Church of Rome
teaches, and will only follow those contained in God's
Word, where we hear the voice of God only speaking,
and the holy apostles who accompanied him during
his ministry. This is our act of faith, and this is
what probably we shall have put into execution before
the competent authority, when you have received this
letter.

" We confess, beloved Manuel, that we have not been given the same energy and decision as you in confessing Jesus. We confess that we have been lukewarm in publishing what we believe. But we trust that you will pardon us in this delicate matter, and we hope that you will perceive that it was only circumstances which caused us to conceal our faith for a time. We feel we have erred ; but now be assured that we are disposed, come what may, to repair our mistake, and we believe that God in His infinite mercy, so loving, so benign, will pardon us this fault. We are led to think this by the many proofs of the Divine clemency we have given us; the Magdalen, that sinful woman, a model of corruption and vice, who had never thought about the salvation of her soul, and had during her lifetime only thought of carnal delights." . . . .

The last letter from the Malaga prisoners shows the important place which Matamoros' faithfulness held in determining them to follow his example. One of them, Señor Marin, of Malaga, was a sculptor of great merit, and, from his long confinement in a damp cell, he had nearly lost his eyesight. He, from his deep devotion to Christ, received the cognomen of the Spanish Andrew Dunn.

On March 14th, the case of the Spanish persecutions was brought before the British House of Commons, on which occasion Mr. Kinnaird spoke at great

length, and also Lord Palmerston, but no results
followed. We give their speeches below:—

THE PERSECUTIONS IN SPAIN.

" Mr. KINNAIRD said it would be recollected that,
during the last session, the Right Hon. Baronet the
Chief Secretary for Ireland on more than one occasion brought under the notice of the House the case
of the persecution of certain people in Spain, solely
on account of their religious opinions. The right
hon. baronet stated the case with great ability, and
he had no doubt that, although he had since accepted
office, the right hon. gentleman still remained true
to his principles. The Spanish persecutions commenced in 1859. In that year a naturalized British
subject (Escalante) was seized, and imprisoned in a
loathsome dungeon, for merely circulating the Scriptures. He was sentenced to nine years' penal servitude in the galleys, but owing to the intercession of
our consul he obtained a remission of the sentence.
The opinions for which he was persecuted had since
spread in Spain, as they had in Italy, in France,
and in other Roman Catholic countries. The Roman
Catholic priesthood became alarmed, tracked the
readers of the Bible through the agency of police
spies, and subjected them to cruel persecution. The
names of Matamoros and Alhama were already as
familiar to the people of this country as those of the
Madiai were ten years ago. Since his right hon.
friend brought the subject before the House, those
two unhappy men had, on the 6th of January of the

present year, been sentenced to seven years of the galleys, while to a third victim (Trigo) had been awarded four years of a similar servitude. An attempt had been made to connect these men with certain political disturbances which had occurred in the district, but they had been twice honourably acquitted of the charge by the tribunal before which they were carried for trial. They had been condemned to the galleys for no other offence than professing those religious views which were held by the bulk of our countrymen. An appeal had been raised from that iniquitous sentence, and he wished to impress on our Government the duty of an indignant and energetic remonstrance against its confirmation. To be sent to the galleys was not only to be stripped of every right of citizenship, but to be doomed to the companionship of murderers and felons, to wear a galling chain for years, to be denied letters or visits even from one's nearest relatives. Already Matamoros' strength was breaking down under his captivity. Originally an officer in the army, he had been compelled to throw up his commission on account of the faith which he held, and was subsequently, in October, 1860, thrown into prison for the same reason. But these three men did not stand alone. The number of victims to persecution had been constantly growing, though he was happy to hear that there were not so many in prison just now as formerly. Within a few weeks or months, thirty persons were arrested and imprisoned at Granada, Malaga, and Seville alone. Many others fled for refuge to Gibraltar and elsewhere. At one time as many as fifty persons in Malaga were left destitute through the disappearance of heads of families.   In one case, a sculptor with his wife and eldest son were arrested in the dead of night, and cast into a dungeon, leaving five helpless children totally unprovided for.   In another instance, the head of one of the best public schools in Seville was apprehended. It was well known that at Granada the vilest criminals received better treatment in prison than the Christians who were convicted of reading the Bible.   By the latest accounts five were still in prison at Malaga, and three at Granada.   The others had been released, and some, if not all, had become refugees.   It might be said that this was a matter which concerned the Spaniards alone, and with which we had no right to interfere.   Others thought that interference was unadvisable, because it would prove of no avail.   Knowing, as he did, what an impression the debates in the House last year had produced in Spain, he was confident that great good would result from a decided expression of opinion on the present occasion, and from cordial intercession on the part of the Government.   One of the prisoners wrote, with reference to one of the discussions of last session, ' I have not yet read the speech of Sir Robert Peel, but I have heard it notably praised.   An extract from Lord John Russell's reply has been translated, but only by the reactionary and anti-liberal section of the Spanish press.   These periodicals have also published long leading articles commenting on the words of the minister, which, unfortunately, appear to be favourable to the neo-Catholic party (of course that was only the distorted interpretation which that party sought to put on the speech of the noble lord), and double anathemas and menaces have fallen upon us.   The speech has been a fertile subject with our foes. I do not know what the spirit of it as a whole may have been, but I venture to believe that it was not that which the enemies of the gospel and the friends of slavery of conscience would represent it. Be that as it may, the clergy have taken fresh life from it; and not a little was expected from England. We, and with us all Spanish Protestants, looked to you, after God, for everything. . . . . Spain has advanced towards religious liberty more rapidly than in many past years. The attitude of England has done much. Our brethren have taken courage. The liberal press, in its narrow circle, has done what it could. Nay, in the Spanish Chambers the other day notice was given of an intended interpellation to the Government respecting us.' The writer says elsewhere that 'all Spaniards look to England in this crisis, and from England only can we expect any help.' That illustrated the moral effect of the discussions in the British Parliament. He would not recapitulate all the precedents quoted last session by his right hon. friend as to the right of this country to interfere in the matter. He would only remind the House of the words of the eminent authority, Vattel, on this question. 'When a religion is persecuted, the foreign nations who profess it may intercede for their brethren; but this is all they can lawfully do, unless the persecution be carried to an intolerable excess. Then, indeed, it becomes a case of manifest tyranny, in which all nations are permitted to succour an unhappy people. A regard to their own safety may also authorize them to undertake the defence of the persecuted.' An hon. friend of his, the member for Galway, the other

evening made an earnest appeal to the sympathies of
the House in behalf of the Southerners who were in
armed secession from the United States of America, and
who demanded liberty to keep 4,000,000 of people in
perpetual bondage; might not he far more confidently
ask their sympathies for those who only exercised the
right to profess what they conscientiously believed, and
sought not to be treated as felons for holding the faith
professed by the majority of the members of that House?
Nor were they without encouragement from the results
of the intercession made in behalf of their persecuted
brethren in former instances. He had had the honour
of bringing before the House the case of the Madiai, and
their release speedily followed. Little did he think
when he brought that case before the House how soon
the Grand Ducal Government which persecuted them
would be swept away. The tendency of these persecutions was to alienate the people from their Governments,
and they were never forgotten when the day of reckon-
ing came. The House would recollect the benefits
which followed the withdrawal of our diplomatic representative from the Neapolitan Court, and the publication of that remarkable pamphlet of the Chancellor of
the Exchequer with reference to Poerio and his fellow-
sufferers. Where now was that persecuting Government? Here was a great moral lesson which should
not be lost on such Governments—an advantage
gained in a peaceable way by bringing public opinion
to bear upon them. And was the idea of religious
liberty in Spain perfectly hopeless? Within the last
ten years the question of right of worship had been
discussed in the Cortez, and was only lost by one

vote. The press, moreover, was not completely subservient to the Romish priesthood. Another fact of great importance was that, since his right hon. friend had brought forward this subject, we did not stand alone in our remonstrances with the Spanish Government. Greatly to the credit of the Emperor of the French, M. Thouvenol had written a very admirable despatch, instructing his minister at Madrid strongly to remonstrate with the Spanish Government on the subject of these unhappy persecutions; and when he remembered the position of France in relation to the Pope's continued possession of Rome, the fact was all the more significant. Prussia, Russia, and Sweden had also remonstrated, and were endeavouring to persuade Marshal O'Donnell of the impolicy as well as injustice of persisting in these iniquitious sentences. The hon. member for Launceston (Mr. Haliburton), with that power of sarcasm for which he was so remarkable, referred the other evening to what Juarez might have said to the Spanish General who had command of the expedition to Mexico. It certainly was somewhat remarkable that Spain, who had often repudiated her public engagements, kept notoriously bad faith with us in her treaties in regard to the slave-trade, and was now disgracing herself by these persecutions, should go to Mexico in order to compel her to pay her debts. He did trust that Marshal O'Donnell, who had great experience in public life, would see the inexpediency of continuing these persecutions. What was immediately wanted was the pardon of these persons. Private efforts had been unable to obtain this. He therefore asked again for the remonstrance of our Government, and he hoped ultimately to see a change in those laws under which these persecutions had taken place, which were a disgrace to a civilized nation, making it impossible to know if any man was honest in his religious profession; for while one man would undergo imprisonment and the galleys rather than deny his faith, 500 others might think him right without daring to face the danger of avowing their convictions. He begged to ask the noble lord, the First Lord of the Treasury, in reference to what took place last session on the subject of the persecution in Spain and the efforts which were understood to be about to be made by Her Majesty's Secretary of State for Foreign Affairs in order to obtain remission of punishment for Matamoros and others, who were undergoing imprisonment and are now under sentence of the galleys, on the charge of maintaining certain religious opinions and practices contrary to the religion of the State, whether he had any objection to state to the House if any and what steps had been taken in reference to this matter; and whether Her Majesty's Minister at Madrid had been able to obtain any satisfactory assurance that a favourable consideration would be given to his representations on the subject."

"Viscount Palmerston,—Sir, I quite admit that my hon. friend has performed a duty which nobody can complain of in bringing this matter under the consideration and attention of the House. And there can be no doubt the expression of opinion in the British House of Commons must have great weight with those in any country in Europe to whose conduct those observations apply. I am sorry to say that I cannot, however, make any report to my hon. friend and the House as to any satisfactory result which has yet followed any attempts or exertions of Her Majesty's Government to obtain the pardon and release of the persons to whom the observations of my honourable friend apply. The difficulties, as he must be aware, are very great. The Spanish nation is a nation full of valiant, noble, chivalrous feelings and sentiments; but unfortunately in Spain, the Catholic priesthood exercise a sway greater than that they possess in any other country; and, however liberal—I believe I may say so—the Catholic laity in most countries are, history tells us that wherever the priesthood gets the predominance, the utmost amount of intolerance as invariably prevails. And although in countries where they form a minority they are constantly demanding, not only toleration, but equality, in countries where they are predominant neither equality nor toleration exists. Well, sir, the case in this instance bears upon law. It does not depend upon the will and action of the Government. There are ancient laws of the most intolerant and persecuting kind which have been called into action by the ministers of the Christian religion, and that action has been the condemnation of these unhappy men to punishment, which must, in its nature, be revolting to the minds of liberal persons. Efforts have been made to obtain from the Ministers of the Crown of Spain the exercise of their advice to the Sovereign to show that mercy which belongs to the sovereign of every country. Those efforts have not yet been successful. Mixed with the admirable qualities

which distinguish the Spanish people, there is one
quality not undeserving of respect, viz., a feeling of
jealousy of foreign interference in their internal affairs.
It is a quality which is connected with one of the
highest national virtues; and, therefore, it is obvious
that, in any endeavour to obtain the reversal, mitigation, or cessation of punishment, great delicacy must be
shown, and great care taken, lest in endeavouring to do
good we should, on the contrary, perpetuate evil. I
can only assure my hon. friend that no effort will be
omitted by Her Majesty's Government which they
think will be conducive to the attainment of the object
which he has in view."

May England not allow the blood of martyrs to be
at her door. God forbid that it ever may be written
of us that we, through our lukewarmness, have seemed
to say, "His blood be on *us* and on our children." It
is not yet too late to alter our hitherto timid and·
humiliating policy; and, no doubt, if a decided course
of action were pursued an end would be put to this
detestable priestcraft and cruelty. "I was a stranger,
and ye took me not in; naked, and ye clothed me not;
sick, and in prison, and ye visited me not." Our position has been sustained and our country blessed before
now by our helping the oppressed, and now we have
another opportunity offered us which, as yet, has not
been taken.

The public press was not silent during this iniquitous persecution; the *Patriot* of Feb. 27, 1862,
took it up warmly, and its brilliant article we give
below :—

"THE LOOK OUT.

"Let the names of Manuel Matamoros and of J. Alhama become household words in every Christian family in these islands. 'Remember them that are in bonds as bound with them.' The Spanish Government, in accordance with Article 128 of the Penal Code, has condemned these noble confessors of the gospel to seven years of the galleys, and to perpetual civil disability, with costs. Spain, which is advancing rapidly in wealth, education, political influence, and military power, remains mediæval, tyrannical, exclusive, spiteful, intolerant in her views of religion. It is sometimes supposed that all national development is co-ordinate, and that advance in every line of progress is equal and parallel. But experience proves that this is far from being the truth. A people may make progress in military power without advancing in arts or virtues; a nation may develop to a marvellous degree the resources of a fertile country, while remaining as to the higher departments of thought and feeling in a state of barbarism. The diffusion of secular knowledge has in itself little effect upon superstition. Why should a nation abandon ancient superstitions as the result of instruction in science when it is seen that an individual great man, who has mastered the whole circle of modern knowledge, remains a bigoted Catholic? Besides, Spain acts in this business, so she imagines, on principle and on experience. In Spain, if anywhere, it has been proved, so she alleges, that thorough persecution is, on the whole, effectual in the suppression of 'heresy,' at least for the time present; and the government appreciates the advantages of unity in the affairs of 'religion.' There is not much ground for astonishment, therefore, at the issue of the trial of the Spanish Bible-readers. If you add together the probabilities arising from Spanish experiences in history; from the wrath of priestcraft assailed in one of its last strongholds; from the demands of a popular superstition friendly to the vices of a self-indulgent nation; from the cold-blooded cruelty of a modern bureaucratic and centralized government aiming at 'order' and quietness, you arrive at a sum total of likelihoods which convert into a philosophical certainty and a State necessity the result which has been realized.

"But MM. Matamoros and Alhama will not suffer in vain. They are accompanied to the galleys by a Power who will cause their detention and slavery to turn out 'rather to the furtherance of the gospel.' The widely-diffused zeal on behalf of religious liberty, which is a characteristic of our times, has somewhat tempted men to a forgetfulness of the fact that the sufferings of Christian teachers have as important a part to bear in the extension of Christianity as the openings for unhindered works liberally afforded by political wisdom and justice. There never was a time, perhaps, when there was more danger than at present of the missionaries of the gospel permitting themselves to suppose that the prospects even of imprisonment and death are decisive reasons for abandoning particular evangelic enterprises. There never was a time when the self-devoting heroism of a few martyrs would produce deeper and wider effects upon the kingdom of darkness than now. We are all too prone to make our own safety and comfort the first condition of Christian soldiership. The extreme antagonism existing between true Christianity and 'all that is in the world,' should prepare us for the frequent practical expression of the deep spiritual opposition to God harboured in the bosom of mankind. 'Political and religious liberty all over the world' will never oblite-rate the strife between truth and falsehood, good and evil, God and the Devil. 'They that are born after the flesh' will persecute, as far as they are able, 'them that are born after the spirit.' There are many who wish to 'live godly' in Christ Jesus, but who, in a sense far different from that of St. Paul, will not 'suffer persecution.' They will not hear of a man's undergoing wrong for his 'religious opinions.' Now, such extravagance proceeds from a miscalculation of forces. Liberty is a good thing, to be much sought after, and to be struggled for by Christian politicians. Meantime, suffering also is a good thing, and ex-ercises a material influence upon the diffusion of spiritual religion. Towards the close of his ministry Paul spent nearly five years of his life, continuously in a state of bondage; yet, in the Roman letter, written during the latter portion of this detention, he always speaks of his 'bonds' as effectual preachers of truth. Chained by the hand, like a dangerous wild beast, to a Roman legionary, he ever speaks of his manacles as of equal value with miracles in the defence and propagation of the Gospel.

"How is this? It is because the spectacle of a cultivated man suffering severe affliction for conscience' sake, affliction which he might wholly escape by ungodly abandonment of his principles, always makes a deep impression on thoughtful observers. When men bring themselves 'much gain by soothsaying,' or by any form of religion, it throws a doubt upon their absolute sincerity. The obvious gain in money, in station, in authority, in reputation, is considered to offer a sufficient *rationale* and exposition of the ruling motive. Doth Job serve God for nought? is Satan's taunt at the prosperous believer, re-echoed by the world, which is always sceptical of fine excellence. But, when a man brings himself into trouble, or hard labour, or irksome toil, or straitened circumstances, by following his conscience; when he sacrifices bright worldly prospects for a spiritual and eternal end, it draws attention to the faith, and persuades men that there is something in it. Some people, indeed, talk as if the world were more likely to be wrought upon religiously, the more influential and prosperous, in a worldly point of view, are its advocates and patrons. It is conceived that the 'upper classes' particularly are more likely to be converted to goodness by a right reverend father in God enthroned in the House of Lords, and having five or ten thousand a-year at his disposal. But, in truth, this is a mistake. A duke or a marquis is just like any other man in the constitution of his mind, and is more likely to be persuaded by the spec-

tacle of self-denial, of disinterestedness, of suffering
borne for the sake of conscience, than by all the
gorgeous trappings of a secularized hierarchy.

"Thus it is that suffering for the truth proves so
powerful an auxiliary in its diffusion. It furnishes
the evidence of a real faith and patience. Men are
at ease in their sins when they see only a 'godliness'
which is 'gain.' But when they see a man burning
to ashes for a principle, or going to the galleys for an
idea of God, it gives them the impression that religion is a reality; and to make it seem real is halfway towards making it be believed. Suffering for
the faith also exhibits God's supporting grace in sorrow. Matamoros says in his recent letter to the
churches in Paris, 'This sentence causes me ineffable
joy.' It represents the comforting action of the
Divine Spirit in the midst of a world doubtful of all
supernatural agencies. It kindles the enthusiasm of
sympathizers, and makes them much more bold to
speak the word of God without fear. Nothing is
more inspiring than a martyrdom. The sparks of
the burning fly and fall in every direction, and raise
fresh 'fires' on earth, such as God delights in—fires
in which truth shall consume error. Suffering
quickens the ingenuity of Christians, and leads them
to devise fresh methods for assailing the fortresses
of superstition. It exposes to public gaze the hateful
qualities of the opposition. It exhibits the essentia
weakness of systems which can support themselves
only by force, not by argument. It brings to light
the tyranny and cruelty of priests, who will leap
through every restraint of right and honour in order

K

to maintain their power. Frequently persecution has widely diffused the gospel by dispersing its confessors, who go 'everywhere preaching the word,' just as Palestine was filled with the fugitives from the persecution at Jerusalem, and American freedom was founded by the exiles of England. And, lastly, oftentimes the imprisonment of noted Christians has turned their thoughts inwards, since all outward activity was forbidden, and enabled them to mature in solitude thoughts and works which have operated to the production of evangelical religion long after their imprisonment was ended. It was thus that Patmos, under a divine inspiration, produced the Apocalypse. It was thus that the Restoration, with its Act of Uniformity, and its Conventicle Act, and its Five-mile Act, produced Baxter's 'Christian Directory,' and Howe's 'Blessedness of the Righteous,' and 'Delighting in God,' and 'The Vanity of Man as Mortal,' and Alleine's 'Alarm to the Unconverted,' and Bunyan's 'Pilgrim's Progress,' and Milton's 'Paradise Lost,' and many other spiritual legacies of that age of sorrow. And thus our beloved brethren in Spain shall not suffer so many things in vain. We shall pray for them in every public act of worship; we shall ask that the solicitations of England, and Prussia, and Russia shall not be ineffectual in bending the pride of the Spanish Government; we shall beg that the warm intercessions of the Evangelical Alliance, so ably presented to the Prime Minister O'Donnell, by General Alexander, may not fail of success. But even if the Spanish hierarchy persist in enforcing the terrible and cruel sentence of the galleys, we shall still confidently expect that one Matamoros will, though in his bonds, chase ten thousand opponents, and one single Alhama, in chains and convict dress, prove stronger for the shaking of the Popedom than all this petty persecution can prove for the extinction of the gospel.

"W."

Few in our country have shown more unceasing sympathy and perseverance in the case of Matamoros than General Alexander, and the record of his mission, which is also from the *Patriot* newspaper, we here insert:—

"SPAIN.

" THE PRISONERS FOR THE GOSPEL.

" The following statement of the result of General Alexander's visit to Spain has been forwarded to us by the Evangelical Alliance:—

" 'Major-General Alexander, who, at the request of the British Committee of the Evangelical Alliance, and as the representative of the Conference of Christians of All Nations, held a few months since at Geneva, visited Madrid, to endeavour to obtain the liberation of the Spaniards imprisoned for reading the Bible, has just returned from his mission.

" ' The object of the mission was not to excite public agitation, or to adopt any course which might wear the appearance of foreign interference with the laws of Spain—a point on which the people of that country are proverbially sensitive—but simply to seek for an act of royal clemency towards the prisoners, especially towards Matamoros, Alhama, and Trigo, who have, solely on the ground of their religion, been condemned to the galleys, the first two for seven years, and the third for four years.

"'Through the kindness of several distinguished persons in this and other countries, the cordial, though unofficial, services of the ambassadors of England, France, and Russia, were enlisted in this work of mercy. The Prussian ambassador, though a Roman Catholic, had already made representations to the Spanish Government. Other valuable aid, Spanish and foreign, was also obtained. At the request of Sir John Crampton, General O'Donnell favoured General Alexander with an interview, at which he entered fully into the subject of the General's mission.

"'At that interview the General frankly stated the circumstances under which he was deputed to lay before his Excellency the expression of the principles and sentiments of his co-religionists, not in England only, but in France, Germany, Sweden, Holland, Switzerland, and other countries; that, although the arrangements for his mission had been made by a particular Society, the cause was common to all Protestants.

"'General Alexander then presented to General O'Donnell a written statement of the object of his mission, and of the pleas adduced to obtain from the clemency of Her Majesty the Queen of Spain the pardon of men who stand acquitted of all political and criminal offences, but who are condemned to the galleys for taking the Sacred Scriptures as their rule of faith, and acting according to their conscientious convictions.

" 'The Prime Minister was most courteous in his reception of General Alexander. He received very cordially the statement above referred to, together with a translation of a Minute on the subject of the Spanish prisoners, adopted by the Geneva Conference in 1861, and of lists of the nationalities represented at that Conference, and of many persons of note in Europe known to be interested in the fate of men now suffering for conscience' sake in prison, and over whom impends the dread sentence of labour in the galleys.

" 'The Duke of Tetuan, while stating the obstacles to General Alexander's object, expressed his satisfaction with the manner in which it had been sought to promote it, and promised to submit the papers presented to him to his colleagues in office. He made some remarks upon Spain being less intolerant than was generally supposed, but said that though she would allow nothing like dictation or foreign interference, still her Government was considerate of moral influences and of fair representations that came properly before them. He observed that, though he could hold out no hope of an immediate favourable result, yet, if the object was to be gained, the course adopted was the best that could have been pursued for the purpose. In the course of his remarks the General alluded in a gratifying manner to his own Irish origin, and spoke in very complimentary terms of the army to which the General belongs, and of the Sovereign whom it is his honour to serve.

" ' The final result of this interview will be anxiously waited for by Protestants throughout Europe and America.' "

If we contrast the conduct of our rulers in this matter with that of Darius, the Persian monarch, when Daniel was in the lions' den, we cannot but see the deepest sympathy and energy evinced in the actions of the latter, whilst supineness and apathy are the characteristics of the former. We cannot but admire the conduct of Darius when we read the words, "*The king was sore displeased with himself, and set his heart upon Daniel to deliver him, and he laboured till the going down of the sun to deliver him.*" Again, "*The king went to his palace, and passed the night fasting, neither were instruments of music brought before him, and his sleep went from him. Then the king arose very early in the morning, and went in haste unto the den of lions.*" The remainder of the story is well known. The deep sympathy of the Persian monarch elicits from us sentiments of grateful admiration for his untiring care and love to Daniel, and we sought in vain for a corresponding line of action from those in power in our Government. "*If thou altogether holdest thy peace at this time, then shall their enlargement and deliverance arise to the Jews from another place, but thou and thy father's house shall be destroyed. And who knoweth whether thou art come to the kingdom for such a time as this?*"

CHAPTER IX.

EXTRACTS FROM THE DEFENCE OF THE PRISONERS AT MALAGA.

THE conduct and activity of the *Roman Catholic* advocates chosen to defend the cause of the Malaga prisoners, appears bold when compared with that of our *Protestant* rulers. In order that our countrymen may judge between the two, we give some extracts from the defence made in Malaga by the learned jurist Don Bernabé Davila y Bertoli, in the month of August, 1862.

DEFENCE OF PRISONERS AT MALAGA.

" D. Roqué Meaño and D. Francisco Mariano Lopez, —in the names of D. José Gonzalez Mejias and D. Antonio Carrasco Palomo, prisoners in the public prison of this city for the supposed crime of attempting to abolish or change the Roman Catholic and Apostolic religion in Spain—appeal against the accusation of the fiscal, in which he demands for our clients the penalty of nine years of penal servitude with accessories, and a payment of a part of the costs of the case.   .   .   .

"It is an eternal principle that a man cannot be forced to believe anything which his reason rejects or his will repels; and the Catholic religion—this religion of pure love, which has been founded by Jesus Christ in the external form of the Christian Church, which has amongst all social institutions borne the precious fruit of salvation on the earth, and to which Europe owes that pure humanity which lies at the root of its civilization—the example and the teacher of all other civilizations, which has awakened, by means of the instructions of its Divine Founder, the sentiment of human dignity in every man, under every sky, and in every social state; which has kindled the heavenly flame of love amongst men; which has drawn closer the bonds of universal brotherhood, and has been the best stimulant to the development of all the physical and moral forces with which human nature is gifted—this religion, we say, cannot be forced upon any one by material force or moral violence, for the eternal designs of God have made it in harmony with the nature of the free and rational man. If there have been limitations and imperfections in the history of our country which have authorised prosecutions and punishments for religious opinions—if fanaticism and dogmatism once found their perfect, genuine, and severe representation in the tribunal of the Holy Office, which was clothed with immense privileges, and armed with an absurd private jurisdiction to defend the sublime principles of Christianity with the weapons of fire and tortures—these imperfections should for ever be put away from among us, and these bygone times should never return, for every religious doctrine, and especially the Catholic, constitutes a subjective relation apart from and above the objective idea, which is the fatal basis of all intolerance, and which springs from an imperfect knowledge of God.

" To-day the scene has quite changed—thanks to the advance of human reason and the salutary conclusions which the philosophy of our day has drawn from the history of the past. Progress has created a new world of ideas more in accordance with that Divine will, which must rule the earth until it be accomplished. Amongst these ideas shines the doctrine of the Divine Unity as taught by Jesus Christ and explained and illustrated fully in the whole life of the Teacher. Toleration is already a dogma throughout civilized Europe, and truly Christian society looks with horror upon slavery, tyranny, and the abominations of the middle ages, which can only be compared to the abominations and miseries of Paganism.

" This, then, is the reason of the just celebrity which this suit, and some others of the same character, have attained in other countries—of the general interest which has been called forth in favour of those persecuted for their religous opinions, and expressed by almost the whole press here and abroad, and which has found a solemn echo of just complaint in some of the Parliaments of Europe.

" When some new symptoms of the old intolerance were remarked in our land—when, in this great age of the earthly life of humanity, the shadow of a half-living apparition of the past fell across the present—immediately the chill was felt by universal and most worthy interests, and since then all civilized nations have kept

their eyes fixed upon us, and wait anxiously for the
definite issue of these proceedings.   .   .   .   .

As by the fundamental code the State established the
Roman Catholic and Apostolic religion as the only one
of the Spanish nation, it is evident that no form of
worship distinct from that consecrated to, and practised
by, the Catholic church can be admitted into our
land.   .

"We are not competent, nor is it our present
business, to examine the causes and the reasons for
this legal disposition, which we simply recognize as
existing ; it is sufficient for us to remark that the law
limits the exterior liberty of the citizen in a very
positive manner under these special circumstances,
its precepts involving a prohibition of all public acts of
any other worship or religious sect.

"But how can our clients be accused of having
violated this law ? We understand why the terrors
of justice should visit the criminal who carries alarm,
consternation, and tears to the heart of a family. We
desire the punishment of him who destroys, usurps,
or injures the property of another. We perceive the
wisdom of inflicting a severe penalty upon those
citizens who scandalously sow disorder and anarchy in
society, upon those who scatter broadcast upon its
surface the germs of evil and transcendental misery ;
but we cannot see how reason or the law can be so
tortured as to be made to accuse any good citizens for
the *sole crime* of not believing what the Roman Catholic
Apostolic Church believes, and for having privately
practised the rites of any other religious sect.

"We concede at once that the intelligence of our

clients is labouring under a lamentable delusion. The spirit always strives to attain truth, and in the heat of its constant thirst, and in the incessant struggle which it sustains, it may often stumble into error or fall into scepticism.

" Truth is not the cup which passes from lip to lip at the festal board, and therefore it would be very dangerous to seek the basis of crime in any of the frequent deliriums of human reason.

" We do not seek here for crime. The measure of the offence can only be the evil done to society— injuries which the public sustain ; and if this sublime principle of science cannot be denied by sound logic, we must acknowledge that though the doctrines held by the accused and their co-religionists are not in accordance with all the dogmas of the Catholic faith, at least, the end which they propose to themselves is one extremely beneficial to society, and its ten_ dency is an eminently moral one. As a proof, we take some articles of the statutes or organized rules of this secret association. The document is found in the 129th folio of the acts.

" ' Article 3. These members must set an example of morality, propriety, and manifested love to the gospel. Each must be a constant observer of these duties ; a good parent and householder, a man without degrading vices, or propensities opposed to the teaching of the gospel. He should be discreet and courteous ; in a word, an example to other Christians.

" ' Article 20. The Council must watch with special care over the religious instruction of those individuals who compose the association, striving to create a family in Christ, which shall be well taught in the gospel, an example to the age and worthy of their profession, to which end it must watch constantly those who have the direction of the congregations.'

" These are some of the requisites demanded from, and some of the duties imposed upon, the individuals of the Directive or Governing Council. We now quote two of the articles which refer to the' brethren in general.

" ' Article 3. Every member (of the society) must remember that when he is received by his brothers in Christ, it is on the ground of his being a man of faith, and having laid aside all miserable ambitions.

" ' Article 4. Every brother must practice evan-gelical Christianity with all assiduity and zeal, and must not look with indifference on the afflictions of his brethren, nor of the rest of mankind; dedicating himself constantly to this duty, and giving by his own example the highest stimulus to others.'

" We have drawn special attention to these passages because they, and all the rest of the rules, show with perfect distinctness the humane and charitable objects of the association, as well as the beneficent tendency and the laudable aim of its members.

" This line of conduct is in strict accordance with the sublime precepts of the gospel. Separation from degrading and corrupting vices, sincere and earnest faith, progressive moral culture, domestic love, the re-nunciation of mean and low ambitions, the continual exercise of Christian charity, voluntary sacrifices for the alleviation of the miseries and sorrows of mankind; — such is the summary of the spirit of those wise maxims which our clients inculcated, and which they practised with scrupulous zeal. . . . .

"We wait now with tranquillity for the decision which will, we doubt not, be the free and complete absolution of our clients.   Can we do other than expect it?   Can we believe for one moment that after all the sorrows and griefs which our clients have already suffered for so long a time, they could be condemned to a terrible and undeserved punishment?   No; the law is above all the shield of the citizens' rights, and in virtue of its precepts the innocent who are unjustly accused can always be defended.

" The punishment inflicted upon an innocent man can never be repealed.   The suffering of the honourable citizen who has not infringed the rights of others, and has not injured them, afflicts and troubles society in all its breadth and depth.

"Behind our clients stands all Europe interested in this case, which involves her own rights and liberties, and waiting with impatience for the *dénouement* of this drama, which seems not to belong to our age.   The august doctrines of progress, the continual teaching of history, and the almost divine inspiration of reason, proclaim with trumpet voice the triumph of this cause, which is the cause of justice and of right, the cause of humanity and civilization.

"We live in a time of conflict.   The field is ever open to contrary ideas, but truth loses nothing in the struggle, but rather gains ground by discussion, and, with its beneficent influence, dissipates the dense obscurity of error, and raises at last the banner of triumph. Finally, let it not be forgotten that the Catholic faith rejects by its first principles all intolerance, knowing that intolerance has been the fatal origin of so many heresies and of some deep schisms in the very bosom of the universal church.

" Away, then, for ever with intolerance and its evil root from our noble and beautiful soil, and flourish here for ever with an absolute empire the fertile idea of the unity of God and the love of all mankind in God."

CHAPTER X.

THE SPANISH PRESS.—LETTER FROM MATAMOROS.—
DEFENCE BY HIS ADVOCATE BEFORE THE TRIBUNAL AT
GRANADA.

THE Spanish Press gave no uncertain sound in this great religious question, of such transcendental importance to Spain. The editor of the *Clamor Publico*, Don Fernando Corradi, supported and pleaded for the oppressed in many excellent articles. In a letter to Matamoros about the same time, he says:—"Because I have defended, and continue to defend, religious liberty, I have been threatened even with death. Because I have supported your cause, they are endeavouring to ruin my family with violent exactions." In one year only, this newspaper was fined to the extent of £800 sterling, but in spite of all it held on its way bravely. Matamoros, in commenting on the rigour of the Spanish Government in his case, says:— " Why does not the Government ask for the official documents in a case where the superstitious and intolerant action of the tribunal is thrown into the balance? That tribunal is entirely composed of Neo-Catholics, and that particular section of them who, in Spain, defend the stake and the Inquisition, and in every

act its intolerant spirit is manifested. Its hatred to
Christians, and the intimate assurance that they are
doing good to their souls by endeavouring to exterminate us, is already contributing, and will contribute,
to bias the sentence passed upon us as Protestants.
To ask from the friends and supporters of the Inquisition justice for Protestants, is like asking the Pope
to canonize Luther. Our Spanish churches are
animated by a noble and generous spirit, which is not
easy to describe, and the Malaga prisoners are setting
an excellent example. The persecuted, who have been
hiding for months from the rage of their enemies, are
now even desirous of appearing before the tribunals,
without dreading in the least the consequences. Oh,
brother of my heart, all this is unspeakably precious,
and assures to us happy results. This discourages
tyranny, although it stirs it up to greater wrath.
My beloved brothers write to me to say that they
wish to imitate my example, that they wish to come
into prison to suffer with me; and the poor people
attribute their valour to my exhortations and conduct. Poor dear people, they owe nothing to me, but
all to God, who gives them His Holy Spirit. Comprehending the weakness of the human heart and the
infant state of the Spanish Church, I have laboured
much more than you could believe, that this church
should be firm in Jesus, and might give a worthy
example to the world. I have prayed much to the
Lord to help me in this respect, and He has heard my
prayer. You cannot imagine how profound are the
sympathies evinced in all parts of Europe towards us;
they are manifested by various acts and under different

auspices. In the midst of all these things the enemy is exhausting all the means of wrath against us, but this gives a contrary result to that which they propose.

"From Amsterdam, the Hague, and Rotterdam, I receive letters constantly, which are eminently consolatory to me, which I answer, and publicity is given to all my communications in Holland. The consistory of the Free Church at Amsterdam, in answer to a letter of mine, in which I begged them to help us in our evangelical labours in Spain, answered me that, though they had neglected to do so up to this present time, they would nevertheless in the future remember Spain. So that even if I do die, I shall die happy when I think that in every place people are taking an interest in the spiritual welfare of Spain. The suffering prisoners of Malaga have again written to me, in such a happy strain. Their letters reveal such a spirit of Christian resignation, and are neither more nor less than the expression of that holy joy that inspires them with such deep love and gratitude to you all, and with the most complete and decided faith. Oh, I am so thankful for all this; it is for me a motive of interminable joy in Jesus to witness the noble spectacle they are giving to the world, of faithfulness in their chains, and I have not words to express my thankfulness to the Lord for this. I bow my knee before our heavenly Father for them, and my heart is full to overflowing with these pure emotions. I am so happy, yes, more than happy; something so wonderful that I cannot explain it, but it is, beloved friend, my rejoicing in Jesus, the fountain of all joy,

L

and superior to all. When, on the other hand, I
meditate on the spectacle presented by the Church of
Christ in all places to the unbelieving world, that
world which rushing headlong downwards loses itself
at last in the dark and solitary valley of death, my
gratitude to God gains strength and humbleness, and
I begin to understand that, grateful as I may have
been to Him, I can never be grateful enough; and
now, while my enemies rejoice in my grief and in that
of all my dear brothers, while they are exhausting the
dregs of their wrath, I see, on the other hand, many
thousand hearts bending humbly before the Lord in
prayer for the poor martyrs, dropping tears of love at
the remembrance of their sorrows, giving an example
of faith, and saying to the world, Do your worst;
we pity you, we pardon you, and not by force, but by
prayer, we shall be more than conquerors. And what
can I say to you about that zeal which is manifested
by you all in supporting the numerous families of the
imprisoned? Oh, beloved brother, I cannot find
words to signify to you all I feel on this head. When
I see so many families who would have been exposed
to the greatest misery, now, thanks to your charity,
enabled to bring their husbands, sons, and brothers
in bonds, the food they so much want, that bread
which the angry hands of their enemies had deprived
them of, by taking from their midst the worthy bread-
earners, who, through the sweat of their brows, provided for them; when I consider that now, though the
father is imprisoned, vexed, and tormented, his heart
is at least not torn by the idea of the misery of his
children and of his wife, that our enemies cannot

rejoice in their complete destitution as they can do in our martyrdom; and when I consider that all this is in answer to prayer, and what a brilliant spectacle this Christian love presents which springs from faith in Jesus, I rejoice with true evangelic joy.

" I am glad to hear that you liked the defence my advocate made in my case. It has been printed, and is a document that has made a deep impression on the minds of Spaniards; and though the advocate is a Roman.Catholic, this seems to have given it more weight, for it is so compact."

THE DEFENCE OF DON MANUEL MATA-MOROS BEFORE THE TRIBUNAL OF GRANADA.

The Advocate, D. Antonio Moreno y Diaz (whom the editor of the *Clamor Publico* calls " a person well known in Granada for his faith in the sacred dogmas of the Catholic religion which we profess, for the moderation of his ideas, and for the independence of his character "), having stated the case in the usual legal terms, thus proceeds:—

" Our position at this moment is critical in the highest degree, delicate beyond belief, and in many respects most embarrassing. We are about to defend a worthy man and a noble cause, but the man is not known, and is therefore all but abhorred by ignorant minds, and the cause is terrifying those fanatics who refuse to comprehend it.

" The ministerial voice has said, ' An attempt has been made to change in our beloved country the

Catholic faith, and to substitute for it that which
Protestants profess; and the very mention of such a
crime causes deep pain to every good Spaniard. The
religious unity of the nation, our most deeply-rooted
and venerable faith—that which our ancestors left to
us—that which has borne our banners from pole to
pole unsullied, and with honour and glory—that faith
which reconquered our land, and rescued it from the
hands of the infidels—that which bore civilization to the
New World —that religion which our fundamental
laws declare to be the true, the only one—some unfortunates have attempted to overturn, substituting
in its place error, disorder, and chaos. Instead of
the Catholic unity, this great blessing, the envy of all,
which we have been able to preserve in the midst of
the perturbations and schisms which have afflicted
Europe, they seek to give us anarchy; and by breaking
the sacred chains of the obedience due to the Holy
See, to destroy that principle of authority, already,
alas! much weakened.'

"How, then, if the crime is so horrible, if the work
in question will lead to such horrible disorders, how do
we dare, notwithstanding, to support the cause of him
whom the representative of the law would no doubt
call the *worst* of the enemies of our past glories, of our
beloved country, and of the religion of our ancestors?
It is true that we, who glory in the name of Catholics
and Spaniards, and who would rejoice to declare
ourselves such, as much to-day as yesterday, by word
and deed, in the secret of our consciences as before the
whole world, we cannot but shudder at the picture of
the crime and its authors, which the official pen of the

zealous functionary to whom we allude has sketched for us.

"But our view of these things is, by good or bad fortune, so totally different from his, and our inexperience or our good faith has caused us to adopt such convictions on this subject, that, terrible as may be the prospect, and many the catastrophes set before us, nothing will make us waver from our point.

"We undertake the defence of Don Manuel Matamoros Garcia not only without uneasiness, but with satisfaction, and though we feel that this noble task may call forth censures which we have not received when we have pleaded for unfortunate criminals who have expiated their guilt on the shameful scaffold, yet we live in the firm hope that, if we succeed in gaining a favourable result, our efforts will have been more truly profitable to the Church and the State than are all these passionate accusations and these terrible sentences which weigh down those who are persecuted in Spain for their religious opinions, to the astonishment and alarm of civilized Europe.

"From a long series of prolix observations which we have made upon the past and present life of our client, we have arrived at the positive conviction that while he resists with indescribable tenacity every effort which is made to overcome him by force, we may hope everything from him if he is treated with gentleness and persuaded with reason. He is still very young, imaginative, ardent, gentle, and of noble sentiments, with a soul, unfortunately, of a class but too rare in the world; and in the heyday of his youth he sacrifices himself at the altar of an idea, which we will not specifically describe, but which, even if realized, would produce neither anarchy, disorder, nor chaos.

" He dearly loves his fatherland, and is interested, as is every good Spaniard, in its prosperity, its renown, and its glory, but he desires to see Spain free in an absolute sense; that is, enjoying the peace, and the benefits, and the admirable harmonies which result in a civilized nation from the knowledge and the practice of the doctrines of the gospel.   This, and no other, is the beautiful ideal of his illusions, as we shall hope to prove.   Those who do not know him—those who, having never seen him, judge of him by what the ignorant vulgar say—may perhaps stigmatize him as a visionary, an innovator, a madman, a heretic, or an apostate.   But we must oppose the torrent of public opinion in this question, and declare our belief that he is a worthy man.   We have several reasons for so believing.   The first, because every one is worthy who, like Don Manuel Matamoros, aspires continually to benefit mankind, presenting constantly health and life with the words and the example of Him who redeemed us at Golgotha.   Secondly, because we believe no other epithet can be applied to him who carries a treasury of goodness within him, and who practises, as if by instinct, the Christian virtues where of we are the admiring witnesses.   And thirdly because, apart from all this, we must remember that more than once he has desired to immolate himself in the place of his companions in misfortune, and has asked for pity for them and their families, while, with chivalrous enthusiasm and sublime resignation, he has proclaimed himself the sole author of the crime for which they are accused, and the only person responsible for all its consequences; and fourthly, and lastly, because it is impossible to withhold respect from a young man who, like our client, has borne with nobility of soul all the hard and constant sufferings which have been his lot in the disgraceful imprisonment which he has endured. . . .

"The majority of enlightened persons of this country for whom toleration is a dogma, and all those neighbouring nations where this precious conquest of modern days exercises all its salutary influence, these have no sooner learned that the prisons of Andalusia are filled with unfortunates who are persecuted for their religious opinions, than they were deeply moved, and have not ceased since then to intercede for them by the press, from the tribune, and even in high official places.

"This case, then, is of such intrinsic importance, and has acquired so much interest, that not only those whose fate will be decided by its results, but also all the nations of Europe, are waiting with anxiety and with impatience for its termination.

"With impatience because they wish to see these unhappy prisoners at once set free; and with anxiety because they tremble lest, in the middle of the nineteenth century, and in a nation so cultivated, so noble, and so generous as that which inhabits the Iberian peninsula, the sorrowful spectacle should be presented of certain honourable citizens condemned to heavy punishments for the single *crime* of professing a religion which is not the religion of the State.

"Our examination must rest upon three points—the existence of the crime, the legality of the proceedings employed for its discovery, and the justice of the penalties enacted for its punishment.

"As regards the first particular, let us hear how the representative of the law argues. He desires to prove that Don Manuel Matamoros unreasonably complains of intolerance. He affirms that in Spain no one is punished for their religious belief, though openly manifested and heterodox, as long as they do not publicly apostatize. Afterwards, comparing the conduct of Luther with that of the prisoners, he says 'But Matamoros and his associates, forgetting the faith of their ancestors, and without any external cause for irritation or exasperation, preached their errors, catechized the incautious, established Protestant churches, each severally and all together forming associations prohibited by the law.' Then triumphantly he continues, 'The prisoners must know and understand that they are not accused for their religious faith, nor for having manifested it; but because they have attempted to change the religion of the State, and have practised external and abstract acts, and of which the direct result would be such a change.' Finally, as if to give a clear and precise formula of his opinions in the matter, he asserts that, 'When one or more persons propagate doctrines contrary to the most holy dogmas of our faith as the Holy Catholic Apostolic Roman Church teaches, they commit the crime which comes under the 128th article of the code.'   .   .   .   .

"In Spain we are no longer in the times of Torquemada! For arbitrary authority can no longer 'call itself law, and the ominous tribunal of the holy offices no longer takes account of offences against religion. If such offences exist now, they are properly classified and punished by the penal code, and the magistrates and judges, whose duty it is to administer justice, must regulate their decisions by its decrees. . · . . . . . .

"Our fundamental law lays down the principle that the only religion of the State is the Roman Catholic Apostolic, and the penal code punishes not alone any who attempt to abolish or alter it (Art. 128), but also all who shall publicly apostatize from it (Art. 136), and also those, who, having propagated doctrines or maxims contrary to its dogmas, shall persist in publishing such after they have been condemned by the ecclesiastical authorities (130). These are the three chief offences against religion which are noted by our code, and of which of these is Don Manuel Matamoros accused? . . . . .

"In the world of speculation an arena is open to all intelligence by means of discussion. To believe or to doubt, to accept as good or to reject as evil, to admit as suitable or to shut out as prejudicial, ideas and theories, are movements and evolutions of our mind which cannot be contained within bounds without tyrannizing over conscience and impeding the necessary onward progress of humanity. Man must have, by an inalienable right of his existence, full liberty to think, full liberty to express his thoughts, full liberty to discuss them, full liberty to adhere to what he thinks best, and full liberty, in short, to associate himself with those who believe as he does.   There is no danger that he will go astray in the path, for all who have studied, known, or thought anything about the mind of man, will recognize that he is not less rebellious against the reason of force than submissive to the force of reason; and thus guided by reason, and shielded by faith, he can go safely forth into the arena where ideas, principles, and doctrines are struggling together, and he arrives at the knowledge of the good, the useful, and the true, in all branches of human wisdom.   Hence, toleration is the rule in every civilized nation.   Hence, there can be no political liberty without free discussion; and hence the need of the distinction between him who attacks any institution, and him who is not its partisan, and who may associate himself with others, to combat it on scientific grounds, to use his influence to reduce the number of those who oppose it, and to desire that it should succumb to, or be modified by, the benefit of public opinion.   .   .   .   .

"The letters of Don Francisco Ruet show us that the writer having announced to the Neophytes that their wish to be enrolled in the books of the Reformed Spanish Church has been fulfilled, proceeds to trace for them the line of their future conduct.

" 'Every Spaniard,' he says, 'who is converted to the true faith must be a real missionary to his friends, and must strive with persuasive words, and by works of mercy, to convince many others.'

"Faithfully following this peaceful counsel, the members of the directive junta of the Reformed Church of Barcelona, in the circular which they addressed to other juntas and brothers in Spain, thus write:—'If mutually and fraternally encouraging one another our faith fail · not, perhaps we may be permitted to salute with hymns of jubilee the radiant aurora of the kingdom of God in our unhappy land. Let us labour then with ardour in the holy work of the evangelization of our brothers, and if our efforts appear barren, let us console ourselves with having done our duty to God and man as good and sincere believers. But no! we will fill the field with seed, and when God wills it shall bring forth fruit.

" 'If we can do nothing else, let us sow the grain of mustard seed, and let us rejoice in the conviction that it is written that "the birds of the air shall lodge in the branches which grow from the least of all seeds." '

"Matamoros and Alhama, thoroughly agreeing with these bases in their correspondence, actions, and words, have constantly taught that the chief, if not the only principles of action which should be used, are the moral and religious education of the people, mutual concord amongst the afflicted, zeal in the preaching of gospel truth, and the constant practice of Christian virtues. Finally, the high praises which in their exposition to the Scotch committee they lavish upon young N—— A——, all and only for his faith, his preaching, and the good fruits of the latter, which drew out a multitude of hearts to the love of Jesus Christ.

"Here, then, is all that Manuel Matamoros and his co-religionists have done, or have attempted--to convince many by persuasive words and good works;

to evangelize—that is, to teach the people the doctrines of the crucified Lord; to encourage one another
fraternally in this holy work, and do their duty as
good and earnest believers, filling the field with the
seed which should bear fruit in God's good time,
and hoping, as the result of all, for the establishment
of religious reformation, so that they might salute
with hymns of joy the radiant aurora of the kingdom of God amongst us. Not one word of menace,
not one subversive sentence, not one remotest thought
can we trace, that they had realized, that they purposed to realize, one material exterior direct action
which should in any way change or abolish in Spain
the Roman Catholic and Apostolic religion.

"How, then, can Manuel Matamoros be accused as
the author of this crime? How can he be supposed
to deserve the penalty of eleven years' imprisonment? .   .   .   .

"Now it will be easy to us to prove that, contrary
to the opinions of the counsel for the Crown, Don
Manuel Matamoros has but too good cause for com-
plaining of cruelty, arbitrary and even inhuman
treatment, practised upon himself and others in the
name of the law.

"There is no penal law in Spain against those who
introduce, keep, or circulate prohibited books. Notwithstanding this, the civil governor of the province
heard that some brought from San Roque were circulating in Granada. He gave verbal orders to a
police agent to inquire and discover who were the
individuals concerned in this. But this agent took
upon himself powers which he neither possessed

absolutely nor relatively, and having at midnight entered the house of Don José Alhama, searched it all through, and seized whatever letters and papers he could find, finally arrested the master of the house, and placed him in solitary confinement.

"By impartial reflection upon these facts—that a simple policeman, to verify a question, may invade the domestic hearth, search at his pleasure, tear away whatever books and papers he fancies, and finally drag away to a solitary dungeon an honourable citizen—are we not convinced that there has been here serious abuse, and the more censurable because its consequences have been so serious? Where are the laws that protect social men? Who ever imagined himself authorized to infringe and break them as this police agent did? And who was this man, to presume, on his own authority, to seize papers and books which were private property, to classify them as good or evil, to discover in them the proofs of the existence of a crime, and to take away to prison their owner?   .   .   .   .   .

"But that is not all. Hardly had the name of Manuel Matamoros been found in these papers, when the civil governor of Barcelona (where our client then was) received a telegraphic order to search and seize him in like manner, and that he should be brought as a prisoner by stages to this capital. Very serious was this order to Señor Matamoros. His health was much broken, and two well-known and highly-esteemed medical men certified that his life would be endangered by the journey on foot of one hundred and seventy leagues, during the rigorous cold of that season. Any one would have supposed that at least he would have been permitted to remain where he was till his health should have improved. Not at all—the order was given and must be obeyed. 'Let him come to Granada, ill or well,' was the only answer which the well-considered opinion of the medical men elicited. What would have happened if he had not been enabled to make this journey by sea? Where would he be now if he had travelled hither from Barcelona, on foot, chained in a gang of prisoners, and lodging with them in prisons on the road? Probably his *name* would have been sent forward—but nothing more.

" And yet the counsel for the Crown is astonished that he should complain! and affirms that complaints are unjustifiable.

"Truly, we would inform this gentleman that the sole reason for the interest which so many thousands are taking in this case, both within and without the Peninsula is, first, upon the very nature of the case itself, and then the luxury of persecution in which the authorities have indulged.

"It was not enough to drag Don Manuel Mata-moros hither at a moment when he needed the most tender care from his family, there was still something to be done, and now one of the many military com-missions, which began to act on their discretion after the affair at Loja, took upon itself to meddle here, and to implicate him. His situation was, for some time, terrible, in consequence of this new accusation. The fiscal-instructor lavished his ' in-communications ' (orders to place the prisoner in solitary confinement);

he resorted to every description of treachery to create the proofs of the imaginary crime; and having placed the fate of our client in the hands of wicked men and vile criminals, at last, fortunately, the case passed from the hands of its author and came before the ordinary tribunals, where it was immediately quashed, so evident, so palpable, so enormous was the injustice with which Don Manuel Matamoros had been persecuted. . . . . . .

"Without desiring to enter into any detail of the errors into which opposing parties run, or to present ourselves before the world as models of perfect Roman Catholic Apostolic believers, we affirm, as incontestible truth, that from the doctrines which our clients teach we should expect anything rather than bad citizens. As the basis of their propagandist labours was ever to teach the maxims of the gospel, we may easily see that though their neophytes might not acquire a pure orthodoxy, they would, at least, receive an amount of religious instruction which is but too rare at present, and which could only tend to make them peaceful and useful members of society.

"And what more could a truly enlightened Government desire? What greater glory could we desire for our dear fatherland, eminently Catholic as it is, but where, we confess with grief and shame, there is so much ignorance, and indifference, and hypocrisy, than to see all its sons converted into faithful and obedient followers of the crucified Lord?

Truly, whoever thinks calmly on these things must agree that, if Don Manuel Matamoros is condemned to any penalty, he will not be punished for the harm that he did, but for the good that he.desired to do. Farther, and this is very important, so unjust a sentence as this would injure rather than benefit the Church. We all know that the Catholic Apostolic and Roman religion is not the only ruling faith on earth, but that there are, unfortunately, not a few countries where it is either persecuted or only tolerated; and with what reason shall we demand that these persecutions should cease, and that under the wing of toleration the most holy dogmas of our faith should be preached, if we make a display and a glory of our intolerance by condemning to prison and the galleys those who incur the guilt of heresy or propagate its errors? We offend against the sanctity of our faith, against the belief which our ancestors bequeathed to us; which has crowned the brow of our country with laurels; which carried civilization to a new world; which is the first and best ornament of the Spanish nation, if we believed for an instant that it was necessary to use in its defence the rigour, the intolerance, and the tyranny of earthly powers.

" No ! Our Mother Church suffices for herself, for she is borne in the arms of a supernatural strength. Seek the proof of this in the words of her Divine Founder ; in the promise of the Holy Spirit, which never abandons her ; in the grand code which contains her doctrines; and remember that a God-man cast the seed of the Church into the earth, that, watered with the blood of innumerable martyrs during centuries of horrible persecution, it should, at last, fill the face of the earth with the fruit of life eternal.

" If, then, in the name of our most holy religion, which is all mercy and gentleness, no tyranny or injustice can be practised ; if toleration is an essential dogma of Catholicism, and a powerful instrument in the development of the Church; and if, on the other hand, the clients in this case, at whose head stands Don Manuel Matamoros, in disseminating the doctrines which they profess, and which are those of the gospel, do society no harm, but rather instruct and improve it, we can come but to one conclusion, that the complete absolution of the prisoners is the only reasonable, just, and equitable termination to the affair."

CHAPTER XI.

LETTERS FROM GRANADA.

MATAMOROS again writes:—" Our Paris friends intend to make the greater part of the defence public, according to a letter they have lately sent me, for, like yourself, they think it so good. Señor Don Moreno Dias is my advocate's name, and he has been complimented by many eminent people, some of whom are known to him only by hearsay, so great is the enthusiasm that has been produced by its perusal. I can assure you that from much experience I can say that you have done notable service to Spain by the translation and printing of the work of Dr. De Sanctis, 'Confession and Tradition,' and when I first heard of it I found it impossible to get many copies, but those I did get have done good service. A fellow countryman, Señor —— Usoz, sent me by Mr. Rew the important work called the 'Epistola Consolatoria,' written in 1560 by the distinguished Spanish brother, Don Juan Perez. It is addressed to the suffering saints in the prisons of the Inquisition at Seville, Valladolid, etc. It is written in the old Castilian language used in those days, and is extremely interesting. It is a treasure of piety and divine love, and one of the best books that

has come within my reach. I must tell you something
of this Mr. Rew, who came all the way to Granada to
visit me, with his wife and niece. When he was here
in my cell, there were present also the wife and
daughter of Señor Marin the Malaga prisoner, my
mother, Señor Trigo and his wife, Alhama, and my
brother Henry. After talking a little together, Mr.
Rew spoke to us most opportunely, and with much
faith, and, filled by the love of Jesus, with much feeling he exhorted us to persevere, to continue instant in
prayer. I had also the pleasure of speaking at this
time to those then present, and of explaining to them
the continual joy I had in Jesus, and the hope I
entertained that this joy would be unceasing, through
a lively faith, much prayer, and the consolations of the
Holy Spirit. I spoke at length on these important
subjects, and many tears fell from the eyes of the
women there present, who were much moved. I read
to them the 1st chapter to the Philippians, as also the
4th of 1st Peter, and happy thoughts came to the
minds of all touching these beautiful passages from
the Book of Life, and there was manifest in the midst
of our little congregation a visible but inexplicable
joy in Jesus. Mr. R. asked me at this time also what
was my opinion as to the education of some of the
children of the prisoners in England, and I gave him
my humble opinion on the matter, which is very important, and ever since I have been reflecting over it
with great pleasure. I told him that I thought it not
only desirable, but that the results likely to follow
would, with God's blessing, be very great indeed. He
seemed to think the same, and left, animated by the

best desires. May God bless him! And finally, dear brother; in my humble cell we all bent the knee to our heavenly Father, and I returned thanks to Him for the joy He allowed me to experience in my chains. I thanked Him for the willingness with which I and the other prisoners would give up our lives for the sweet name of Jesus, and for His love. I thanked our Father for the Christian activity displayed by the body of Christ, and begged of Him to give to it constantly the presence of the Divine Spirit. I pardoned in His sight all our enemies, and finally I gave thanks to God for permitting me to suffer for the divine name of Jesus. Certain other subjects I embraced in my prayer, and was almost exhausted as I finished, for I am so powerfully moved, so deeply impressed when I am engaged in this delightful exercise, that the pleasure I feel is immeasurable, and on the coldest winter's day I perspire profusely."

In a letter from Matamoros in June, 1862, he says the following:—" I have received four copies of the small but important tract against the traffic of negroes in Cuba, against that horrible, that dishonourable traffic in human blood, that terrible stain to humanity, that execrable blot on my country, and on all countries that continue to allow this page to remain in their history.

" I have sent the tract to various towns in Spain, and if I had some hundreds of them I would willingly pay the postage, so as to have the pleasure of forwarding it to various friends and important personages. No one has ever been able to make me give up my opinion, which is that Europe can never expiate the crime of allowing the continuance of this traffic. I can't understand how modern society can permit that the father be torn from the bosom of his family, and the son from the father, the spirit of destruction pandered to, and all for the sake of sacrilegious gains to a few hundred ambitious and privileged individuals."

In the month of August I had a long letter giving much information, a copious extract from which I give below:—

" Prison of the Audiencia, Granada, Aug. 11, 1862.

" My dearest and ever-to-be remembered father in Jesus, my indefatigable, my zealous, and beloved brother, in the hope of our future life. Your highly appreciated and beautiful letter of the 25th of the past month, received the 5th of the present, and the longest of all I have had the comfort of receiving from you, reached me in all safety, and how cheering and edifying to my spirit it has been!

" When I had the joy of receiving it, one of mine was on the road, with an inclosure for the Rev. Mr. Magee, and in it I told you of the petition of the fiscal, against the dearly-loved friends and brothers in Malaga.

" Your letter contains two things eminently beautiful, and of unlimited consolation to me; one is the almost entire re-establishment of your most precious health. Oh! this is of such importance to me; this is more to the poor prisoner than his own personal health, more, a thousand times, than his liberty. The second, my beloved, are the eloquent proofs of love that you give all through your country (and likewise beyond it), unequivocal expression of incomparable esteem that the body of Christ gives us, in recompense of your great ˜ zeal. This said, I am going to answer your letter, although I shall do it indifferently, as usual.

" I rejoice greatly that you have written to the Rev. Señor Ruet; he also tells me of it to-day, in a letter, that is like a heavy tear falling from his overwhelmed heart.

" Poor Pastor ! in every place grief pursues him. What a sad exile he is suffering. In short, my beloved, believe me truly, I have a most vehement desire to see you, and to talk with you. I have a very strong persuasion that you are chosen by the Lord to open to my poor country the path of its triumph ; I hold as a certainty, that the Lord will grant you this distinguished favour, this precious page in the history of your Christian life. I pray to the Lord that He will grant me to see you, to embrace you, to speak much, much with you of what relates to Spain, and then, that God may show me the road I have to follow. May the will of the Lord be done !

" I would say much to you to-day, much about this great work to which you are called; I would initiate you in the best means, that, in my humble opinion, are the most opportune for arriving soonest at the desired end, for gathering the spiritual fruits, of so much sacrifice, so many efforts, of so much labour ; but I think the moment has not yet arrived. At the present, there is a most important question that opens to my country the desired road for its triumph in the gospel; and it is necessary that this should come to a conclusion. When this is settled, be it in what way it may, we will think with indefatigable solicitude upon the rest, for I think there is now doing for Spain a thousand times more than one could calculate, and with better success than could have been accomplished, perhaps, by the work of many years. Each day I note a greater enthusiasm for the evangelical cause in Spain. Now I do not see that dread of tyranny—everything presents itself before me now, firm, decided, and hopeful in Jesus; the shield of Jesus, stronger a thousand times than steel, makes it impossible for the sharp weapons of tyranny to wound the heart of our holy work. Tyranny only in appearance triumphs, but its triumph is like that of the tiger with the poor sheep, drawing forth his claws filled with innocent and inoffensive blood; it has no other triumph, this is its miserable victory.

" I note, dear friend, a certain terror in the enemy's press—I note a certain panic amongst our enemies, and I see much love, much life in Jesus, in all the beloved brethren. Oh! a thousand times blessed be the sweet name of Jesus, fountain of all consolation, of all resignation, of strength, and of hope.

" As soon as I have an unoccupied moment, I mean to write a letter to the *Clamor*, giving a general idea of all that has happened, and is now taking place in Spain, in order that public opinion may have a true and full impression, under which it may study this great cause, which eminent men call the first cause of the globe. The picture it presents is assuredly more important than appears at first sight, and I think Spain ought to know what it is.

"From what I have said to you in the beginning of this letter, you will understand, my beloved protector in Jesus, that my days have been greatly occupied; besides what I have already told you, I have had to reproduce new and numerous data for the committee of Paris, that they may be published in connection with the religious persecution in Spain. From Madrid I have had a number of letters from different friends and people there. I have had some from Malaga, from Gibraltar, from Holland; and, in short, each day my occupations increase more and more, and this has been the cause that I have not yet written my letter to the Roman Catholics; but do not fear, it shall be written on the first occasion, and probably very soon.

"It would be almost impossible for me to explain how much I am occupied. I rise to write, and I am writing all day, and I finish doing so late at night; this is a great consolation to me, it gives me life, dear friend.

"I have received an excellent letter from Dr. Capadose, of Holland, deeply and profoundly touching. Dr. Capadose is an old man, but with a vigorous imagination, a heart full of life and health, and very deeply instructed. He loves you much, and he knows all your worth; he knows and admires your eminent zeal. I had very strong desires that you two should be in direct communication; already, some time since, I mentioned it to him, and he assured me he would write to you; and now, I see with joy that he has done so, and that it has given you Christian pleasure. Oh that this mutual correspondence of beings, so much loved by me, that this kind of double link between two of God's beloved sons may give to the world the worthy fruit of the virtues of both, of the Great Captain Jesus, under whose glorious banner they serve with so much enthusiasm.

"In some of my former letters I think I told you of his wish to publish a pamphlet upon this question, and he asked permission from me a short time since to publish all my letters in it. I replied that he might use them in whatever way he thought would most advance the Lord's holy cause, nevertheless, I had never expected that my humble letters would see the light. But how could I refuse this to a dear brother who thinks such a publication is beneficial to the Lord's body? It is now many months since I received a letter from the venerable Mr. Dallas; perhaps my last went astray, or his occupations have prevented him; at any rate, I think I will write very soon to him.

"The signatures to the letter from the Presbyterian Church in Dublin, St. Mary's Abbey, I have not been able to make out entirely; two only have I understood. If you find any mistakes, correct them in the translation, I pray you. Both of them are worth very little, rather, I should say, nothing, coming from my feeble pen; if they have anything that recommends them, it is because my heart speaks in them.

"I have read with much gratitude the words that

Mrs. Sturge dedicates to my humble self; if I have
time I will send her a few lines in this, trying to show
her the great value in which I hold hers.   They are a
great consolation to me ; but Mrs. Sturge will know
that nothing is due to me ; no man can do any good
thing; whatever is acceptable in me is the work of
the Holy Spirit, the work of God ; Matamoros is worth
a thousand times less than nothing.

"These proofs of divine love that are manifested by
all the brethren, and that offer to my sight the sacred
spectacle of the most holy union in the divine name
of Jesus, make me happy a thousand times more than
one can imagine ; and as this consoles me in Jesus, so
does it disquiet me little or nothing whether the Roman
Catholics ask my liberty or not from the Spanish
government or the queen.

"I have already told you more than once that my
future fate does not disturb me.   My prison is no cause
of sadness to me ; it is a sweet cause of joy and
rejoicing in Jesus ; and my liberty, except as granted
through the powerful influence of prayer, affects my
heart very little.

"I know that God watches over me, and how
little can the enemies of saving faith do ! of that faith
that He left us, as the only path to life.   But the
way of God is different from our way and I often
say to myself, ' If it is the will of the Lord that the
Roman Catholics ask for my liberty, must I not
respect the designs of the Most High? who knows,
if He permits this, that through my very enemies
the injustice of my imprisonment may be shown
forth ? '

"I will not ask for it; but neither will I refuse it. It is indifferent to me, however, as in all this matter my liberty is not the first object; but the necessity of showing the injustice of these attempts against conscience. I leave to the day the anxiety that belongs to it.

"But permit me to tell you one thing. It appears to me that I see in this what I read in the Book of Life respecting Jesus under the judgment of Pilate (Matt. xxvii. 19). His wife writes to Pilate, under the impression caused upon her by a dream, and frightened, prays her husband to have nothing to do with the case of that Just One. Pilate washes his hands; but he sends him to be scourged, and gives him up to the rage of the people in spite of knowing his innocence.

"I am not just; there is but one man to whom the 'being just' belongs, and He is Jesus Christ. I am a miserable sinner, but I am innocent; and if before the laws of the world I am criminal, it is because men agree it should be so, that they may better serve Satan. Other men besides those who believe me guilty, ranged under the same banner might warn, and even supplicate them not to punish me, and to cease their rigour; but for this they would invoke the laws of wordly expediency. They calculate an evil in all this, and like the wife of Pilate, they desire, through fear of the world, to avoid it. But in all this do you see the work of the Holy Spirit in the Catholics? I think not, it is mere wordly expediency. Notwithstanding, I believe that my Pilate (the Queen and her government will give me up to the convict overseers of the galleys. I think they will allow all the fury of that clergy to fall on me; who embitter the laws, irritate the conscience of the judges, and in every way work against Christians.

"Pardon me, dear friend, for having taken the liberty of making this poor, humble comparison to you. I think the charity of Catholics would be the charity of Pilate.

"If you can send me by R——, Valera's Bible, recently published in London, I shall be greatly obliged; it may be useful to me in the galleys.

"This moment I have received a letter from Seville, containing very interesting details, which I shall now give you a brief sketch of, and at greater length hereafter.

"In Seville, nineteen persons have been proceeded against; for four of this number only has the fiscal demanded seven years at the galleys. The judge asked pardon for all the nineteen.

"The fiscal of her Majesty demanded pardon for seventeen, but the superior tribunal begged that the penalty of seven years at the galleys should be passed upon Señors Don Diego Bordallo and Don T. Mesa Santanella. The audiencia of Seville or superior tribunal approved entirely the petition of her Majesty's fiscal, and they have sentenced Bordallo and Mesa to seven years at the galleys.

"When the sentence of the judges in the inferior tribunal differs from that of the superior tribunal, the parties sentenced have the right of appealing. the third time; and as this has occurred in the case at

Seville, Bordallo and Mesa have appealed, and the cause is now running the usual course; there is still a hope of pardon for these two victims of tyranny.

"In the cause nothing has been proved; but Bordallo and Mesa are sentenced on the ground of moral evidence, and by the 45th rule of the code the judges are authorized to impose penalties for moral evidence, although proofs may be wanted.

"This is a sketch of the spectacle presented by the cause in Seville. But, there is something more. Bordallo writes to me that he has been seventeen months in prison, and he has not received a single real from anybody to help him. I believe it, but I do not understand it; for I had been assured from different sources that the prisoners at Seville were succoured, and now I see it is not so, at least with Bordallo and Mesa, the only ones at present in prison there.

"As soon as I was aware of this, I wrote to Bordallo, telling him to let me know immediately to whom I might send some relief for him from the sum that I have for my own necessities. This letter goes out to-day, and within three days I -shall have the answer, and I will send him 200 Rs. (£2), which is all I can spare.

"Henceforward I shall put myself in direct communication with the prisoners at Seville. I do not abandon any one; whilst I have a loaf, three parts of it shall be for my brother prisoners, be they Spaniards or not. The All Powerful will do me justice. Henceforward, dear friend, the prisoners at Seville shall have a place in my poor letters; you shall know all about them, for I think my duty is not only towards a certain set of prisoners; all are equal in my estimation.

"These sentenced at Seville have not been found out through the papers that were taken from me, but through some documents that the post-office authorities intercepted; in short, when I receive your answer to this, I shall give you fuller particulars.

"Let us turn to Granada; there is no news here; Trigo's wife has been very ill, but is now much better; indeed, I may say convalescent. Alhama continues well, and so are all his family. The alcaide has gone to a bathing-place for two months, and on this account we are enjoying more liberty.

"I send you, inclosed in this, some of my likenesses, as an humble proof of gratitude to those dear brethren.

"I am going now to finish, after having detained you so long. My letters are archives, and it requires patience to read them; but, friend of my heart, you must bear my failing with resignation. I hope, when writing to your respected father, that you will offer him by humble remembrances.

"My mother salutes you, and all your family, with gratitude and Christian joy, as also does Enriqué. The Christian remembrances of all the brethren, and the heart of your humble brother in the Lord,

"MANUEL MATAMOROS."

"N.B.—The missionary, of whom I spoke to you, for Oran, has been entirely approved of by the committee at Paris."

Granada, September 10.

"I think that in fifteen days my trial will be public, for I observe an unusual activity, and, as I believe, because they are desirous that I may be condemned before the arrival of the queen at Granada, which will be on the 8th or 9th of October, and just two years since my imprisonment. What is most likely, when I receive your answer to this, my case will be settled, and I shall be able to tell you about it. I am completely tranquil, and if my sentence is severe, I shall sing songs of praise to my Lord. I intend to be present at the public trial, and to speak before the tribunal—not to ask their pardon, for that I do not need, but to ask that all the weight of the law may fall upon me alone, and not on my companions."

After two years of " wearing out of this saint of the Most High," the oft-mentioned and long protracted trial was brought to a close; and the letter. following, giving some account of the same, was received :—

LETTER FROM MANUEL MATAMOROS.

"*Granada, Prison of the Audiencia, Oct.* 5, 1862.

" My dear and zealous brother in Him who is our life and hope, two years ago the governor of Granada sent the order for my capture, and for the examination of my house. I was seized, was taken to a miserable prison, and from that time till now, you know what a chain of suffering has bound me; you know how much honour has been put upon me; for it is a glory and a joy to be permitted to suffer for Jesus' sake. Well, now, my enemies, not yet satisfied, have condemned me to suffer eight years of the galleys, to inhabilitation, and to the judgment of all the costs.

"I am twenty-seven, and I am going to the galleys; to a horrible place which is intended for the shame and sorrow of those who dwell there. But there is neither shame nor sorrow for me! My soul rejoices in Jesus. I, a poor miserable sinner, have been chosen by the Lord to suffer; and in this there is no shame, but honour; wonderful honour for me; for I do not deserve this distinction, and I am very grateful to my Master who has granted it to me.

"This horrible suit has at length come to an end, having been carried forward with a most tyrannical spirit for two years—two years of grief, and tribulation, and tears—two years of the patient resignation of a dear mother, whose son has been torn from her side, and placed under the ban of a terrible sentence. Oh, my poor mother! She was attacked with illness when she received the news. Mother, thou art also a victim to this cruelty, but thou also canst rejoice in thy tribulation for Christ.

"The time has come, dear friend, when I, deprived by men of all rights of citizenship, must enter upon my punishment—must go to the place which society has set apart for those wretches who are unworthy to continue in its midst. The voice of my dearly-loved mother will, perhaps, never again reach my ears. I shall know that she suffers, but shall not be able to comfort her with my presence. I shall be there altogether at the mercy of a fanatical governor, who will visit me with all the force of popish cruelty. There, at the merest caprice of the officials, the unfortunate convicts are beaten, and buffeted, and abused, even when inoffensive; and I shall be exposed, perhaps, to the cruel blows of some vile criminal, who has been chosen as overseer chiefly because his terrible antecedents are such as to inspire his fellow-prisoners with terror.

"The blows of such an one may fall upon me and hasten my death. I shall never hear the voice of my dear brothers. Your precious letters, my much-loved friend, will never reach me; and this will be my life for eight long years. But for all this, my cross I take up joyfully and follow Jesus. If I have not been permitted to carry the Word of God from village to village throughout Spain, I will publish it in prison. God rejoices over the conversion of the most abject, of the most sinful, and to those criminals I will show the way of life. There I will be, if the Lord allows me, just what I was when free. My hearers will not be honourable citizens, they will be miserable convicts. But, perhaps, these very convicts may see how horrible their past life has been, and will begin to live a new one, and will respect and will follow Jesus; and you can fancy how I rejoice to be able to dedicate myself to such a glorious work; and I must not fear the rod of punishment. Jesus sought out his death for our sakes.

"His apostles went everywhere preaching the word, through sorrow, tribulations, torments; they are my example, I follow them. And all this is not in my own strength, I am worthless, am nothing, can do nothing, by God's strength only I shall be enabled to do this; yet my heart tells me that I shall be permitted to carry out my earnest desires, as I have prayed for the sake of Jesus.

"Alhama has been sentenced to nine years. The additional year of punishment is given (amongst other reasons) because he wrote and acknowledged that letter, directed to me, which was seized, and which, bearing my name and address in full, and containing important intelligence, was the cause of my imprisonment also in Barcelona; which, you remember, was commanded by telegram. The judges believed that Granada was the chief seat and origin of these troubles, of which they suppose me to be a victim. Notwithstanding, they condemned me to eight years. The Lord pardon them!

"Trigo has been pronounced not guilty, and will soon be set free. He will return to the bosom of his family. I do heartily rejoice. Dear Trigo, may the Lord enlighten and protect him for the future!

"As our sentences do not exactly correspond with those of the inferior tribunal, we may again appeal against them. It is a matter of indifference to me whether an appeal is made, or whether I go at once to my doom. The appeal would keep us still for some months in this prison; but this offers nothing to be wished for, as the immediate commencement of my term of labour has no terrors.

"I have, however, consulted my respected and revered friends, B., W. N., and Dr. B., and yourself.

I will do as you advise, but have no choice in the matter myself. Alhama will appeal, but I need not therefore. I will fulfil my eight years, and he may obtain commutation. Believe me, dear friend, I am very happy. The continued illness of my darling mother is my only real trouble; but my Lord gives me strength to bear all with patience.

"I shall address a letter to the queen on her arrival at Granada, not to ask for mercy, which I do not need from her; no, for my crime, if it existed, would only be judged by the God who judges the consciences of all men, but I will represent to her our inoffensive lives, the liberty of our brothers in Seville, Malaga, and Granada, and the inalienable right of Christians to meet together to worship round the household hearth.

"I forgot to tell you that all the rest of the prisoners have been, or will immediately be, set at liberty. My most loving remembrances to all dear to you. Salute all my brothers in my name. Your affectionate brother in the Lord,

"M. M."

About this time, the other Granada prisoner, Señor Trigo, writes as follows:—"Respected Sir, and beloved brother in Christ, after nineteen months of untold sufferings, the tribunals of this world have absolved me from the eleven years of penal servitude that was petitioned for against me by her majesty's fiscal, and in a few days probably I shall be set at liberty. Conscientious motives of eternal gratitude impel me to write these few lines to you. My heart is so filled to you

and all the rest of your magnanimous and sympathizing
countrymen, that I wish I possessed the eloquence of
Paul, in order to express to you as I should desire my
deep and earnest gratitude for the many benefits received from you all, and which have helped in no small
degree to sweeten the bitter cup of sorrow mixed for us
by the hands of tyrants, for the sole crime of loving
and propagating the blessed gospel of the Lord Jesus
Christ. And as I have taken the liberty of addressing
you, I cannot help mentioning in my letter how much
the Spanish church owes to that eminent, decided, and
resigned champion of the truth, Don Manuel Matamoros.
Without him and the Divine help dispensed to him,
the persecutions we have undergone would have destroyed the Spanish Christians; and what can I say of
his excellent mother—of that worthy lady whose ma-
ternal love is only equalled by her many virtues, by her
heroic resignation, and by the distinguished gifts that
adorn her, and which are the admiration and the
respect of all who know her. I say all this, though I
feel that already you are aware of these facts, but a
sacred duty of conscience impels me not to be silent.
The labours of the son bring him into prison. He is
condemned to eight years of servitude, but nevertheless,
all is resignation in them both, all is rejoicing in Jesus,
all is Christian decision. Manuel has the pleasure of
receiving innumerable visits from people in every rank
of life, and letters of sympathy; even his enemies cannot help paying a tribute of respect to his virtues.
. Yesterday he was visited by an ecclesiastic, who, moved
by a desire to know him, found his way to his prison,
where he remained for a long time, talking and discus-

sing; and he finally told him, that he had come to see him, moved as he was by his energetic and dignified deportment, although walking himself in quite a distinct path from Matamoros. But I must conclude. Manuel, placed at the head of all correspondence concerning the Spanish prisoners, has watched over all with unceasing care, and, as far as I am personally concerned, I can say that he has done for me far beyond what I could ever have contemplated. I say this, for I have never known him indifferent to. my wants, but ever endeavouring in every way to mitigate my sufferings. I conclude by wishing that the Most High may grant to you and your family His heavenly grace, and that being sustained by it you may enjoy that felicity which your humble brother in the Lord desires you.

" MIGUEL TRIGO."

CHAPTER XII.

VISIT OF AN ENGLISH CLERGYMAN.—LETTER FROM MATA-
MOROS.—CONCLUSION.

An English clergyman visited Granada latterly, and
gave an account of his journey, which I extract from
the *Christian Observer* of December, as follows:—

"We reached Granada on the 11th of September last,
and on the following day went to the Prison of the
Audiencia. It is at the back of the Palace of Justice,
a pretentious stone building, at the foot of the hill on
which the Alhambra is built, and, though somewhat
gloomy, not more sombre-looking than such places
usually are. A few soldiers were lounging in the door-
way as we went in, but they did not appear to take much
notice of us, and we were instantly admitted when it
was known that we were friends of Matamoros. Inside
the prison we were met by one of the Protestants, who
bore in his face evident traces of a long imprisonment.
We followed him up a stone staircase, and into a
corridor, where several other prisoners were idling
about, smoking, eating, sleeping, or playing at cards;
and then he led us into a good-sized airy room, with a
window looking out into a court, three beds, a table
and some chairs; and where, from a photograph I had

seen in England, I instantly recognized, in the man who rose to meet us, Manuel Matamoros.

"He is in the early summer of manhood, slightly above the middle height, with jet black hair, and finely chiselled features, Italian rather than Spanish. His face beams with intelligence. I confess he took my heart by storm, and I speedily found in him a most beloved brother, whom I shall know instantly if we shall meet in heaven. My first and last impression of him was, that he is a prince among men. There was a force and an authority in his very way of expressing himself, that, to our mind, stamped him with the stamp of genius, and our guide said to us that his language was so sublime, he had the greatest difficulty in translating it. He gave me the notion, moreover, of being a man of strong affections, for the love in him seemed to kindle into a white heat as he showed us photographs of friends, among which I recognised Dr. and Mrs. Tregelles and Mr. Dallas. . . . . There were several others in the room. José Alhama, a hatter of Granada, who was present, has since been sentenced to a more severe imprisonment than Matamoros. He is quite unlike his friend, both in appearance and cast of mind, but there was an air of quiet strength about him, that showed he knew in whom he had believed, and that if he could not confess his Lord with excellency of speech and wisdom, he could at least suffer for him. . . . . I can never forget how Matamoros read the eighth chapter of the Romans, which seemed to open up to him a new mine of gospel promises, how grandly it sounded in the majestic Spanish tongue; what em-.

phasis he laid on the passages that touched on the fulness of the gospel liberty, and on the certainty of the coming glory; how, ever and anon he would lift up his voice, and look round on his fellow-prisoners, his whole face beaming with radiance, until the climax of the apostle's appeal, in verse thirty-one, almost overcame him; and he asked in a tone of ecstatic triumph, 'Who shall separate us from the love of Christ?'"

There remains but one more letter to complete those received and printed, which we give below.

" Granada, Nov. 8, 1862.

"BELOVED BROTHER,—I am happy. I live in the joy of Jesus. Liberty will never be to me more sweet than my prison has been, through the divine name of Him who on Golgotha sacrificed his life to snatch us from eternal death. No suffering, no sorrow, clouds for a moment my Christian gladness. God has granted me this blessing, for his goodness is inexhaustible. In my letter of the 30th I gave you the details of our present position. This ministerial fiscal is very bitter against us. He has demanded the augmentation of my sentence. He is not content with that of eight years of the galleys, perpetual inhabilitation for all instruction, rights, or political position, and the payment of the heavy costs of the suit! He has also appealed against Trigo's acquittal, and his present liberation. In fact, the whole case stands as it did the day after the sentence of the inferior tribunal. All must be done over again. The fiscal has appealed against us all, except Alhama; so that it is quite possible that those who have been acquitted may now be condemned.

"Dearest friend, you know that my health has been poor and weak for a long time. The sufferings of prison or of the galleys cannot but hasten the day of my death; but I look forward with joy to that day. Eternal death is not for those who love the Lord Jesus. . . . .

"I thought it right, in my address to the queen, to vindicate our common right, and to demand from her permission to worship God according to our consciences, and to ask from her, if not perfect religious liberty, at least toleration.

"You write to me of my sufferings, dearest brother. I see that they occupy your heart and memory, sadly and constantly. But, dearly-loved brother, let your mourning on my account be turned into joy. I, your poor brother in Jesus, whom you love and with whom you suffer, I suffer not. No! I rejoice unspeakably. This cruel sentence, these appeals, these two years of captivity, these doubts and delays on the part of foreign governments to speak a word in favour of our Christian liberty, and the opposition of the queen and the government to our release, all seem to my memory as causes for rejoicing.

"If I perceived love and kindness in my enemies, that would indeed seem strange! but their anger against me is natural, is consequent; and this anger causes me to raise my heart continually to my Lord, thanking Him for this eminent honour which He has been pleased to lay upon me, a despicable, useless, all-unworthy sinner. Oh! believe me, dearest friend, not alone in prison could I rejoice; not alone in the sufferings of the galleys; the stake, the scaffold, the axe of the executioner, would give me only fresh cause for gladness. I am ready not only to suffer for the divine name of Jesus, but also to die for Him.

"Do not let the indifference of the European governments affect you. All their power is as nought if the will of God is contrary to their will. Our weapon is only prayer—a powerful and mighty weapon, of which the world knows nothing; but the prayers which ascend to the throne of the Eternal bring forth fruit; for the goodness of God our heavenly Father is inexhaustible and infinite. I should rejoice to see these governments do all they could to procure liberty and toleration for all nations; but the Lord must do it, or nothing will be done. He wills that all shall be obtained by prayer; and therefore, whatever happens, I shall rejoice in Jesus. The liberty of my body is nothing to me; for this reason I said nothing of it in my address to the queen.

"That which really interests me is the salvation of my soul. I entreat you, dear friend, and all my brothers, to pray for me, that I may be faithful to the end. I have been told that a European deputation is about to visit Madrid. I rejoice! for by the might of prayer the doors—not of my prison, that is nothing—but of my country, may be thrown open to religious liberty, and I fain would hasten the dawn of that approaching day. This was one of the reasons of my address to the queen.

"Farewell, dearest brother in the Lord. Receive

this letter as a token of the constant love and gratitude of your brother in Christ,

"MANUEL MATAMOROS."

And now, in conclusion, I pray that this little work may be prospered by Him whose foolishness is wiser than men, and whose weakness is stronger than men. Has England no lesson to learn from Spain? What was it that helped so much to lull the voice of God's Spirit in that land in the sixteenth century? Was it not the gold of Peru? And with what is Satan seducing the hosts of the Lord in this country now? Is it not with the golden cup of Babylon, full of abominations and filthiness of her fornication? Is not our commercial pride, of which our Exhibition is the exponent, the Delilah that has kept Samson spellbound? and is not the fierce anger of the Lord revealed against us nationally, and smiting us sore in the very heart of our stronghold, by what is occurring now in our manufacturing districts?

Shall we continue to be silent? Saints of Christ, awake. Behold the Judge standeth at the door. Witness the good confession of the young Spaniard whose letters you now have before you, and arm yourselves with a like mind. A greater evil than Romanism is eating out the vitals of our populations. But the Lord will appear to " destroy them that destroy the earth," though they give to their sorceries the pleasing name of civilization. The enemy has come in like a flood, but the Spirit of the Lord shall put him to flight. Nothing else can stand before Satan. In this alone has been the secret of Matamoros' strength. It was this made Samson more than conqueror. Does the young lion roar against him? *The Spirit of the Lord came mightily upon him, and he rent him as he would have rent a kid.* Do the Philistines shout against him? By the same Spirit *the cords that were upon his arms became as flax that was burnt with fire, and his bands loosed from off his hands; and he found a new jaw-bone of an ass, and put forth his hand and took it, and slew a thousand men therewith*—a most unlikely weapon for such a warfare, but none other than the sword of the Lord when wielded by the brawny arm of a lively faith.

𝕸emorials

OF THE

LAST DAYS AND DEATH

OF

MANUEL MATAMOROS.

—o—

"He being dead yet speaketh."

THOSE readers who have followed us in the previous narrative, which detailed the conversion, the subsequent "bonds and imprisonments," and the "good confession" of Manuel Matamoros, will linger with a saddened interest over these "MEMORIALS," which tell of his labours of love during the period after his liberation from the Prison of the Audiencia, at Granada. "For the space of three years he ceased not" to spend his strength in that cause so dear to his heart—the evangelization of his countrymen.

In these concluding pages will be found the particulars of our beloved friend's declining days, and the record of his departure to that better land concerning which he said, "I shall live in the midst of that joy unceasing, of that peace, and of that love, which I have sought in vain on earth."

W. G.

CHAPTER XIII.

A VISIT TO THE PRISON AT GRANADA.—THE DEPUTATION
OF THE EVANGELICAL ALLIANCE.

It was arranged by our loving Heavenly Father, that
in the spring of 1863, and about two years and nine
months after our beloved brother had been imprisoned
at Barcelona, I was enabled to pay him a visit in the
prison at Granada. A short time before this his confinement had been made a little less irksome by the
goodness of God, who, as in the case of Joseph, caused
the jailor to become favourable to him. It appears
that the wife of the jailor was very sick, and in his
trouble the husband came and humbled himself to
Matamoros, who, touched by his sorrowful story, promised to pray for the poor woman. The Lord
graciously heard the prayer, and she was soon restored
to health. This occurrence was the means of bringing
about a great change in his conduct to Matamoros, who
from this time had liberty within the prison. The
prisoners used to take off their hats to him when he
passed, and he was respected and beloved by all, but
by none more than by the jailor himself, who, desirous
of showing him some special act of favour, offered to
give him any one of the prisoners as a servant to wait

on him in prison. He chose one of the greatest criminals for this service, and before long this man, who was imprisoned for murder, heard from the martyr's lips the wondrous story of the love of Jesus, which touched his hard heart, and he became a believer in that blood that cleanseth from sin, even when of the deepest dye, and he was from that time not only a happy man himself, and enabled unmoved to look forward to his severe punishment at the galleys, but he also became a faithful and loving attendant on our afflicted brother, and relieved the tedium of his solitude.

On arriving at the prison I was at once admitted to the cell of Matamoros, whom I now saw for the first time, after a correspondence which had lasted nearly three years. The time that we spent in that never-to-be-forgotten cell was, as can be well imagined, a period of extreme joy to us both. We were soon in each other's arms, experiencing the happiness that loving hearts feel under such circumstances—hearts joined and made one in Jesus, brought to know each other through the agency of God's Holy Spirit, and sustained in that relation by the same Spirit.

Through the kindness of English Christians, I had had the pleasure of alleviating his sufferings; and large sums of money had been sent for him and the other prisoners at Granada and Malaga by myself and other friends. This amount during the long period of their imprisonment cannot have been less than two thousand pounds, and was intended also to pay a part of the law expenses, and to help the families of the persecuted.

Knowing as I did, that this money had all passed
through Manuel's hands, I was prepared to find in the
prison some few comforts; but in this I was quite
mistaken. I pictured to myself our Christians in
England, who many of them are in affluent circumstances, and in many cases surrounded by luxuries;
but, thank God, the religion of Matamoros was more
in conformity with the type presented to us by the
Christ of the Evangelists. His beautiful hair was
neglected; his trousers, which had been much worn
at the knees through kneeling on the rough flags of
his cell, were mended by his own hands; there was no
sofa, no easy chair. On a small table was a huge pile
of letters, papers, etc. Seldom have I been in a more
melancholy apartment, yet never in a more hallowed
one. All I saw was more apostolic than anything that
I have witnessed before or since, and preached a sermon
not easily to be effaced from my mind.

When, afterwards, I asked the families of the persecuted if they had received sufficient for their wants,
they quickly replied—

"Oh, we have all had enough. You do not know
Don Manuel; he has given all to us, and kept nothing
for himself."

I am constrained to say, that in all his ways he
more closely imitated the blessed Saviour than did any
other man I ever knew. Let us thank God that He
has permitted us, in these days of formality and dead-
ness, when selfishness seems to have taken such a
strong hold on our hearts' best affections, to see, in
this dear disciple, some few living traits and characteristics of Him who said, "The foxes have holes, and the

O

birds of the air have nests, but the Son of Man hath not where to lay his head."

The short time that I was enabled to be with him in the prison was most precious and profitable to us both. I found out that he scarcely ever ate anything with appetite. His tears were his meat day and night. I fancied that if I could join him at his dinner he might eat with more comfort. I therefore had some food brought from the hotel, and, after a long and most interesting morning of sweetest communion, we sat down to the table which our blessed Father had spread for us in this memorable spot. How it rejoiced my heart to see this dear afflicted one forget for a time his sorrow, and eat, as he told me, with more appetite and relish than he had done for many a day before. I am one who believes in the *communion of saints*, the *forgiveness of sins*, and the *life everlasting*. I believe and enjoy all these things *now*.

After this, our time was spent in going all over the prison, speaking with many of the prisoners, visiting the cells of Alhama and Trigo, and seeing in the upper part of the prison the place where Matamoros had spent such weeks of terrible solitary confinement as nearly cost him his life. He paused long in telling me all about this; impressing on me what it was for one like him, with a heart full of love, to be shut out for weeks from all who were dear to him; to have his correspondence intercepted; to be seized with a burning fever, and have no doctor to attend, no friend to soothe, no one to give even a cup of cold water. But such was his lot, and he dragged this chain for many weeks alone. No Silas was with him during this period, but One was there who more than supplied his place, even Jesus, the Faithful Promiser, who has said, "Lo, *I* am with you alway, even to the end," and who kept his word.

While here, and in great bitterness of spirit, Matamoros wrote on the wall some verses of poetry, which I read with deep interest. They had the fire, the zeal, and the talent that characterized all his correspondence, and many times since have I regretted that I did not take a copy of them. Alas! what is our life but a great *blank* of duties neglected, of sympathies unheeded and refused, of dry eyes where tears were called for, and of hard stony hearts when tenderness was needed! Alas, alas! what unprofitable servants we are, and how far, O Jesus, from the standard of Thy bright loving example!

We were permitted to have Alhama and Trigo, Matamoros's mother, and two others, with us in our brother's cell. We read the Scriptures together, and he prayed with extraordinary fervour. Prayer with him appeared to be a mighty struggle, a continued supplication, into which he threw the full powers of his mind, and soon convinced the friends who were present of the immense difference there was between it and the formal petitions which many of us offer; as, indeed, there is also between our lukewarm lives and his burning, unceasing zeal and activity. Our chapter on this occasion was Romans viii., which was his favourite portion, and on which he seemed to feed continually. We obeyed our dear Lord's command at the same time, and, in remembrance of his love to us, celebrated his supper.

On the whole, the two days I spent here were delightful to myself, and most profitable to dear Matamoros and to all; but my visit was short, for, from prudential motives as well as from other causes, my time was limited; but I had *seen* the man whom I loved and admired so much, and truly there is nothing like seeing. God keeps this great joy in store for us, to *see* Jesus, whom having not seen we love, and to see Himself and the lovely place He has prepared for us.

After the last loving embrace, we parted, and as I descended the hill from the prison, I saw this dear witness for Jesus stretching out his arms between the bars of his window to wave to me his last farewell. Oh, how indelibly is impressed upon my memory that noble countenance, beaming with love, from behind that grim, lugubrious grating. The contrast will be all the more striking to those who have come out of such great tribulation, and have washed their robes and made them white in the blood of the Lamb. " Therefore are *they before the throne* of God, and serve him *day and night in his temple.*" God shall indeed " wipe away all tears from their eyes."

LETTER RECEIVED FROM DR. CAPPADOSE, OF HOLLAND.

"To Mr. W. Greene.

" *The Hague*, 25 *March*, 1863.

" DEAR BROTHER IN HIM WHO IS OUR LIFE AND HOPE,

" To-morrow, please God, I leave with my dear wife this city, and make a journey into Spain. But I will tell you regularly the antecedents. I expressed my anxiety that a deputation might be formed, and the London Committee of the Evangelical Alliance was in the same feeling. On both sides we made some exertions. Here I called many friends of the good cause together, and exposed to them at length the whole history of Matamoros and his companions, communicating to them the blessing God had given to us some years ago on our efforts in a similar case in Sweden, when some female members of the Catholic church have been oppressed, and finally banished, in accordance with the then and still existing law of the land, and how by our efforts and deputation they have not only been recalled and liberated from all punishment, but after a lapse of several months, this persecuting law is set aside, and since freedom of conscience is introduced into Sweden. My narration to them was a complete success; the great majority of the assembly entered into my views as to the necessity of a deputation, and it was decided on the election of deputies there and then.

" By acclamation three gentlemen then present were elected, and I myself first. But our English friends have taken a resolution that the deputation should wait till the final sentence was known. I, for my part, fearing that perhaps in this case I could no more see our friend Matamoros, so resolved to go before to Granada. To-morrow then I hope, under the lovely experience of the presence of my true Conductor, whose face I constantly and ardently seek, to depart for Neuchatel, in Switzerland, in order to remain there under the roof of my oldest friend, and then through Geneva, Lyons, Marseilles, to Malaga, and so to Granada, a long

and fatiguing voyage for my age and constitution—
bodily; but I am in the hands of my Lord, and go
with confidence. The advocate of M. wrote to me that
once at Granada I can see Matamoros every day. Now
this is one of my great desires.

"From Granada, I hope to go to Madrid, in order to
join the great deputation; but I suppose a pretty long
time will be taken by the judges in preparatory work,
so that I fear the case will not be decided before the
end of April.

"It is uncertain if the Queen will admit the deputation, and perhaps she will defer time after time.

"However, it may be that the very presence of the
deputation will strengthen the public opinion, which
begins to be more and more favourable to our cause. I
have heard that the Queen has received more than one
note from other queens appealing to the royal privilege
of pardon. I hope, my dear friend, you will have
received a copy of the two little pamphlets I published
on this subject. You have seen that I have dedicated
the second to yourself, as the constant friend and
benefactor of our dear Matamoros. The sale of the
first publication is still continuing. I have been so
happy as to transmit a new sum of £30 as proceeds
from the sale for the needy families.

"Now, dear brother, you will be so kind as to follow
me with your prayers. Oh that the blessed Lord,
whose glory I seek in all things, may sustain us with
the right hand of His strength, and may His spirit also
be with you and all the children of God.

"Most faithfully in the Lord,
"DR. CAPPADOSE."

THE DEPUTATION OF THE EVANGELICAL ALLIANCE.

The Evangelical Alliance, finding that the efforts of the British Parliament had no effect in obtaining from the Queen of Spain the liberation of Matamoros and his companions, and that the mission of General Alexander was alike unproductive of fruit, determined on sending to Madrid a European deputation, composed of some of the leading Christian men from the following countries, whose names are affixed below :—

NAMES OF DEPUTIES.

AUSTRIA .... Baron Von Riese Stallburg.
BAVARIA .... Pastor W. Tretzel.
DENMARK ...... M. A. L. Brandt.
ENGLAND ...... Samuel Gurney, Col. J. G. Walker, John Hodgkin, Esq., R. W. Fox, Esq., John Finch, Esq., Joseph Cooper, Esq., Rev. Dr. Steane, Rev. H. Schmettau.
FRANCE .... Count Edmond de Pourtales, Pastor G. Monod, M. George André, Baron L. Bussière.
HOLLAND ...... Baron K. F. de Lynden, Dr. A. Cappadose, M. Van Loon.
PRUSSIA .... Capt. Von Kluber, Henry XIII. Prince Reuss, Count Von Behr Negendauk.
SWITZERLAND ... M. Adrien Naville.
SWEDEN .... Baron Hans Essen.

But before reaching this stage in its organization months were consumed in meetings, consultations, and the interchange of communications between the committees of the Protestant and Evangelical Alliances, until at length the time drew on when

the case would be finally disposed of by the Spanish
Judges. About this time, the Rev. Dr. Steane addressed to Major-General Alexander a remarkable
letter entitled " The Persecution in Spain," which
was published by Messrs. Nisbet, and which increased
the sympathies of many in this interesting Mission.
The local committees of the Evangelical Alliance at
Edinburgh, Glasgow, Carlisle, Dublin, etc., met and
sent resolutions to the London committee, protesting
against further delay. The Foreign Secretary, the
Rev. H. Schmettau, whose unwearied diligence in
corresponding with individuals and committees in
almost all parts of the Continent entitles him to the
highest praise, was continually receiving letters to
the same effect, showing that foreign Protestants
were everywhere expecting the summons, and holding
themselves in readiness to obey it. And it was at
this period, that Sir Culling Eardley published his
letter to the Earl of Roden, in which he explained
the cause of the delay, and the course intended to be
pursued. That course was at length adopted, and it
was determined to organize the deputation. A special
committee was appointed to carry the resolution into
effect, Sir Culling Eardley being the chairman, Lord
Calthorpe treasurer, Revs. Dr. Steane and H. Schmettau
its secretaries, and everything was done which the
emergency required.

This work was commenced and carried on through
all its stages with prayer. Often the difficulties were
so formidable and the discouragements so great, that
the only hope which could be indulged, lay in the
belief that importunate and united prayer would not be

offered in vain. It was not forgotten that it was while the church was praying that Peter was liberated, and as that fact stands in the sacred page to show to the followers of Christ in all ages where, amidst the furious persecutions of the ungodly, their great strength lies, so let the story which these pages record find a place for the same blessed end, and as a further testimony to the glory of God, in the annals of the modern Church.*

On Tuesday, May 19, 1863, with the single exception of the Earl of Aberdeen, the English members of the deputation had all arrived at Madrid, as also had the majority of the deputies from the other European nations. The English members lost no time in waiting upon Mr. Edwards, the Chargé d'Affaires at the British Embassy, Sir John Crampton, the English ambassador, being then absent. The strong impression left by the interview was, that the deputation had little to expect from this quarter, and it was afterwards found to be shared by the deputation of "Friends," to whom Mr. Edwards had also stated his strong disapproval of the course which the prisoners had taken, that of appealing against their sentence—and especially of the independent tone with which, in their appeal, they had commented on the persecuting laws of Spain.

Two of the deputies had also a private interview

---

* For a full account of all the proceedings of the Evangelical Alliance in the matter of this deputation, see the pamphlet entitled "Narrative of the Proceedings of the Deputation to Madrid in behalf of the Spanish Prisoners. By Edward Steane, D.D." Nisbet.

with the Duke de Montpensier, who gave them some good advice as to the best course to pursue, and who said that he himself was an advocate for religious liberty, and that in consequence of his conduct in this business, he had been charged by his friends about the court with being a Protestant. He was nevertheless a sincere Roman Catholic, but as in England, which is a Protestant country, he himself enjoyed perfect liberty of public worship, and was treated with full consideration in all that affected his faith both by Queen Victoria and by her subjects, so he desired that Protestants in a Catholic country might enjoy like privileges.

Soon after this the deputation met to consider the propriety of seeking an audience with the Queen of Spain, and also as to the mode of making their desire known to her Majesty. On the latter point, the meeting was much guided by Count Stallburgh, Chamberlain to the Emperor of Austria, and Baron Von Lynden, Chamberlain to the King of Holland, who stated the usages of their courts; and as there seemed little probability that an audience would be asked for the deputation through diplomatic channels, it was resolved to ask for it through the Queen's Major Domo. On this very evening, however, as M. H. Schmettau was returning home, hearing an evening paper called *La Correspondencia* cried in the streets, he bought one, and there read the announcement that the Government had commuted the sentence on Matamoros and his companions to banishment, for the same length of time as the prisoners had been condemned to imprisonment with hard labour.

On finding this sudden and remarkable change in the sentence, much discussion arose as to what should be the line of action now taken by the deputies, and they decided that first an address to the Queen should be prepared, to be signed by all the members of the deputation, stating, that while they felt thankful to God that Her Majesty had mitigated the sentence under which our brethren were suffering, they had much more to claim respectfully at her hands, and that they begged to be allowed to leave with Her Majesty the petitions they had brought with them, in which the views and principles of the large bodies of Christians, in the different countries of Europe who had sent them, would be found deferentially and explicitly stated. Secondly, that a letter should be written, in the name of the deputation, to Matamoros and his fellow-sufferers, congratulating them on the mitigation of the terrible punishment to which they had been sentenced, and offering them affectionate and Christian counsel and sympathy. Dr. Cappadose and the Rev. H. Schmettau were requested to draft a letter to Matamoros, and M. A. Naville, M. Van Loon, Count Kanitz, Pastor William Monod, and Dr. Steane, were appointed to prepare the address to the Queen.

After the meeting broke up at which these measures were adopted, a telegram was received, communicating the distressing intelligence of the death of Sir Culling Eardley, president of the Evangelical Alliance, who from the first had taken the deepest interest in the case. It is as impossible, as it is unnecessary, to describe the deep gloom which this event threw over the deputation

Many tears of sincere affection and sorrow were shed; many prayers of profound submission to the holy will of God, and of sympathy with the bereaved family were offered up; and the subsequent meetings for business and for devotion were all shaded as with the solemnities of the eternal world, and saddened with the sense of an irreparable loss.

At the next meeting the draft-letter for the Queen was produced, carfully considered, and approved, as well as the one for Matamoros, which was ordered to be forwarded to him. Just at this crisis, Count Edmond de Pourtales and Baron de Bussière arrived as deputies from Paris. These noblemen waited at once on the French Ambassador, and placed the whole matter of the deputation before him. He undertook the difficult and delicate mission of presenting the letter to the Queen. Thus the last difficulty was in a most unexpected manner removed. Nothing could have been more opportune than the coming of the two French noblemen just when they did; and it will always stand as one remarkable proof, among many others, of God's gracious smile on that errand of love which had taken the deputation to Spain, and of his providential guidance of their measures.

The Prussian members of the deputation had been in communication with the Government on the subject of their being admitted to the royal presence to deliver the message and letter from the King of Prussia, and from the Prussian Queen Dowager, and in this they ultimately succeeded, though under restrictions as to any reference to the object of the deputation. They mentioned that when, during the interview, Prince

Reuss seemed as if approaching the obnoxious subject, the Marquis of Miraflores immediately interposed, and turned the conversation to another topic. It appeared also that the commutation of the sentence had been hastened, in order that it might be accomplished before the presentation of these distinguished persons to the Queen could take place. It should further be stated that as a token of respect to the deputies, and as at least an implied recognition of their part in the matter, the act of commutation, signed by the Queen herself, was sent by the Premier to the Prussian Deputies for their more entire satisfaction in reference to the attainment of the object of their mission. They were also assured that the prisoners at Malaga, as well as those in the city of Granada, were included in the mitigated sentence.

Soon after this the letter of the deputation to the Queen was conveyed by Baron de Bussières and the Count de Pourtales to the Marquis of Miraflores at Aranjuez. He promised to lay it before her Majesty, and consented to receive at his house at Madrid the various petitions and addresses from different countries, and to inform the Queen of their contents. A copy of the letter to the Queen appeared in *The Times* of June 3. In the meetings for worship held by the deputation at Madrid, and scarcely less in those for the transaction of business, they were often constrained to acknowledge the manifest presence of the promised Comforter, for to his divine power alone could they ascribe it, that their hearts were so drawn together, that their embarrassments were so gently cleared away, and that their conclusions, though previously discussed with unrestrained liberty

of opinion and of speech, were ultimately adopted with
perfect unanimity.   And as they thus met in the charity
of the Gospel, so they at length parted with augmented
mutual respect, and cherishing that love for each other
which is the greatest of the Christian graces, and the
most precious because the most enduring fruit of the
Spirit.   Nor, finally, can the fact be suppressed, that
they were thus enabled to realize and to manifest in
Spain, that most intolerent of the Papal nations, and in
the face of the whole observant hierarchy of Rome, the
true unity of the Church of Christ—a unity not more
blessed in itself than it will ultimately be seen to be
powerful, when in that universal manifestation which
it is one day destined to attain, it shall overthrow every
antagonistic force and hold forth the crowning demon-
stration that Jesus is the Christ until, in His own words,
"the world may believe that *Thou hast sent Me.*"

It was eminently characteristic of dear Manuel's
large-hearted unselfishness that when the news of his
own safety from his severe sentence was telegraphed to
him, he instantly flashed back the question—"And the
brothers at Malaga?"

CHAPTER XIV.

MATAMOROS'S RELEASE FROM PRISON.

In a memorandum which our brother has left among his papers we find some interesting notes on the manner of his release from his long confinement at Granada, which we give in his own words:—

"In the month of May, 1863, I was sentenced to nine years at the galleys. It was afterwards thought that this sentence might be changed into nine years of banishment. My own wish was not to have any alteration at all in the original sentence, nor to ask for pardon from Queen Isabella. An excellent friend to me and my work in Spain wrote to me some months before, saying, 'You ought not to ask for anything, nor to admit of any alteration in the sentence pronounced, as you have been now finally sentenced to the galleys,' and my own sentiments on the matter were entirely in accordance with this advice. Nevertheless, the general opinion of my friends was of a contrary nature. All wished that I should accept the commutation of the sentence, so when the royal order was communicated to me I accepted the matter, so as not to place myself in opposition to my friends' wishes and not to prejudice my dear fellow-prisoners.

" The immediate consequence of this commutation in the sentence was that my liberation from the prison of Granada took place at five o'clock in the morning of the 29th May, 1863, and I was accompanied by the Sergeant of the Civil Guard, Antonio Perez Oriviola. My journey from Granada to Malaga I accomplished by the diligence, accompanied by Trigo, Alhama, and their two daughters, and by the wife of the former. The conditions that the Sergeant of the Civil Guard fixed before consenting to allow us to travel by diligence were:—*First*. That a carriage should take us from the gates of the prison to the distance of half a league from the town, and that another should wait outside Malaga, so as to prevent any public manifestations in either of these towns. *Second*. That we must take all the seats in the diligence. *Third*. That I should pay for the seats of the Civil Guard to Malaga and back to Granada. *Fourth*. That once in the diligence I must not get out before arriving at Malaga, and if I was hungry I must eat in the diligence. *Fifth*. That none of the public papers of Granada, or of any other part of Spain, should mention about our deliverance. Such were the principal conditions, and there were other unimportant ones not added.

We arrived at Malaga at half-past seven o'clock the same evening. The Sergeant of the Civil Guard behaved very well to us, showing us much attention. He apppeared to be a worthy and educated man, never unnecessarily displaying his authority, but doing all in his power to be agreeable to us, and at the same time to fulfil his obligations. Indeed, on the whole he appeared to sympathise with us. We arrived safely, but dreadfully tired. Nothing important happened by the way, with the exception of the conduct of the last guard we had when entering into Malaga, who was drunk and was very impertinent to us; but this was of small importance."

After sleeping at the prison of Malaga they proceeded to Gibraltar, according to orders received from Madrid. From the same paper we extract the following:—

"At four o'clock in the evening the public prison of Malaga was filled with police. The commissary and the turnkeys were waiting for us. Our sortie from the prison was managed with much prudence on the part of the authorities. We were each one of us led to the port by a single policeman, and each one through a different street in the town of Malaga, and thus arrived at the place where we were to embark. The Mole was filled with people; many were waiting for us there. The boat left the shore at six in the evening, and I left my beloved Malaga; but oh, how my heart bled as I left the shore of my fatherland!

"At nine o'clock in the evening the ship of war 'Alerta,' in which we were, started on her way to Gibraltar. They gave us good places on board, and during the journey we received many kind attentions. We arrived at Gibraltar on the 31st of May, at nine in the morning."

After passing a few days there he determined on visiting England, and embarked for London on the

22nd June, 1863, at an early hour of the morning. Of this he says:—

"The first day on board ɪ passed tolerably, but on the second I found myself unwell from head to foot, and with this many sorrowful recollections came into my mind, as well as lamentable meditations and impressions, making my fatiguing journey sadder still. Yes, but all this was necessary; it was indispensable to sacrifice *all, all, all*, for that holy work, the evangelization of Spain, for the temporal and spiritual wants of my dear friends, and in connection with everything that had to do with my poor and unfortunate country."

After a rough passage along the coast of Spain and Portugal, they experienced finer weather across the Bay of Biscay, but nevertheless he appears to have suffered much. He adds:—

"Finally we came in sight of England. What joy! what profound delight for all the Englishmen on board! The most unspeakable delight was painted on the countenance of each one, and they all, as if drunk with pleasure, came to point me out that speck of land that loomed in the distance, exclaiming, 'England! England!' We gradually neared the shore. I had formed a very unfavourable idea of the vegetation of England, fancying that it was poor and feeble; but my surprise was great when I discerned from the vessel that, on the contrary, it was luxuriant, healthy, and very lovely. On entering a little further inland we saw the country more clearly. It was the Isle of Wight; and now for the first time I saw an English town. On the 30th June we reached the

mouth of the Thames. What a lovely aspect presented itself before me; what a delightful impression it made on my mind; and what poetry filled
my soul on that beautiful morning! As we proceeded up the river the stream became narrower, and
every turn brought before us something agreeable to
look upon."

At length our dear brother arrived in London, and
remained there about a fortnight. His reception was,
unfortunately, very far from what his true friends
wished to give him, but all was permitted by Him who
giveth not account of any of His matters.

We cannot look back to this period of dear Manuel's
history without feeling that the fire of. persecution was
hotter—or, at least, the fogs of intolerance and mis-
understanding were darker and heavier around him at
this time—than ever before. It is a mournful page in
the history of our English Christianity, and we gladly
turn it over, leaving to Him who hath said "There is
nothing hid that shall not be revealed," to show in his
own good time how pure and single-eyed was dear
Manuel in all his dealings, and also how severely he
suffered at the hands of some from whom he expected
love and support.

CHAPTER XV.

WORK AT LAUSANNE.—PREPARATIONS FOR EVANGELIZING SPAIN.—WORK ORGANIZED AT PAU, BAYONNE, AND BORDEAUX.

To give some idea of the labours of our brother after his release from prison, an extract from a statement of his own is here introduced. This will put the reader in possession of many facts that will show the nature and importance of the undertakings which were commenced in France and Switzerland, and carried on with most blessed results.

" When once the prison doors were opened to the prisoners, and when persecution ceased in Spain, the first thought that occupied the minds of the exiles was to continue the work begun, profiting by the experience of the past and preparing for the eventualities of the future. As there are many appearances that the day is near at hand when liberty of worship will be granted, we have been led to prepare ourselves, and also to prepare our youth. When I left Spain the first thing that was laid on my mind in a particular way was the creation of a Spanish college for that portion of our young men who should feel disposed to prepare themselves by theological studies; a fitting place was soon fixed upon in France, and we commenced with six young Spanish pupils. At the same time one of our young persecuted brethren went to Switzerland, where, being already far advanced in knowledge, he was enabled to devote his time to the more serious studies ; while in France I began to prepare myself for everything that my future position might call me to undertake.

" During this period the work in the interior of Spain advanced with fresh vigour, and its results were visible in many ways; and now this implacable persecution, by means of which our enemies expected entirely to destroy our work, had, on the contrary, only opened a new future, by preparing public opinion (which generally is favourable to toleration) to re cognize the cause of the persecuted, and to take an interest in them. Our beloved brothers at —— boldly put themselves at the head of the work, which began to be extended and consolidated. Besides this, the creation of a college in France filled them with joy, which was increased when they learned that some were thinking of founding, at Lausanne, an institution which was intended to afford opportunities for supplementing and completing the studies of the youth from Bayonne, where the teaching was more of an elementary character. The work at Lausanne was inaugurated at the beginning with only six young people, but afterwards its numbers were increased.

" The well-disposed among our youth in Spain appeared to vie with one another in their emulation to be among the number of the future preachers of the gospel in their country, and fathers and children both gave many manifest proofs of this fact. It is not difficult to observe the rapid progress that the Spirit of God has given to this blessed work. The number of converts in Spain has increased considerably, as have also their means of labouring, and the interior organization of the churches has guaranteed solid and positive progress. But in order that you may have a good idea of the same, I will cite some passages from an important report made by Pastor Currie to the Paris committee, of which he was the representative, subsequent to his visit last year to the churches in Spain. The following is a part of his report:—

" ' On arriving at ——, all the friends there received me with the greatest cordiality. Everyone, from the directing body down to the humblest Christian, appeared desirous of being useful to me, and of anticipating my wishes. Often from morning till evening have I been engaged in receiving and paying visits, my friends wishing to accompany me wherever I went. There exists in this place a congregation of .three hundred members, whose names have been given to me. This congregation is thoroughly well organized, as you will hereafter see. A committee composed of six individuals, who are all sincere Christians, and who are both capable and prudent, manage the work, under the superintendence of our brother Matamoros, who is recognized and loved as the founder, the father, and spiritual director of this body. This committee holds its regular sessions, which are opened and closed with prayer; its acts are duly registered in a book, which I examined. Political discussion is strictly forbidden.

With the exception of ten evangelists or missionaries, who are labouring for the dissemination of the Scriptures and of Scripture truth, the remainder of the congregation are quite ignorant of the names of the persons who form the committee. Sometimes, in cases of emergency, the committee invites the other evangelists to be present at their meeting, so as to obtain their advice and to have the assistance of their judgment. These missionaries are, for the greater part, young men of exemplary conduct, intelligent, and filled with zealous and noble sentiments. These, after their daily avocations are finished, seize every propitious occasion to combat the errors of the Church of Rome, and to preach the truth. These dear friends have as yet but a limited knowledge of the Scriptures; but, nevertheless, such as they are, the evangelists of —— interest me much, for while they do not dishonour the name they profess, they act faithfully to the extent of their light and their faith.

" 'These young men are, so to speak, self-taught, for they have neither a pastor to instruct nor books to enlighten them. Every Sunday morning they form small gatherings in different parts of the town, where they preach the truth; and afterwards, when among their audiences they observe people sufficiently convinced of the errors of Romanism, and who are living a good life, they ask them to join the Reformed Church. Indeed, sometimes the demand is spontaneous on the part of the listeners, and needs not to be provoked. In such cases, the person who wishes to be received has to sign a request to that effect addressed to the committee. The evangelist presents this, and if there be no opposition the applicant is admitted.

"'During my sojourn at —— I sometimes assisted at the committee meetings, and on each occasion, two, four, six, and even seven propositions for admittance were presented. In receiving these new members, I believe that the committee makes few mistakes. They know that the faith and walk of the neophytes are still weak, and that they need instruction ; but being once convinced of.the sincerity of the step they have taken, of the fervency of their desires, and uprightness of their conduct, the course of the committee is easy. These brethren are received, and the committee look forward to seeing them progress in their spiritual career, and in the love and knowledge of their Saviour. Every Sunday evening, the members of the committee, together with some evangelists, meet for reading and worship, when the Word of God is studied and prayer is offered. All the functions of the committee and of the evangelists are gratuitous, and among them simplicity, brotherly love, and peace abide. They seem to out-rival each other in zeal, and display the greatest activity. These churches are as yet quite in an incipient stage, and much is wanting; yet, nevertheless, even as matters now are, they have pleased me greatly, and I ever wish to see them increased more and more, not only in numbers, but also in that spiritual life which is hid with Christ in God. The doctrines of the gospel appear to have taken such deep root at ——, that from three to four thousand persons, it is believed, would join the Reformed Church on the day that religious liberty was proclaimed in Spain.

" ' Besides the many visits that I paid to these friends, I was also enabled on many occasions to celebrate divine worship, first with the members of the committee and the evangelists united, and afterwards with sundry individuals from among the groups to whom the evangelists were in the habit of preaching. On all occasions 1 remarked the most sustained attention, and a great thirst after truth on the part of the hearers, who numbered from fifteen to twenty individuals. I also had the pleasure of having meetings composed entirely of females. One evening there were seventeen present, and had all who wished been able to attend we should have had twenty-five. This fact is, to my mind, most comforting; for not only do they form the most living part of the Church, as was explained to me, but, besides, as wives, mothers of families, and Christians, they may, by God's grace, do much good, not only at home, but all around.' These were M. Currie's words, written in October, 1865.

" I shall now say a few words about an institution which I some time since had the pleasure of founding here at Pau. Some years ago I had the idea of forming an institution for young Spanish women, the daughters of our Protestant brethren, and to give them the education necessary to fit them to serve the Lord in the different vocations he might call them to occupy, whether as governesses or as wives and mothers. Different propositions from Spain made to me in regard to this matter confirmed me in my conviction that this project was approved by God in connection with the work in Spain, and would have His blessing. Consequently, immediately after my arrival at Pau, I communicated my idea to Miss C——, who sympathized with me, and who made it, from that time forward, the subject of her constant prayers, as I did also; and it frequently formed the subject of our conversations. I soon after left Pau, filled with this idea, which occupied my thoughts, and I wrote a long letter to her from Eaux Bonnes, touching lightly on the different points of the work in general. Part of my letter was as follows:—

"'*Eaux Bonnes, on the Rhine.*

"'The habits and customs in Spain are very different to what, I am happy to observe, prevail here, and they do not allow the same freedom in social intercourse. On this account, and from other circumstances, there is a difficulty in obtaining access to females in Spain for the purpose of announcing to them the gospel of God's grace. For this reason, this great and delightful task (whose importance is such that we would willingly call it the heart of our work) can only be carried on by females. But, through the grace of God, this branch of our labour may become one of the most solid bases on which our work of evangelizing our beloved country may have its foundation; for in all places doors are open to women, and they are always well received, whether they come to sit down at the domestic hearth, or to address the wife, the mother, or the unmarried female. They have access everywhere, which is far from being the case with the men.

"'I believe, then, dear sister, that it is not only

useful, but indispensable, that this special establishment should be founded, for the purpose of receiving a sufficient number of young Spanish girls, and of giving them a solid Christian education, so that they may acquire not only sound Scriptural instruction, but, at the same time, all the general information which pertains to a solid education, and which will by-and-by open a way for them among the many different classes of society. Under proper direction, and above all with a view to serve the Lord, they should be taught what are the duties of the daughter, the wife, and the Christian mother; they should be initiated into all the exercises of Christian charity, and be led to visit the sick and the poor. Indeed, by giving them an opportunity of living for some time in a Christian atmosphere, where spiritual life is *a fact*, and where faith is manifested by works of love and self-denial, we should be commencing a holy and blessed work, whose results may have, through God's grace, an incalculable influence on the religious future of Spain; and I cannot but recommend it to your notice, in the divine name of our Blessed Lord.'

" Such were the considerations which decided Miss C——, after a season of prayer and inward conflict, with full confidence to begin this work of faith, which already has given such happy results, and has made us joyful in the thought that the blessing of Jesus is resting upon it."

I lately received a letter from a brother in Spain, who takes a lively interest in our work there. From it the following is extracted:—

" We feel, from day to day, that the Lord is blessing

us in this town abundantly. A few days back, being
the anniversary of the death of Torrijos and of his forty-
eight companions in misfortune, I was walking with
C——, and, as we felt tired, we sat down to rest. The
seats on this promenade are double, so that the persons
who sit down are seated back to back. Well, as we
were sitting on one of these seats, there came two others
to sit down also. One was an honourable old man;
his companion a man too, of mature years. Three
others soon joined them, and commenced a conversation.
The youngest, speaking of the recognition of Italy by
Spain, said, amongst other things—

"'This was a want of our age, in the presence of
which the will of the Queen and the clerical party have
been obliged to bow; and those who to-day recognize
the unity of the kingdom of Italy, will also be forced
to submit to the other conquests of this century, not
bloody conquests, as the event we to-day are celebrating;
and in due time we shall have liberty of worship posted
over the door of every dwelling.'

"'Quite true,' replied the other. 'You remember
the persecutions of 1860 and 1861? That is a blot on
the history of Spain that must be effaced by asking for
liberty of worship.'

"'Yes,' said the old gentleman.

"'But perhaps you are not aware that there are in
this town now many Christians like those who suffered
persecution, and that their number daily increases. A
man comes to our house twice a week to read to us the
Bible, and a tract entitled "Andrew Dunn." What
pleasure we experience in listening to him, and in
seeing that these people only seek after peace. More

than once I wished to introduce politics, but he always replied that it was not about earthly things he wished to converse, but on divine things alone. He said, also, that the Church of Spain must be reformed, and return to its primitive standing, for then only would all things go on well.'

" ' That would be for the true welfare of the people,' replied the younger man. 'I also have had some serious conversations with one of these primitive Christians, and when I expressed my desire of entering into communion with them, he replied, " Yes ; but you must first of all enter into communion with Christ." '

" Such was the conversation of these sincere men. We said nothing, thinking that thus they would speak more unrestrainedly; but we seem to have perceived in their words a spark of that divine light which rejoices Christians here, and so we were made truly glad."

Much more of a still more interesting nature is contained in the same letter, but we cannot at present reproduce it. A little farther on, however, we have a few lines of much importance, and, as they are from Matamoros's own pen, they are well worthy of our consideration:—

"The counsel that I give to my fellow-countrymen is, not to allow themselves to be governed by anyone in the development of their work, but by Jesus only. Let us be neither of Paul, nor of Apollos, nor of Cephas, but of Christ, and may His Spirit be our guide. This is the best recommendation that I can at the present time give to the church in Spain. May she apply herself to the study of the Word, and with the help of the

Lord, that Word alone shall be her guide.   Let us seek
to belong only to Christ, to walk and to increase in
Him.   Let us labour in the evangelization of the
people, and let us be directed by His Spirit alone.   This
is my counsel for the present.

"MANUEL MATAMOROS."

The above will give some little insight into a portion of the labours of our brother when in France, but
presents only a very superficial glance at the immense
activity and unceasing care that he took of everything,
and every individual, in any way connected with this
most interesting work.

At Bordeaux, three other of the persecuted brethren
were located, and, through his assiduity and attention,
they were enabled to support themselves and their
families.   The young men established in Lausanne
were most comfortably lodged in an excellent house,
and attended the instructions of the College of the Free
Church of the Canton de Vaud.   Funds on a large scale
were required for all these things, and the activity and
prayers of our brother have supplied them all.   Two
missionaries labouring among the Spaniards at Algiers
and Oran were placed there at the suggestion and request of Matamoros.   But it was necessary to know
him intimately to comprehend how his whole life was
a living sacrifice to Him who has sacrificed His life for
us all, in order that we might be His purchased people.

During the whole of the time of his exile, Matamoros's health was very feeble, and he was scarcely
a day out of the doctor's hands; but in the midst of
all this, when strength permitted, his lips and pen

were never quiet. Such activity for Christ I have rarely witnessed, and such generosity of disposition I have seen in none. He was very much beloved in Holland, Switzerland, and France, and received innumerable presents of various kinds from the saints in all these countries ; but his joy appeared to manifest itself more in giving than receiving, and he kept scarcely anything for himself.

A part of his three years of exile was spent at Bayonne, but at Lausanne his heart seemed to have been more at home than anywhere else, thanks to the loving sympathy he found in the house of those warm-hearted, earnest Christians, M. and Mme. Bridel. He was in journeyings oft, sometimes to Holland and sometimes to Paris. England saw but little of him, though he sighed to be among us, and looked to us as those from whom he expected all. *Spain calls at present, with as loud a voice as ever Macedonia did,* " *Come over and help us. Come over and give us Christ's gospel. Come over and give us your sympathy in a cause which is the greatest of all causes, because it is for eternity.*" I cherish a hope that, in spite of much lukewarmness, in spite of much to mourn over, these words will enter the hearts of some who love Jesus, and that they will hear. In such a case my book will have answered the purpose I have in view, not merely to give a faithful picture of God's faithful servant, but to rouse others to imitate his bright example.

CHAPTER XVI.

A WOMAN'S REMINISCENCE OF MATAMOROS.

In the summer of 1865 we had been obliged to leave our home in Mallorca, for change of air and rest for my husband and children, whose health had suffered from repeated attacks of Mediterranean fever, and we were staying at Montpellier (Hérault), when I saw for the first and last time the subject of this memoir.

Before his arrest at Barcelona we had been interested in him, and all through the weary months of his imprisonment his letters had been read, translated, and circulated by us, and had called forth appreciative sympathy and energetic assistance from friends in many places.

The motives for that sympathy and the need for that assistance are fully set forth in other chapters of this book. I only allude to them now in order to make a kind of confession as regards my own feeling towards Matamoros, whom I had so far only known in his semi-public character. Personally, then, I was inclined to think that he had been too much talked about and bepraised. The inflated and exaggerated style of Spanish correspondence, so far from impressing me with a true sense of what he had done and suffered, had reacted upon my mind, till I undervalued both, and when I knew that he was coming from Pau to spend a day or two with us, I anticipated little more than a confirmation of my fears that the vulgar fame of a patronized ex-victim must have destroyed the glory of his martyrdom and that self-consciousness, which is self-conceit, could hardly have failed to mingle with and damage the simplicity of his heroism.

But my recollections of the short hours of our personal acquaintance go to prove that I was quite at fault.

He had passed through the long grief and pain of his imprisonment unembittered, through the ordeal of European notoriety undisturbed, and through the crucible of côterie admiration unspoiled.

Surely this is much to the glory of the grace of Him who, Himself lowly and humble of heart, kept His servant from faults all the more insidious and dangerous, because they do not always look like sins, and because they are often encouraged and fostered by the injudicious affection of Christians themselves.

I first saw Manuel Matamoros one evening, early in December, 1865, at the Hotel Nevet, at Montpellier.

Our sitting-room was on the first floor, and my little daughter's nursery was on the second. By some mistake of the servants, he had been directed to the upper floor, when he had asked for our rooms.

My children were in various stages of preparation for bed, when we heard a sound at the door and saw standing at it a figure which looked almost gigantic in the dim evening light, with coal-black hair and beard, and bright, amused, kindly eyes, gazing down at the pretty group of half-dressed babies.

Q

My first glance at him seemed to sweep away clouds, and to reveal the man as he really was. I jumped up from the ground where I had been sitting, and said, "Is it Manuel?" To which he answered with a hand-clasp like that of a friend, and I hurried with him down to the room where my husband was waiting, and where the two friends were soon locked in one another's arms.

I wish I had at the time made some notes of the long conversations which took place between these two, both so earnestly desiring to ascertain the best means of spreading, in the land which was dear to both, the knowledge of the love of God. But I did not do so, and though some of the trifling occurrences of those days are very vivid and clear in my memory, I dare not write down here what I believe to be my recollections of things said then. So much has happened, I have seen and heard so much of Spain since, that I could not be assured of my own accuracy. The peaks of distant mountains seem merged into each other when the evening sun shines on them, and the sense of the leagues which separate the nearer from the farther ranges is lost in the vague blue mist which rises from the plain at their feet.

We dined at the *table d'hôte* that day. Manuel was in very good spirits, and I remember our noticing that at the long table, where we were the only foreigners, the proverbial characteristics of the different nationalities seemed for the moment changed. The vivacious, loquacious French people were dining in silence and with gravity, while the sombre Spaniard and the reserved and cold-blooded English people chatted and laughed over the meal like three children.

Manuel's manner was very frank, genial, kindly and simple. He was quite ready to receive any suggestion, advice, or criticism concerning his work or himself. The impression made on the first evening and which lasted and grew was—"He is quite unspoiled." We attended a Sunday evening service which M. le Pasteur Recollin held in a room, hollowed out of the rock, beneath a part of the town, and which he loved to call "The Catacombs of Montpellier." Schools and week-day services were held here, and after the service on this especial evening, a few friends were invited to remain, and Manuel gave a slight sketch of what he had done, and what he hoped to do. M. Recollin's judicious questioning drew out most lucid and interesting details, and Manuel felt how much he had been helped "to say his catechism," as he called the account he had given us.

The little audience was thoroughly delighted and sympathetic, and full of brotherly feeling.

Next day, a much larger meeting was held in the house of one of the rich families of Montpellier, whose name is on many a page of Southern French History.

The external contrast between this gathering and that in the "catacombs" was very great, but it was chiefly in externals, and the welcome to the servant of Christ, for His Master's sake, was equally cordial in either place.

Manuel himself was far "too great a man," as a great American has said, "to know how he dined or how he dressed," and was perfectly at his ease in his simple well-bred way, with people of every class and rank of society.

The easy courtesy and stately simplicity which characterise the manners of his countrymen lost nothing of their grace and charm in his person, and the refinement which accompanies Christian grace, and which sorrow and suffering bring forth in elect natures, thus trained and moulded, distinguished and ennobled him, supplying defects of education, and correcting errors of early training.

He spoke long, earnestly and ardently to the crowd of cultivated and critical hearers, and carried them all with him by the faith and fire with which he told his story. He spoke in French, with facility and fluency, though not quite correctly. Not eloquently, except so far as every Spaniard is eloquent, but with so much personal feeling, coupled with such self-forgetting modesty, that I think the effect produced was greater than might have been made by a more finished orator.

At the close the audience manifested much kind and sympathetic feeling, congratulating, applauding, and encouraging him.

He received all the homage with quiet dignity and gratitude, laughed a little, when it was all over, at some point-blank praises which were more direct than tasteful, and ended with—"If they will only help our Mission !" . . . .

On the fourth morning he left us. The diligence started early, but we breakfasted together, and commended him to the love and care of the Father who had brought him out of prison and was leading him onward by a way that we knew not to his heavenly home.

My personal recollections of him end here. They are very pleasant ones in every way. The handsome, intelligent, meridional face; the cordial, affectionate manner, tempered by a kind of wistful deference which was very touching and attractive; the heroic simplicity and modesty; the transparent innocence, and the unshaken endurance and resolution of his life were all legible in his words and ways.

The games he played with my little children; the imitations of cats, birds, and dogs with which he delighted them; the stories he told them of his tame canaries and the mice he used to feed in his prison, are well remembered still by them, but cannot be described or repeated here. He left us, blessing us and them, and I saw him no more.

CHAPTER XVII.

FAILING HEALTH.—LOVING FRIENDS.—LAST DAYS.—
ASLEEP IN JESUS.

AFTER organizing the work at Pau, Bayonne, and
Bordeaux, Matamoros went to Paris to make some
arrangements. The long journey by railway from
Pau, much speaking and exertion while at Paris,
but principally the unkind slanders coming from
England, and circulated afterwards in France—all
these combined, were too much for this great tender
heart, which seemed to. live only to love and to be
loved. This inclement clime of human life was no
longer suited to a nature ripe for the " better land."
After a short visit to Paris in the beginning of the
year 1866, he returned to Lausanne, in Switzerland,
where he had founded one of the establishments for
the preparation of the Spanish youth for service in
the gospel in Spain.

He reached Lausanne on the 3rd May, 1866. An
American lady in affluent circumstances had met him
at Pau, in the previous summer. She had suffered
the loss of all she held dearest on earth, and was
led by the Lord to sympathize with and finally to

devote herself to the noble cause which was so dear to Manuel's heart. Having ample means at her disposal, she quickly entered into his views concerning his much-loved country, and helped him in bringing twelve more young Spaniards to be educated at Pau. During the month of May they arrived at Lausanne, where they were first placed in certain pious families for a few months, so as to enable them to obtain some knowledge of the French language before commencing their studies at Pau.

This lady was happy in being able to supply all the wants of her dear adopted son; and thus, through the kind providence of God, he was during the last year of his life in very comfortable circumstances. His arrival at Lausanne was the cause of great joy to all his numerous friends there, and to himself. His home was for some time with his good and faithful helpers, M. and Mme. Louis Bridel, at La Borde, in the immediate neighbourhood of the town, by whom he was received quite as their own son. Although he often complained of being much fatigued, yet at the commencement of his visit the state of his health did not alarm them. While with them he expressed a desire to be consecrated by the synod of the Free Church of the Canton de Vaud, and in spite of the irregularity of the case, this body decided on granting his request, as they considered that he had, through the sufferings and persecutions he had endured in his long imprisonment, received from the Lord a higher consecration than theirs.

But he now daily appeared to be gradually sinking, and from the beginning of June his friends became seriously alarmed for his health. Many combined causes brought on low fever, accompanied by want of sleep. He received afflicting intelligence about the state of the health of his dear mother. This was a time to him of much trial and inward struggle. He said to Mme. Bridel, "No doubt the Lord is causing me to pass through all this in order to prove to me once more, that in all things I must trust in Him, and in Him alone, and that to Him only must I look to bring all hearts to be favourable to me and to my country."

He also wrote to a friend, saying "I hear my poor mother will probably lose her sight. Alas, my mother! She suffers sorely, but it is not thought that her life is in danger, though she is seriously ill. She is much supported by God, and evinces a sweet and heroic constancy. Oh, who can tell how much I love her! But I am sure that God Himself will take this care into His own hands, and tell her that I love her beyond all bounds. May God support thee, mother of my heart, and may He bless thee with His choicest blessings !"

On Saturday, 26th May, he held his first meeting for prayer and reading of the Word with the young Spaniards at La Borde, and these meetings were repeated twice a week till the 23rd June, when, being too fatigued, he was obliged to retire ; this caused all his friends the most serious anxiety.

I was enabled at this time to leave my usual occupations, and to spend nearly six weeks at Lausanne. As the good Lord had. brought me to cheer my friend in prison, so now He sent me to console and comfort him in his dying hour. The very day he was no longer able to feed the flock of God, I was sent to take his place. The Lord was very present at our little gathering. From this time forward it was thought for many reasons desirable for Matamoros to be at the Hôtel Gibbon, where Mrs. McE——, the American lady before-mentioned, was staying. Until the moment of his death, she rendered him constant and invaluable attention. This pleasure of ministering to an heir of glory was also afforded me for many weeks. Manuel often said, during his last illness, that God had gathered round him his best friends to comfort him, and we all thanked God that it was His good pleasure thus to solace his loving generous heart. There were others that loved him dearly, who longed to be in the privileged place that we felt we were holding by the dying bed of this dear saint, but the great Orderer of all our steps did not call them to this honoured post.

The decline of our beloved friend's strength was very rapid, and in spite of the attention we rendered, and of every care that medical aid could afford, we found nothing could arrest the progress of the disease. The lungs were much affected, and his breathing daily became more difficult. For a month he passed very restless nights, almost without sleep, being frequently obliged to sit in an upright position, with his head supported on pillows, unable to lie down, and in intense pain. The lungs, heart, and liver were completely disorganized, and a great quantity of water having now collected round the heart, we deemed it prudent to have a consulation without loss of time.

The eminent medical men called in gave it as their opinion that, if the features of the case became aggravated, he might be carried off in a few days. I felt it a duty to apprize him of the nearness of his end, and when I told him that within a week he might receive the final summons, he replied very calmly—

"Bueno ! Al cielo !"—"It is well ! To heaven !"

He requested me to go at once to La Borde, where his letters and papers were, and to bring them to the Hôtel Gibbon, which I did. The amount of correspondence and documents was so great that it took us the best part of two days to sort and arrange them, and when this was done, he was enabled quietly to leave all in the hands of his heavenly Father, though he had many hours of struggling and of prayer. On the same evening that he heard the doctor's opinion, Pastor Bridel read and prayed with him. Matamoros himself also prayed with a remarkable warmth of emotion and elevation of soul, and asked particularly that if God wished to call him home, He would enable him to obey the summons; not in the spirit of a servant who knows not the will of his Master, but as a child, who knows that his Father is doing what is best for his child; and he thanked God for bringing his loving friends about him at such a moment. But even after this he was able to go out a little in an open carriage as far as La Borde, where he was able to breathe the sweet fresh air, and where he enjoyed perfect tranquillity.

On Monday, the 16th June, he was very weak, and the Lord's Supper was celebrated in his room, about ten people being present. Pastor Bridel, who presided, addressed to each of us two verses of Scripture. Those for Matamoros were, "My grace is sufficient for thee," and " All things work together for good to them that love God."

In a letter he addressed at this time to Mme. Bridel Matamoros says—

"I am very weak, though the doctors say I am better, but be that as it may, the Lord is my all. In beginning to struggle with the agonies of death, I desired life, but now I alone desire the perfect realization of the will of God. A few days ago, certain matters connected with my work engaged my attention, but now I lay down my work at the feet of Him who gave it to me. He will make a perfect use of what is His alone. I should have liked to labour yet a little, but under these solemn circumstances it is no question what I like, but what is the Lord's will."

Amidst their deep sorrow it was yet to his friends a source of joy, and a cause for gratitude, that they were permitted to see him enter into this complete rest and detachment from all earthly things. This grace was granted to him, after much striving and anguish on his part. He wrote a few lines to the young Spaniards in the town and neighbourhood, as follows :—

" With what sympathy do I write to you and with what love do I address you ! In these solemn moments I wish to speak to you to tell you that I love you, and that your spiritual good is the burden of my prayers. Take notice of my position. Still young and in the

first year of my Christian activity, the thread of my
life is about to be severed. What would become of
me if I had not such a Saviour as Jesus Christ now?
Jesus in this hour of sorrow is my friend, my help, my
strength; as He is also my salvation. Adieu, my
dearly beloved ones. May the Lord bless you with His
choicest blessings.

"M. MATAMOROS."

He invited the young Spaniards at Lausanne to
come to his room and sing to him his favourite hymns
in Spanish and in French, when he spoke most
touchingly to them, telling them in his ardent and
loving way all the affection that he bore them; and
how he hoped that they would be earnest and
faithful in the blessed work they were beginning.
He also expressed himself to them most tenderly and
touchingly about his probable speedy departure from
this world, saying, "Leaving you all appears to me
as if pieces were torn from my heart." After they
had sung the sweet hymn, "Venid Pecadores," etc.,
he remarked, "How lovely and how true are those
words, 'El cielo es del alma la patria mejor,'"—
"Heaven is the better country of the soul," adding
that the sweet melody of their voices had seemed
to him like the music of a choir of angels; and such
indeed it had appeared to us all who were present at
this memorable farewell scene. At an earlier period
of the evening he prayed earnestly, sweetly, and de-
voutly for Mme. Bridel, Mrs. McE——, and myself,
that we might be faithful to the cause he had so much
at heart.

SPANISH WORDS OF VENID PECADORES.

I.

Venid pecadores, que Dios por su amor
Al cielo nos llama, que es patria mejor,
Do nunca la aurora—Perdio su fulgor
Do brilla la gloria—Del Dios creador.
Si, si, venid ;—si, si, venid ;
El cielo es del alma la patria mejor
Alli son eternos la paz y el amor.

II.

Dejemos, hermanos—aparte el dolor,
Que arriba en los cielos—el coro cantor
De espiritus puros—proclama Señor
A Cristo, Dios hombre—nuestro Redentor.
Si, si, venid—si, si, venid
Los angeles cantan—la gloria y honor
De Cristo, Dios Hombre—nuestro Redentor.

III.

Trabajas y sufras, aqui pecador
Y el pan que te comes—rego tu sudor
Mas Dios te reserva,—por suerte mejor,
Primicias celestes—de eterno valor.
Si, si, venid—si, si, venid
Primicias celestes—de eterno valor
Si sigues la Senda—De tu Redentor.

A celebrated doctor of Lausanne was called in at
this crisis. He gave us some hopes that if we could
find a suitable private dwelling-house on an eminence
in the neighbourhood of Lausanne, his breathing
might be improved, and his sufferings be rendered
less intense. Mrs. McE—— requested me to search
for a house so situated, giving me *carte blanche* as to
expense, so anxious was she to do everything possible
to save such a precious life. A Scotch lady then at
Lausanne volunteered to accompany me in the search,

which appeared likely to be no easy task. I was truly helped by this Christian woman in the accomplishment of what appeared to all so desirable.

After seeing a very nice villa in an elevated position, but which we were unable to secure, we proceeded to another that appeared to us to combine everything that was required by our dear sufferer. We were ushered into a beautiful drawing-room which over-looked the placid Lake of Geneva, with the majestic Alps beyond. The walls of the apartment were hung with costly paintings, and the *tout ensemble* of the room bespoke at once comfort, taste, and refinement. As I looked round it, I was constrained to say to myself, " It will be hard work for the flesh to give up these nice things," not remembering at the time that the hearts of all men are in the hands of the Lord, and that He turns them whithersoever He will. In dependence on Jesus, who is indeed a very present help in time of need, and who in a special manner proved Himself to be so on this occasion, I stated the object of our visit to Mme. G——. She appeared desirous of assisting Matamoros, and offered to receive him, and even herself to help in attending on him ; but when I explained that we wished to rent the whole house just as it stood, with all its conveniences and dependencies, the case appeared to be altered. She did not see her way very clearly, and appeared not a little surprised at our rather extraordinary re-quest. " The Lord had need of it ; " and He had sent us there to ask it in His name. Soon after she had left the room to consult her aunt, she returned with a face shining at once with pleasure and deep sym-

pathy, and announced to us that we should *at once*
have her beautiful villa, servants, linen, carriage, etc.,
etc. We returned with her to the drawing-room, where
we found her aunt, and we all four sat down.

After asking the lady the terms on which she
would rent her house, and receiving from her the
unexpected reply, that we were to pay *nothing*, oui
hearts were filled to overflowing, and we did indeed
rejoice with abundant tears of joy and thankfulness.
I told this lady how she had by this act refreshed
the saints; and I felt indeed the force of those words,
"Inasmuch as ye have done it to the least of these
my brethren, ye have done it unto Me." O glorious
faith of Jesus, that leads to acts of self-denial such
as this; and, O blessed Spirit of God, that gives
grace to perform such noble acts! We had been very
anxious about this matter, which had been recommended by the physicians, and was considered by
ourselves as so desirable, and it was no light cause for
gratitude that we had met with such complete success
in so short a time.

This arrangement took place on Saturday. On
the Monday following, at an early hour, our beloved
Manuel was safely installed in the new abode provided
for him by the same Friend who said, "In my Father's
house there are many mansions. I go to prepare a
place for *you*."

The noble act of this lady reminded us of the
breaking of the alabaster box of ointment, exceeding
precious; and the fragrance of this act of love may
waft its sweet perfume abroad now as did the spike-
nard of the Magdalene.

But many were the incidents worthy of notice that we witnessed during the sickness of our Manuel, and a long and interesting book might be made from the little details connected with our beloved sufferer. A Roman Catholic servant, who attended him at the Hôtel Gibbon, appeared to spare no pains in smoothing his dying pillow, and doing all in her power to make him as comfortable as she could. I thanked her frequently for her self-denying attention, as did also dear Manuel. When he was removed to the new habitation, she expressed a desire to go and attend on him there also, but as she was the principal housemaid in this large hotel, where they have two hundred beds, her services could not be dispensed with. On leaving Lausanne, I had some conversation with her, and asked her if I should see her again? She asked what .I meant. I replied, "*Au grand rendezvous.*" (" At the great rendezvous.") To which she immediately answered—

"*Oui, monsieur, je l'espère.*" (" Yes, sir, I trust so.")

I asked her, "Do you believe in Jesus?" and was answered in a very unmistakable way in the affirmative. I had in my pocket a copy of St. Luke's Gospel, which she received with tears of joy; and I look forward to see this dear woman with our beloved Manuel on the resurrection morning, now so near at hand. The servants of the hotel appeared all to vie with one another in serving him, and the sweet impressions he has left behind him in Lausanne will not be soon forgotten.

But I am diverging from my subject, and must

retrace my steps to the Belvedere, the name of his new abode. We there procured an invalid's carriage, in which he was drawn about on the green turf, so abundant in this sweet garden. This little exercise, and the lovely view, and the pleasant flowers, were all most precious to the dear saint, and much alleviated his sufferings.

I had now remained with him for about five weeks, and fully purposed remaining to the end, but had two unmistakable proofs from God that it was his will that I should go to do a little service for him in Holland, which was also connected with our dear brother. My decision to depart was finally formed after receiving a letter of farewell that he penned at three o'clock in the morning after a night of pain and acute suffering. It was as follows :—

" Lausanne, July 23.

"REVERED AND DEAREST FRIEND,—The noble, constant, and Christian aid which, in these last days of my earthly suffering, you have rendered both to my soul and body, is the lovely continuation of the history of our friendship, in which your part has been one sustained sacrifice. You are about to leave me, and I desire to assure you that you are right in so doing. You have given up a long and precious period of time to me, but now your fatherly duties recall you to your family. It is I who remind you that you ought to go, and yet it is I who will suffer the most deeply from your absence. The loss to me will be irreparable, for your holy and edifying position at my side has been at once that of a father and a friend. But in heaven, in those mansions which are already

R

ours through Jesus Christ, we shall meet again and spend eternity together. The Lord is very near me. His presence strengthens me. I feel that Christ is my friend, my Saviour, my all. My peace is perfect. I am only awaiting the will of God.

" Your son, your friend, your brother, in prison as at liberty, in days of health and on the brink of the grave, am I, friend of my heart, friend in Jesus. Embrace all who are dear to you in my name. Until we meet in heaven, in the Lord, your

" MANUEL."

This letter left no doubt on my mind as to what the Lord wished me to do, so on Tuesday I started on my journey for Holland. My separation from Matamoros cost us both a severe pang, but it was the will of God. I much dreaded the farewell, fearing that it might hurry on his decease.

On the day before his death Mme. Bridel was with him, encouraging and directing him. She spoke to him about the intense joy that awaits all the faithful servants of Jesus Christ, when they can contemplate what eye hath not seen nor ear heard. He answered her with a child-like confidence of manner, so character- istic and so indescribable, which those who knew him can never forget, and those who did not know him can hardly imagine. Soon afterwards he proposed prayer, and prayed in nearly the following words:—" My God, God Almighty, I call on Thee. Jesus, my Saviour, and Thou, Holy Spirit, do I invoke. Thou knowest that I know the joys of heaven, but oh, give me to enjoy them in a deeper degree. Do Thou thyself prepare me for heaven. Enable me to make those around me feel the joy that fills my heart. I bless Thee for the Christian friends Thou hast given me in this land of exile. I bless Thee for the happy moments we have been able to pass together. Cause them to know how much love and respect I feel towards them. Give them, too, to be daily more encouraged, in labouring for Spain."

On the morning of his death, and after passing a troubled night, having had painful dreams, he said to Mrs. McE—— and to M. Carrasco, who were near his bed, "From earth to heaven, by the way of Golgotha. It is a beautiful journey." At eleven o'clock in the morning he asked for all the young Spaniards to be called together. He wished to hear them singing, which they did in the adjoining apartment, the doors being open. They sang the French cantique, "Vers le Ciel," and the Spanish one, "Venid Pecadores." Afterwards they came into the large drawing-room, where Matamoros was, and he said to them, "Avançons-nous."* This was a hymn which he greatly liked. The young Spaniards sang it, and he endeavoured to accompany them with his dying voice. He afterwards said to them, "Live very near to God; yes, *very*, *very* *near*. May God bless you *much, very much.*" He was exhausted, and his head fell on his breast. All around him were bathed in tears. It was mid-day. The young people had left, and only the elder ones had remained with Mrs. McE——. Matamoros appeared to be asleep. After a few moments he awoke, and

* A hymn translated from the English, "Joyfully, joyfully, onward we move."

addressed to Mme. Bridel some words of blessing and farewell. After this he was again troubled a little, and spoke of some dreadful things he saw in his dreams· Mme. Bridel said to him, "The Lord is my Shepherd." After these words, pronounced slowly, he became calm, and nodded assent. A moment later he said, "Like my Saviour;" to which Mme. Bridel replied, "Yes, at thirty-three years of age." These words arose from a conversation which he and Mme. Bridel had had a few days previously, when she remarked to him that his labours on earth had been short and were soon to be terminated, and that our Lord had finished his great work at the age of thirty-three. After this conversation he appeared to sleep peacefully.

Some passages of Scripture were read to him, and one of the Swiss pastors, M. G——, prayed by his bed; but we do not know if he was enabled to hear these consoling words at this time, or whether his soul which was now parting from his suffering frame, was not already contemplating his Saviour's face in the heavenly city. Oh, how sweet and consoling was this sleep. His death was very tranquil, for towards the end, God in his infinite mercy took away all pain, and restored to him facility in breathing, from the want of which he had suffered so much. At length he breathed quite naturally, and soon afterwards he fell asleep in Jesus.

Oh, how blessed this sleep! The thunder rolled in the distance, but on the sleeper's placid face rested a heavenly calm. At about half-past two in the afternoon there was no sign of earthly life remaining; the heavenly life in Jesus' bosom had commenced. A few minutes elapsed, when a terrible peal of thunder seemed to announce the departure from this earth of a great soul who had entered into eternity.

On Thursday, August 2nd, a number of friends from Geneva, Lausanne, and other parts of the Canton de Vaud, accompanied his mortal remains to their last resting place. In the drawing-room at the "Belvedere," and standing by the coffin, Pastor Bridel (after a short prayer had been uttered and a Spanish hymn sung by the young friends and countrymen of the departed) gave his testimony to the faith, the devoted activity, and the Christian death of Matamoros, reading some passages of the new testament at the same time. The faith of our brother was expressed, he said, by Titus ii. 11—14 and iii. 4—7 ; the aim of his life and his zeal for God's kingdom by Acts xx. 24 and 2 Tim. iv. 5—8 ; the struggles of his heart during his illness and his peaceable farewell and quiet respose in God by Phil. i. 20—24. After the reading of these passages the large assembly, drawn together by a feeling of deep love and sorrow, united in prayer from their hearts' depths with Pastor G—— : another verse of a hymn was sung by the Spaniards, and they then moved forward to the burial-ground. Over the grave, and after some remarks on Phil. i. 21, Rev. xiv. 13, and John xi. 25, Pastor Bridel gave a rapid *resumé* of the life of Matamoros :—

"Born at Malaga, October, 1834 ; converted at Gibraltar in 1857 ; imprisoned for the Gospel in 1860. He remained in prison three years, during which time his zeal for God won many souls to Christ ; but it was also during this harsh imprisonment that his comparatively strong constitution gave way. He was condemned to the galleys, but in 1863 the sentence was commuted to one of exile. After some journeyings, and visits to England, Gibraltar, and Bayonne, he arrived at Lausanne in the year 1864, where, during twelve months and with blessing to his soul, he followed his theological studies. He went to the south of France in June, 1865, and passed the winter at Pau, returning to Lausanne in May, 1866. He enjoyed while there but a short period of health and activity, suddenly becoming ill, and falling asleep in Jesus on the 31st July, 1866, at half-past two o'clock in the afternoon."

M. Bridel added that "Matamoros, by the ardour of his zeal, redeemed the time, and by the entire consecration of himself to his work he multiplied his years. Let us imitate his example, and sustain by our efforts and prayers that work, the evangelization of Spain, which he had so much at heart."

This funeral ceremony, at once touching and solemn, was closed by M. Duprat by prayer. While making himself at once the organ of the grief of all who were present, he thanked God that the poor exile had reached home at last, had reached the House of the Father of the family, that possession and that inheritance that can neither be removed nor taken away.

Our Brother was buried at the cemetery called "La Salaz," a lovely, quiet resting place. On his tombstone of white marble are written the following words:—

MANUEL MATAMOROS

DE

MALAGA.

8 Octubre, 1834.   31 Julio, 1866.

—o—

Porque yo me resuelvo, en que lo que en
este tiempo se padece, no es de comparar
con la gloria venidera que en nosotros
ha de ser manifestada.

Rom. viii. 18.

——

Y nos gloriamos en la esperanza
de la gloria de Dios.

Rom. v 2.

——

Por la obra de Cristo he llegado
hasta la muerte.

——

CHAPTER XVIII.

RECOLLECTIONS OF OUR DEPARTED BROTHER.

WE are members of His body, of His flesh, and of His bones. The *Head* of the body, when in the flesh, was despised and *rejected of men*, a man of sorrows and acquainted with grief, nevertheless, "The *chosen of God and precious*." Is it any wonder that the members should share the fate of the Head? I have learned from good authority that on Matamoros's last visit to Paris he was received by French Christians with coldness. This was owing, I believe, to unkind reports and suspicions then current in England, which, in his enfeebled condition, he felt acutely, and he came to Lausanne to die of a broken heart. Thank God, he is now far above the strife of the tongues of men. God has given a faithful picture of the children of Adam in the third of Romans, and the longer we live the more we prove the truth of that word. He there says, "Their throat is an open sepulchre ; with their tongues they have used deceit ; the poison of asps is under their lips ; their mouth is full of cursing and bitterness ; their feet are swift to shed blood."

But we have the satisfaction of knowing that if Matamoros had enemies he also had many good friends, who loved, esteemed, and valued him as he deserved. Among these Dr. Cappadose, of Holland, and a Christian lady at Amsterdam, hold a foremost place. On my way to London in July I visited these friends in passing through Rotterdam, and found that the Lord had very graciously directed my steps to the houses of both these saints, and by his help I was enabled to comfort them when they received the sad intelligence of Manuel's death. I had left, for their perusal, a diary which Matamoros gave me on his death-bed, and I soon after received a letter from the lady, from which I extract the following :—

"Many, many thanks for your kindness in lending it to me. I only wish I had had it in England last year, when I was hunting for justifying evidences and proofs to vindicate our friend's integrity and honour. But it was not to be, and Matamoros had to bear to the last a cross which was the most painful of all to the uprightness of his soul—that of being misunderstood and misjudged by his brethren in the faith. It was the kind of martyrdom he would least have chosen, but that which his heavenly Father appointed as the purifying process by which he was to be made fit for the holiness and happiness of heaven. And now the diamond, being thoroughly polished, is set as a precious jewel in his Master's crown. He has gone straight to his heavenly home, and who among us could wish to call him back? Oh no, rather let all the good purposes of God's infinite love be made manifest to him as soon as he was able to bear the weight of glory and felicity prepared for the beloved child : the faithful servant of a righteous Master, who deemed that his task was

finished and that he was ready to enter into the joy of
his Lord. If we could have been present and felt the
raptures of his soul when brought into the presence of
his Saviour, how we should wonder and adore!"

M. Roger Hollard, of Paris, an eminent Christian
writer, has given to his countrymen some interesting
details of Matamoros in an article which appeared in
Le Chrétien Evangélique of the 20th Sept. 1866,
published at Lausanne by M. G. Bridel : from it we
make some extracts. These further details of his
conversion are not general known in England:—

"When at Gibraltar he was engaged in some
literary pursuits that gained for him general appro-
bation and marked applause at the theatre. His
mind was preoccupied with a poem which he had
been asked to write on a given subject, and while
walking one evening in the principal square at
Gibraltar he heard the church bell summoning to
worship. He at first felt disposed to enter, for from
his infancy he had been taught both by father and
mother to respect religion; nevertheless his literary
pursuits seemed to take the upper place in his mind,
when he heard the bell ring a second time. And
when that solemn sound was heard the third time he
could no longer resist. He entered the church, which
to his great astonishment he found was a Protestant
one, in which English Christians supported the
preaching of the Gospel in Spanish. He was quite
surprised with all he saw and heard, for he had strong
prejudices against the Protestants, who, up to that
time, were in his mind classed with the Jews. What

produced the strongest effect on him was the prayer of M. Ruet, the Spanish evangelist; and what most impressed him in the preaching was the advice given to search the Scriptures. He immediately procured a New Testament, and read it all that night in bed; and when the cannon of the Rock* announced the dawning of a new day, a new day had also begun to shine in his heart. Soon after this he had the pleasure of seeing many members of his family join with him in believing in the Gospel of Jesus, to which he bore, ever after his conversion, such a faithful testimony in the midst of his own people."

M. Hollard commences his article, which I strongly recommend to my readers, by saying—

"Manuel Matamoros, one of the most powerful and loving Christian individualities which has appeared in our midst for a long period of time, is lost to us. Even among our religious men, Matamoros was little understood. When death came and called him away at thirty-two years of age he was already for many only a reminiscence. They remembered him indeed as the young Spanish soldier converted some eight years before to the Gospel, and who had suffered in the dungeon for the ardent zeal he displayed for the faith he had embraced. They knew that, condemned to the galleys, after three years of close confinement, he had seen, through the intervention of a deputation of all evangelical Europe, his sentence changed into that of exile. Nor were they ignorant that he had, while confessing his faith before the tribunal, displayed a

* At Gibraltar a cannon is fired off at daybreak,

courage which called to mind that of the early martyrs of the Christian Church, and that when called upon to retract he determined to write with his own hand the expression of his faith, that is to say, to write his own condemnation. But what was Matamoros at heart? Born of persecution, the hero of a day, and one whose heroism would die with him? Or a man, a Christian, born to leave an unmistakable footprint wherever he passed? What was he in exile? What effect will his death produce? This is known only to a comparatively small circle, and is that of which I wish to convey some idea.

"It was not difficult to know him; it was sufficient to love him; and it was so easy to love him. There was an indescribably noble, yet child-like, candour in him that was irresistibly attractive. He met men and circumstances with the fresh confidence of a child, and faced them with the brave determination of a strong man, who has found in his religious faith an immovable foundation. All that he had to suffer did not shake his confidence, and it is needless to add, that trial appeared only to strengthen his determination. We have often admired how many dangers Matamoros was preserved from by the candour of his nature and of his faith. We do not mean by this to allude to the trials he underwent in his persecution; they were not the greatest he met with; but in religious matters how happily did he avoid the many rocks that he might so easily have been dashed against. Perhaps it was the natural reaction against the ecclesiastical system in whose bosom he had been educated, or, perhaps the affection that he owed, and with good reason, to

Christians of different denominations who sustained him in his captivity or received him in exile. But the fact remains the same : his faith enabled him to preserve to the end his own peculiar style, as well as his original and apostolic simplicity. And the same may be said of his private character. Over those in Spain who shared his convictions Matamoros had acquired a moral ascendancy, the measure of which we shall be able to appreciate by and by. He was received in his exile by numerous tender, powerful, sympathizing hearts, and in all this there was for him a double danger. But over all he triumphed gloriously, for he was as humble in what for lack of a better word we might call success, as he had been strong in the midst of persecution and obscurity. This is saying much. But I express now not merely a personal conviction, but that of those who were most intimately acquainted with this great witness for the gospel, but who at first asserted that because his danger was great, his fall was certain."

M. Hollard continues his interesting account by giving an extract from a letter of Manuel's noble mother, whom the son resembled both in appearance and in heart :—

"This lady, in a letter to Dr. Cappadose, says : 'With joy do I watch him treading that thorn-covered path, which the enemies of Jesus have prepared for my son ; but I see him strong and unmovable in his career : I see with infinite satisfaction that he is aiming at nothing short of the crown of life ; and forgetting his sufferings, I rejoice with him. Had I beheld him weak or wavering, then his poor mother would have died, not from the fear of his imprisonment but of his ultimate salvation.'"

On one occasion, the director of the prison found Matamoros's mother in tears by the sick bed of her son. The report had been spread that his powerful enemies had poisoned him, and the director had come to hold an inquest.

"You weeping?" he said to his mother.

"How can I help it," she replied, "when my son is sick and nigh unto death?"

"If your son," replied the director, "was not as bad a son to you as he is to his mother the Church of Rome, it would be easy for him to dry your tears."

At these words his mother arose quickly, and left the prison, remarking, "If my son were to deny his Saviour, Jesus Christ, I, in my turn, would deny him as my son."

The director, not a little surprised, turned to Matamoros and said, " You have a noble mother."

Further on M. Hollard remarks,—" There was one joy that Matamoros could not do without, the joy of being understood and loved—both himself and his cause, for they were inseparable. Alas, even in his exile he was sometimes deprived of this joy. He came to us out of prison full of confidence and hope, doubting not but that soon he would have inspired us all with pity for his poor country, and inflamed us with love for the work he lived for. Matamoros knew little about us; he did not understand that one of the misfortunes and one of the first impulses of a generation without heroes, is to look with suspicion on heroism wherever it appears.

" They called him imperious : he was only determined to sacrifice all to his mission, beginning by sacrificing himself. He was accused of imprudence : he had faith. They said he confided too easily : he only loved. But let us be silent about all these miseries. They were more painful to him than his captivity or his exile, and 'caused' him to shed many a tear ; but no uncharitable wish or word escaped his lips. Let us call to mind sweeter thoughts. We have said that he lived to be loved ; and he was loved, and deeply. If there was anything on earth that could have caused him to forget his exile, undoubtedly it was the sympathy that he enjoyed in his last days. Above all, there was one little spot to which he clung with deep affection. He thus wrote, a year before his death, to some of the best friends he had during his exile.

" 'As far as I am concerned,' he said to M. Louis Bridel, ' do what you think best ; I will go where you say, and do what you like. But withal, Lausanne has been to me such a consolation, so pure and so holy in times past, and has answered so completely all the wants of my spirit, that just as, if in Spain, I should choose Malaga as the spot for my tomb, so, out of Spain, I would select Lausanne.' And in June, 1866, he wrote to Mme. Bridel, ' On the day that your poor adopted son shall leave this world, gather around you all the others of your adopted family, and make them sing a song of eternal thanksgiving. My tomb must not be watered by tears, but compassed with a song of triumph. My tomb will only be a shadow, a dream. I myself shall live in the midst of that joy unceasing, of that peace and of that love, that I have sought in vain on earth. And though I have experienced it with a few of those noble beings who love me, and whom I have loved with a heavenly love, yet even then, here below it has been ever watered by tears of separation and of suffering.'

" Such was the man we lament. The void that he leaves in the hearts of his friends is deep, and that which he has left in the heart of his Spanish brethren is immeasurable; but when men like Matamoros fall, broken down by labour and suffering, they not only leave behind them a great void, but also a great work which cannot perish; a great example, more needed to-day than ever. And what they find in the presence of that God whom they have served, is—a great repose, the very thought of which dries the tears of those whom the affliction had caused to mourn."

I may safely let the curtain fall at this part of my narrative. He has fought a good fight; he has finished his course; in a Laodicean and degenerate age witnessed a good confession; and, by God's grace, he has left us an example well worth imitating. " Let me die the death of the righteous, and let my last end be like his."

May God bless my little book. May He make it acceptable to those of His blood-bought flock who shall read it. May they be stirred up by it to live a little nearer to Jesus, and to pray and labour a little more for Spain.

CHAPTER XIX.

CONCLUSION.

IN the month of July, 1866, dear Matamoros went to his happy home in Jesus' bosom. He had told me in one of our interesting and intimate conversations that he had asked God to give "Libertad de Cultos" (freedom of worship) in Spain, and that soon, very soon, I should see it with my eyes, for God had heard his prayer. In the year 1868 occurred the memorable revolution undertaken and carried out by three of Spain's best men, Prim, Serrano and Topete. The two first Generals in the army, and Topete Admiral in the navy. The men who had suffered like Matamoros, and who had been liberated at the time of his release, were some of them in Bayonne and Bordeaux, some in Gibraltar. General Prim being in Andalucia at the time of the great victory obtained by his troops over Queen Isabella's in the Valley of the Guadalquiver, not far from Cordova, went soon after to Algeciras, a Spanish town opposite Gibraltar, and had there an interview with the three

s

principal religious leaders who had suffered bonds for Christ's sake. Their names were Cabrera, Alhama and Hernandez. General Prim received these gentlemen with the greatest kindness. In reply to their remarks that their only crime had been, that they did not profess the Roman Catholic religion, General Prim said, "From this day forth there shall be liberty in our country, real liberty; every man shall be master of his own conscience, and shall profess the faith which seems best in his own eyes. You gentlemen," he added, "may return to your country at once, and you are at liberty to enter Spain with your bibles under your arms, to preach its doctrines." Afterwards these gentlemen were sent for by the administrative Junta of Algeciras and informed that they were at full liberty to take up their residence in that town, or that they should be provided with passports if they wished to proceed elsewhere. It is generally well known how, not only these three refugees, but all those from Bordeaux and Bayonne at once entered Spain, and the majority of them went to Madrid, and during several years great activity was displayed in preaching the pure Gospel of Christ. A large bible depôt was opened in one of the principal streets, minor ones in other places; colporteurs employed in numbers to carry the Word of Life into the provinces; halls erected for preaching in all the large towns, and schools established in connection with many of them. Indeed, seldom has such an impetus been given to the spread of evangelical truth in any place in such a short period of time. At the period of which I am writing great improvements were being made at Madrid, new roads and streets being laid out all round and about that city. In cutting through one of these which passed through the " Quemadero de la Cruz," the celebrated spot where the wicked tribunal of the Inquisition had burnt so many of God's saints some 300 years ago, the amount of human bones and other remains brought to light was appalling. Among other horrors were found two bony hands, transfixed by a large nail, and clasped in the attitude of prayer, and the ribs of some victim, with the spear still protruding by which they had been pierced. The effect of the discovery was immense. Rome was revealed more clearly than ever before the eyes of Spain. A speaker in the Cortes said that while there were strange *geological sections* and *strata*, there were also strange *theological sections* and *strata* declaring the history of the past. There was a public meeting held on the site, attended by multitudes. On one side of the excavation there was a high bank, halfway down which the long black strata was exposed to the light of day. Their contents crumbled beneath the touch, and were found on examination to consist principally of the *débris* of fuel and human bodies burned and buried together. God has truly said in his word, " The earth shall disclose her blood, and shall no more cover her slain." The devoted missionary, Mr. Grattan Guinness, accompanied me to this celebrated " Burning place of the *Cross!* " where the *Autos da fé* (acts of faith) were executed. His spirit was moved within him, and he, without loss of time, wrote the following appropriate lines.

Ye layers of ashes black, and half-burnt bones,
Ye monuments of martyr's stifled moans
Of human agony and dying groans,
Cry out till every ear has heard your tones!
Cry till the murderess trembles, though her brain
Is drunken with the blood of millions slain
She did not mean to show you; 'twas the spade
Of simple workmen which your horrors laid
Unearthed and bare, before the light of day;
They only dug to open a new way.
As they advanced, the ground before them grew
In patches softer, changed its wonted hue,
And with the smell of death defiled the air.
They dug, and they discovered, layer on layer,
Black bones, and rusted chains, and human hair,
And iron nails, and bits of melted lead,
And the burnt fuel of unnumbered dead.
They cut the heap across; it crowns a hill.
Its length is shown—its breadth lies buried still.
Doubtest thou reader? I was there to-day;
I saw them at the work; I brought away
Some horrible remains, which while I write
These very lines, are lying in my sight.
A piece of paper on this table holds
Some of this martyr dust within its folds.
I pause, and gently touch it with my hand:
It is not common earth; it is not sand;
I look at it; the tears have filled my eyes;
My God, what is it that before me lies?
The ground beneath was gravel and was red,
But this is dark, and formed a separate bed.
How soft it is, and light; it feels like soil
That has been saturated once with oil;
'Tis full of small black cinders, most is grey
And ashen; here is something burnt away
Black as the blackest coal; this was the meat
Of some relentless and devouring heat.

A little box beside the paper stands,
Its relics I collected with these hands.
I take a something from it like a stone;
'Tis grey and light; ah! 'tis a piece of bone;
This was the side on which the muscles grew,
The other side its chambers are burnt blue.
These four are lumps of iron, they are red
Like fetters that have rusted off the dead.
This was an iron bolt, 'tis long and curved,
To hold a chain or cord it doubtless served;
This is a hollow bone, burnt through and through,
It leaves upon my hand a dusky hue.
That was a bar of iron, now mere rust,
And this is indistinguishable dust.
Oh Rome, thou mother of a cherished race,
Blush not to show the world thy kindly face!
Thy bosom—hide its demons, hush thy breast,
'Tis there alone that suffering men find rest.
How mild the chastisements thy love has used
Whene'er thy children have thy laws refused!
Gentle coercion! Pity's tender tones!
Tell me, thou murderess black, what mean these bones?
These bones before me, those upon the hill,
Who, what were these thus slaughtered by thy will?
What did these helpless women? these poor men?
Why did'st thou shut them up in thy dark den?
Why did'st thou pinch their flesh and starve their frames,
And cast them bound into devouring flames?
True they reproached thee for thy crimes and lies,
And prayed for thee with sin-forgiving sighs.
Thy multiplied idolatries abhorred;
Nor mediator honoured but their Lord;
Condemned thy priestcraft and thy love of gold;
Clung to God's word, and for its truths were bold
Adorned by blamelessness the name they bore;
Loved not their lives to death. What did they more?
Were they adulterers, these prisoned saints?
Or murderers—these who died without complaints'

Hush, for they sleep in Jesus, soft their bed.
His suffering saints their Lord hath comforted!
Hush, for the sevenfold wrath of God grows hot!
Hush, for her deep damnation slumbereth not.

G. GUINNESS.

Madrid, January 14, 1870.

Latterly I again visited this celebrated burning spot, but much pains had been taken to cut away all the ground that was in any way blackened; but though the ground has been removed, the fact remains, and these lines, too, will remain to testify of Rome's treachery and unchangeable character, as recorded in holy writ—*drunk with the blood of the saints.* In the present year, 1881, I visited Spain, passing through Barcelona by Saragossa to Madrid, and returning to London by Bordeaux and Paris. During the last ten years great progress has been made in developing the railway system and the other branches of her industry. I remember in 1855 making the journey from Bayonne to Madrid by the diligence; it occupied seventy-two hours, and I arrived at the capital exhausted and fatigued beyond measure. In the month of May, 1881, it was comfortably performed in nineteen hours, without any fatigue whatever. The same was the case in passing from Perpignan to Barcelona by the Catalonian railway. The railways have been a great help to the introduction of the Gospel into Spain, and frequently, during their execution, the words of the prophet, as quoted by Luke, came into my mind: "Every valley shall be filled, and every mountain and hill shall be brought low, and the crooked shall be made straight, and the rough ways shall be made smooth, and *all flesh shall see the salvation of God.*" Yes, man has been busy in executing these railroads for his own convenience in carrying his merchandize more easily; but God had his plans in view for his own far more important and blessed ends, even for the gathering out of his elect church in Spain, and this, His purpose, is in course of fulfilment evidently.

The sufferings of Matamoros have not been in vain. The Gospel trumpet has been sounded now on her hills and in her valleys by numbers of God's faithful witnesses, and that trumpet has given no uncertain sound; and it is very interesting and worthy of note that the *seven* principal witnesses called out and fitted by God in his infinite wisdom, after they had finished their glorious testimony, were caught up to God and to his throne. Their names were Matamoros, Cosido, Carrasco, Astray, Ruet, Gould and Gladstone. How mysterious are God's ways. Truly we must say with the prophet, They are higher than our ways. Yea, past finding out. Humanly speaking, these excellent *seven* were almost indispensable to the progress of the Gospel in Spain; but we are taught by their removal that God can dispense with the best of us, and that at the best we are but "the *worm* Jacob" in His eyes. He is ever proving to us in such dispensations of His providence that all flesh is grass. It is not by might nor by power, but by My spirit, saith the Lord of Hosts, that all My purposes are accomplished. Would that we were not so slow in learning the lesson.

Other faithful men are labouring unceasingly and indefatigably throughout Spain, and those centres I visited gave proof to the untiring zeal of the Lord's servants at each post. In Barcelona I learnt that there are some thousand children in the schools; eight hundred in Madrid. By a recent change of ministry a better state of things is expected with regard to liberty of worship, which for some years had been curtailed ever since the reaction which was gradually inaugurated after the assassination of the liberal General Prim. Poor Spain needs the sympathies and prayers of God's children as much as ever, and how much my visit encouraged the dear labourers was quite evident to me. Oh that there was more earnest prayer offered by the saints for this deeply interesting field. In a letter just received from a friend I visited on my journey, he says, "God be praised for sending you here. How precious is the flower of Christian sympathy; but, alas! how rare in this poor world of sin." I had the great privilege during my short stay at Madrid of hearing the glorious Gospel preached in all its life-giving and consoling power in the fine old Castillian tongue to a numerous and attentive audience, who were visibly drinking in every word of the preacher. The words were words of power evidently felt by the preacher and also by his congregation. The hall was well filled, and I observed many a tear in the eyes of the listeners, for which I praise God. I must say that, for my own part, the words were precious to my soul as ever Spurgeon's or Guthrie's have been, and all this occurred within gunshot of the burning place of the heretics mentioned above.

Much of the wine growing district I passed through

in the south of France has been a prey to the Phyloxera, and consequently for hundreds of miles no more vines are grown, and the land is turned into pasture or arable land, so the French people have been obliged to send to the south of Spain for the wine that used to be grown on their own territory. This has enriched Spain to an extent hardly credible, as I was told at Barcelona, and this new capital is being invested in new railways and several other ways, and a new life is observant in Barcelona and all along the southern coast. The iron trade in the north, zinc, coal, copper, lead and silver, with many other precious metals, in the south, have brought the energies of Spain into new life as far as commerce is concerned, but, much as we may approve of this material progress, yet it is the careful labours of the men of God and the praying groups up and down the land that are more blessed in the eyes of God than all human activities. Our Lord tells us what to do to meet the emergency. *Pray ye the Lord of the harvest that He would send labourers into His harvest.* Let us obey His command, believing that as He has given us this command He will certainly answer our cry, and this new edition of this book will answer the end I have in view if it stirs up once again the sympathies of the Christian Church to labour and pray for Spain.

The publication of these letters some twenty years ago was much used by God in directing attention to the wants of the Peninsula. Their reproduction at this time will, with God's blessing, give a fresh and blessed impetus to the same holy cause. God can do it and I believe He will. "*Call upon me* in the time of trouble, I will hear thee and thou shalt glorify Me."

I have been much encouraged in my efforts for the circulation of the Gospel in Spain when constructing the railways in that country, and in order to encourage those who are desirous of working in a similar way I must just recite a short story to show how abundantly our God does bless our feeble and unworthy efforts for the advancement of His kingdom. An interesting Spaniard in La Mancha had executed a portion of the railway between Madrid and Alicante entirely to my satisfaction, and from many interesting conversations with him, I found great honesty of purpose in him, as well as other lovely qualities as a natural man. I had with difficulty smuggled into Spain a beautiful large copy of the New Testament at this time (1852), bound in red morocco, with gilt edges, and I had kept it for a long time so as to place it in good hands at last. The man of La Mancha mentioned above was the person I thought of as the one most likely to give it a careful perusal, and I was confirmed in this judgment by a circumstance which happened. I had a new section or contract of the same railway to give in his neighbourhood, and proposed it to him because of the clever and rapid way in which he had executed his first work, but, as he had a large family, I suggested to him to undertake this work *alone* without having any partners to share in the profits, but he refused, and said he did not want to have it all for himself, but wished his friends to share. This act of unselfishness decided me in bestowing on him the true riches contained in the lovely volume. He treasured up the Book to his dying hour. He had been a diligent student of its sacred truths; it had brought joy and peace to his honest, noble heart. At his death he handed the volume to his sons, telling them that it contained the truth, and leaving it to them as the greatest and best gift he could give them. This Book was the means of the decided conversion of the two sons, who brought another interesting man to join them, who was also converted. They three became among the best of the Spanish colporteurs, and have gone through many and great dangers in the propagation of the truth, one of them having lost his eye by a stone lately thrown at him, when defending the doctrine of his Lord. Who can tell the results that the giving of that one red testament may produce? Eternity will reveal the hidden things that we see not at present. "Cast thy bread upon the waters, thou shalt find it after many days." About the year 1856 I passed through Bayonne. There lives there an earnest Christian French pasteur, Mons. Jean Nogaret by name. He had the dark state of Spain laid upon his heart, and had an ardent desire to do something for the spreading of Gospel light in that country. He proposed to me to accompany him to Paris in order to form an association of Christian friends for the proclamation of the glad tidings there. I did so, and we succeeded in getting the cordial co-operation of Pastor Fisch, Valette, Fred. Monod, and others for this important work. The first labourer they sent there was named Pinto. He brought dear Matteo Cosido to the Divine Saviour, and afterwards they helped dear Matamoros in his glorious mission, until he had the great honour to suffer bonds for Christ. Eternity will tell by-and-bye the result of this Paris journey—but one result manifested at present is the existence of some sixty congregations in Spain where idolatry is banished. Where God's word is read and where prayer is wont to be made; but there is still much land to be occupied. We want now men of the stamp of the writer of the letter at page 87 of this edition, to help forward this work by their prayers and sympathy, and I trust God will find them; precious Phebes, "who was a succourer of many," and such holy faithful women whose labours have been and are being owned of God in Spain now. We have some there, I say, but may our God send many such, and may He abundantly bless those who are at present at work, whose praise is in all the churches. America has given us two dear labourers, the brothers Gulick, one stationed at Santander and one at Saragossa. Little did Finney think what would result when Mrs. Gulick was converted through his powerful appeals—a whole family of missionaries. Oh for more Finneys, and more converts like this noble woman.

I now terminate this second edition, commending these pages to my dear Lord and compassionate Saviour, beseeching Him to use them as He did the previous ones, to the edification of His precious blood-bought family, and to the stirring up of the wise virgins of our day to obey His Divine command, "Go ye into all the world and preach the Gospel to every creature."

Awake, awake, for night is flying,
The watchmen on the heights are crying;
Awake, Jerusalem at last!
Midnight hears the welcome voices,
And at the thrilling cry rejoices;
Come forth ye virgins, night is past!
The Bridegroom comes, awake!
Your lamps with gladness take;
      Hallelujah!
And for His marriage feast prepare,
For ye must go and meet Him there.

THE END.

LONDON: ALFRED HOLNESS, 14 PATERNOSTER ROW.
GLASGOW: R. L. ALLAN, 143 SAUCHIEHALL STREET.

www.ingramcontent.com/pod-product-compliance
Lightning Source LLC
Chambersburg PA
CBHW020338030726
47496CB00007B/1934